The
Bewitching
of
Sherlock Holmes

A Truly Holmes Mystery

Jia Hartsiva

ISBN: 978-1-7771660-3-8

Also by Jia Hartsiva

The Arrival of Sherlock Holmes

Table of Contents

CHAPTER 1

Holmes' Sorceries

"My dear Holmes," said I, "this is too much. You would certainly have been burned, had you lived a few centuries ago."

—Sir Arthur Conan Doyle, *A Scandal in Bohemia*

"I DOUBT THE DEVIL MADE HIM DO IT, WATSON," SAID Sherlock Holmes one evening, wearing a faint but mischievous smile. "He is either lost in a world of delusion, or he is a very clever man with a flair for theatrics."

The newspaper fell from my hands, and I gaped at him. It wasn't possible; there was simply no way he could have divined which article I had been reading. There were plenty of features on the page: a three-vehicle collision in our own downtown Toronto ... the death of a German opera singer ... a storm that toppled a wall and graves in an old Jewish cemetery in Beirut ... The piece I had been reading had been tucked into a corner and given a measly two paragraphs.

"A remarkable case," he went on. "Just when I was starting to think there are no interesting crimes and criminals these days ..."

Was I surprised by Holmes' uncanny abilities considering all that had happened since the start of the school year? Somehow, yes, I was. I tugged at my ponytail, perplexed.

Sherlock Holmes was the strangest person I had ever had the pleasure — displeasure perhaps? — of living with. One couldn't grasp his eccentricity simply by observing his lean six-foot frame, his dark hair that alternated between brown and black depending on his mood, or his hawk-like nose and prominent chin. His old-fashioned, dapper style and quaint mannerisms may raise an eyebrow, but it was those deep-set grey eyes that chilled a person. They were his most disturbing feature; they were the source of his genius for surveying and dissecting all that he saw. A single, ephemeral gaze could make one feel naked, and when he opened his mouth to divulge something great or terrible — or even just petty and mundane — one felt disgracefully half-witted for not having noticed what he had noticed.

Holmes, as he liked to be called, had deduced a great many things in the four months I had known him. I had met him in September at the start of my second year of university. We were two of twenty who called home the beautifully restored Baker House. The novelty of moving into the Victorian-era student residence, in the bustling heart of downtown Toronto, had soon dissipated though, ousted by the curious inhabitant of unit 2B.

Holmes and I shared a wall, and this proximity was unfortunate at times since he tended to play the violin at odd hours; pace fervently to and fro late into the night; smoke from the comfort of his armchair, having disabled the smoke detector in his room; and experiment with odious chemicals using equipment he had "borrowed" from the chemistry department. He had a penchant for amassing exact knowledge about select topics, with a particularly concerning fixation on crime. His was an intellect that astonished even his professors, so it wasn't that I felt simpleminded around him. Instead, it was his eerie ability to read one's mind that proved to be a great source of nuisance.

He had performed this sorcery a few times before, but none had been as bewildering as the demonstration he offered that snow-clad day in December, the day after Christmas … which then put us at the mercy of a series of calamitous events.

About half of Baker House's residents had left for the holidays, which was why those of us who remained were now seated comfortably in the parlour. Although it was the largest room after the adjoining dining hall, a century's worth of mismatched furniture made it seem small. Still, it was a homey room with its raised wood panelling, carpeted burgundy floor, and incongruous sofas, armchairs, coffee tables, and lamps. It was a space that radiated so much comfort and warmth that I hardly wanted to stir.

Holmes had commandeered the best seats in the house for us—plush sofas by the electric fireplace—although the effect was a bit diminished, in my opinion, by the phony flames. My caramel complexion likely looked orange in the light; even Holmes' usual pallor had a glow to it. I appreciated the illusion though, listening to the cruel wind bellowing outside. Our housemates, a pleasant lot more or less, occupied the various nooks and corners and filled the room with murmured chatter.

It was out of desperation that I had picked up a newspaper someone, probably Holmes, had tossed aside. I rarely read the papers; there was something dismal about the happenings of the real world where satisfying endings were never a guarantee. I preferred something chilling from Collins or an Austen romance instead, something classic with a thicket of dense words and yellowing pages that smelled funny.

Unfortunately, my volume of Christmas stories by Dickens lay finished by my mug of chamomile tea and retrieving another book from our little in-house library in the basement would require me to get up. Avid reader though I was, my movements became sloth-like when my belly was full. I was suffering from the fatigue that comes when one does nothing but lounge and eat. I was still digesting the hearty Christmas dinner from the day before, though that hadn't stopped me from indulging in leftover roast beef and washing down bûche de Noël and sugar cookies with too much peppermint mocha.

And then Holmes had broken that foggy spell with that sly, irritating smile of his. As was usually the case, I was intrigued; I straightened my spine and leaned forward, suddenly very much awake.

"How could you have known what I was reading?" I asked, one brow raised.

My friend shrugged nonchalantly. "You are an open book, my dear Watson."

Holmes addressed me like that often despite our housemates' smirks, rarely using my first name, Janah. He insisted that I looked more like a "Watson" than a "Janah." I had grown accustomed to both it and his directive that he be addressed by his surname. I hadn't the foggiest idea why he hated his first name so much. The rest of the Baker House residents ignored this request; an unruly few saluted him with a mocking "Mr. Holmes," using an exaggerated imitation of his London accent.

"This is the part where you explain yourself," I said impatiently.

"You know my methods. Apply them."

I sighed. "Did my nose twitch in a weird way? Maybe my pupils dilated or something?"

Holmes smiled. "Very good, Watson."

I tried to hide the surprise from my face. Had I truly guessed correctly? But how could dilated pupils tell him *what* I had been reading?

"You are very good," he went on wryly, "at being wrong, and you are constantly wrong! How can one be wrong so often! Dare I say logical thinking is not a prerequisite for English majors?"

Only my growl, too low for anyone else to hear, halted his flow of insults, but Holmes' acute hearing picked up what most didn't. "Oh, don't look so ferocious. You have a wonderful face, Watson, when your inner animal doesn't surface and distort your features. Ah, faces ..." He wore a dreamy expression. "They provide such a wealth of information. Yours told me what you were reading, although it was the tremor that shook your body—an indication of shock—that first attracted my attention. Were you not aware of The Augury stabbings? They happened in January of this year."

"I vaguely remember hearing about a doctor going nuts in a tea shop on Queen Street, but I didn't realize he'd stabbed eight people and killed one." This time I managed to suppress the tremor that threatened to shake me again. I wondered if I had walked past The Augury during one of my long walks after moving to the city last year. Perhaps I had even bought some tea there. I shuddered despite myself.

"Well, that explains your shock then. You ought to read the papers more often. You would have been less shocked had you been following the case, but I doubt you will trade your books of fiction for news of the real world."

"Yes, I'm a lost cause," I said, rolling my eyes. "I don't think I'll pick up a newspaper again for a long while."

Holmes laughed. "Well, I too am not familiar with all the details since the incident took place before my arrival. I have only just started perusing the older articles." He gave my phone, which lay on the seat next to him, an affectionate pat. His was nowhere to be seen, of course. "Anyway, shall I carry on with my assessment of your face?" As was usually the case when he talked, he strung together sentence after sentence without pause. "Your initial shock quickly became incredulity. You stared at your own cup of tea, forehead scrunched and one cheek quirked, as though pondering how something so violent could happen in a tea shop of all places. Then you felt sadness as you thought of the victims. The shake of your head and the purse of your lips, corners turned down, made it all quite clear. All that was done automatically and in quick succession, of course. The final clue was where you were looking: the upper left corner of the paper. If my recollection is correct, and it normally is, there is no other article there that would illicit shock, incredulity, and sadness." At last, he drew breath, looking satisfied.

"You have the layout of the newspaper memorized?!" I exclaimed.

Holmes shrugged modestly, which was a rare gesture for him. "Only the pages I consulted. Most of the features were rather dull. Sensational things ought to happen more often." The sly smile returned. "So, what do you think, Watson? Is Mr. William Kerfoot a clever thespian, bringing the devil into it with no logical basis as he did, or in desperate need of a psychiatrist?"

"There's no way he was acting," I said. "He walked into a tea shop in the middle of the day and started stabbing everyone within reach. He critically hurt the owner and killed someone else. It was a heinous act, not acting. Why would you think such a thing?"

"I wasn't referring to the deed itself but to the explanation he provided as to why he did it, his claim that he was ridding the world of devil worshippers."

Needless to say, I was perplexed by both Holmes' fascination with this case and his doubts. There had been cases like this in the past, perhaps not here in Toronto as far as I could remember—though one shouldn't trust my recollection since I rarely consulted the news—but elsewhere and around the world. I could hardly understand why Holmes was trying to dismantle William Kerfoot's motive.

His eyes shone ominously as he said, "Because he managed to kill *only* one person."

"Haven't you already filled your mind-reading quota for the day?" I asked irritably. My complaint was blatantly ignored, of course.

"Approximately three years ago," he began, "Mr. Kerfoot's medical licence was revoked due to allegations of professional misconduct, an affair with a patient or something of that sort. Hence, he is a medical man; that is key, Watson. He stabbed nine people in a short span and in a small space, yet he managed to kill only one: an unfortunate shop employee." He paused. "He knows which kind of cut can kill and which kind can save."

The incident seemed rather suspicious now that Holmes had pointed this detail out. "Are you saying his intended target was the shop employee, and having done her in, Kerfoot played the devil card to appear insane?"

Holmes nodded eagerly. "After all, what evil could lurk in a tea shop—"

"Actually, the place isn't a tea shop in the conventional sense," interrupted a nervous voice.

I hadn't been aware we'd had an audience, but the parlour was small enough that anything louder than a whispered conversation could be overheard. It didn't help that Holmes tended to project his voice when he was excited about something.

I looked over at the armchair where our fellow housemate, Arthur Gastrell, was sitting with a large book on his lap. It looked enormous in his hands; he was so small and thin that a rough wind could knock him over. Arthur was the last person I would have expected to interrupt; he didn't speak often, and hardly ever to me or Holmes, although he was always quick to smile when our paths crossed.

The room had gotten rather quiet suddenly. "What do you mean by that?" I asked. "Don't they sell tea there?"

"They sell a lot more than that," Arthur replied, slowly turning red under our inquiring gaze, the effect all the more intensified by his copper-cherry hair. Even his scarce scatter of freckles seemed to glow with colour. Yet his shyness didn't stop him from leaving his armchair to join us. He hovered hesitantly for a moment though before taking a seat next to me. He had absentmindedly brought his book along: *Principles of Food Engineering*.

"You see," he began. "I grew up in the Queen Street West area, and that shop's been there for over two decades, handed down from mother to daughter. I passed it every day on my way to school. Even then, there'd been wild rumours. Apparently, they sell all sorts of things and, er, services."

It was clear he would need some poking and prodding to keep him talking; I gently inquired about the "services," my anticipation building.

"Tea-leaf readings and seances, among other things," Arthur said. "The place is basically an occult shop. The owner is Wiccan."

Holmes leaned in with interest. "Oh, I am surprised the nature of the shop wasn't reported in the papers. These sorts of details make for a relishing story."

"It was initially," Arthur said. "But that soon led to chatter about whether the attack should be considered a hate crime against the Wiccan community. There was also an argument that the emphasis on the occult was stealing the limelight from the victims. I think it's become less problematic to forget the occult angle."

A thought suddenly hit me: Holmes had been wrong; William Kerfoot hadn't brought the devil into it with no logical basis. He'd had inspiration. I was quick to bring this to my friend's attention, of course, and was secretly pleased to see him frown.

"I suppose we shall see," he murmured moodily as he sunk back into the seat, his arched back conforming to the plush sofa. His hooded eyelids slammed shut, effectively ending the conversation.

Arthur shifted uncomfortably as he eyed his armchair and stroked the cover of his book with a distracted air.

He was clearly contemplating returning to his chair, perhaps relieved that his brief moment of mingling had been cut short by Holmes' dozing.

But Holmes wasn't asleep.

In fact, the speed at which his eyes sprang open again made me realize that his mind had been soaring as his body reposed. Fingers clasped, back now straight as a wall, he stared at Arthur for a moment before speaking.

"What troubles you, Gastrell?"

CHAPTER 2

Drebber's Demise

"Oh! A mystery is it?" I cried, rubbing my hands.

—Sir Arthur Conan Doyle, *A Study in Scarlet*

SILENCE FILLED THE AIR AS ARTHUR STARED BACK, although not in the scrutinizing way Holmes often did. Rather, with his mouth agape and large blue eyes magnified by his glasses, he looked like a dumbfounded child.

"Oh, I-I'm just thinking about my courses for next semester. I heard most people fail *Food Microbiology* and—"

But Holmes wagged a finger. "Perhaps academic woes preoccupied you for the past hour as you tried to get an early start on your readings but were utterly confused by the first chapter and found yourself unable to progress any further. I was referring to your less trivial troubles, specifically the one you were reminded of as you eavesdropped on our conversation."

Our poor housemate coloured once again, his freckled cheeks now perfectly matching his red hair. "I didn't mean to—"

"Don't worry about it, Arthur," I interrupted. "My friend here doesn't realize how loud his voice gets when he's showing off."

Normally, this would have been followed by a snide remark from Holmes, likely on the topic of my comparatively limited intellect. Today, however, he ignored me. His eyes remained fixed on Arthur, and his fingers started drumming on the armrest.

"Despite living in the same house for the past four months," Holmes said, "you and I have not exchanged a single word, although in all fairness, I seldom see you conversing with anyone. Not that I blame you. They are a mundane lot." He didn't bother to lower his voice as he said this, of course. Luckily, most of Baker House's ruffians-in-residence, who especially enjoyed hectoring Holmes when he spewed insults, were on holiday.

He went on, "Despite your solitary, timid nature, something compelled you to speak to us. If you were longing for company, you could have joined us one hour ago when we all settled here. Instead, it was the mention of an atrocious act—and devil worshippers—that brought you to us. So, I ask you again, Gastrell, what troubles you?"

The room was remarkably quiet, possibly due to Holmes' commandeering voice … or perhaps everyone had been listening all along, feigning conversation only when the stillness became noticeable.

"I was just thinking about something that happened at work," Arthur admitted. "We're not, er, supposed to talk about it."

"Well, you've already started talking about it, so you might as well continue," chirped a high-pitched, girlish voice.

I grimaced internally as a tall young woman with shimmering white-gold hair and eyes the colour of grass in the summertime glided toward us. It wasn't a good idea to make a sour face in the presence of Christa Bretti since she had a talent for making people feel small with a single glare. She wore that same glare now as she joined us, garbed as usual in something expensive. I, preferring a simple shirt and jeans, usually found Christa ridiculous to look at and mostly ignored her. She returned the favour, and as a result, I knew little about her, apart from her being a theatre major and having an incessant need to taunt Arthur. Even the holidays hadn't softened her spirits; she stood looming over him, arms crossed and fingers tapping impatiently on her cashmere sleeve.

By this point, conversation had stalled completely. It was obvious that everyone in the room had tuned in to Arthur's story. Some had the courtesy to gaze elsewhere, like the well-mannered twins, Kofi and Kwame Makutsi, the eccentric Marieta Charr, and Elodie Willis—or as I liked to call her, Christa's shadow. In appearance, Elodie—with her braided hair, ebony skin, and stick-like frame—was the opposite of her best friend. She was an impressionable girl who existed, or so it seemed to me, only to serve her high and mighty friend. She was far kinder than Christa, and I had always wondered how those two had become the thickest of friends. Apparently, Elodie was also friendly with Arthur; when he glanced at her helplessly as she gave a quick, disguised peek our way, she gave him a faint nod and smiled.

"I work for Crooked Forest Adventures," Arthur began, "which offers outdoor activities like snowshoeing and dogsledding. I've been working there since last winter. Some of the mushers there like to horseplay." His face hardened, and I suspected that *he* was the subject of said horseplay. "But apart from that, it's a great place to work. There are acres of evergreens, and the Humber River is nearby. Nothing out of the ordinary ever happened until about two weeks ago." He paused as though hoping his audience would leave out of boredom. No such thing happened, of course.

"Some of the staff were doing safety checks on the dogsledding paths one morning when they found a dead Alaskan Malamute in the woods near a path. It was one of our dogs, an older dog named Drebber. He'd been a bit sick the past couple days, so he wasn't supposed to be on the trails. But there he was—" Arthur shuddered, apparently recalling what I imagined was a dreadful scene. The death of a dog was a terrible thing—I had grown up with two myself, both long gone now—but there was something peculiar about Arthur's reaction that instilled in me a sense of foreboding.

"Wait, wait," interrupted a heavily accented voice. "Are you sure you should be disclosing this? I hope you're not breaking a secrecy agreement." The light roll of the *r*'s and the undulating pitch almost made it sound like Gwilym Lestrade was singing as his rat-like face and short, slight frame materialized next to Christa.

Holmes groaned loudly. "Willie, my boy, you have a knack for picking the worst time to interrupt."

There was no affection in these words. Holmes openly despised Gwilym, who in turn took pride in besting Holmes, not that he could often. Gwilym hailed from a speck of a town in Wales, not far from Holmes' hometown of London, and I often wondered if their animosity had taken root before they had crossed the Atlantic. Like Holmes, Gwilym was pedantic and often regurgitated facts from his textbooks on psychology and criminology. He was also a stickler for the law, which fit well with his ambition of joining Scotland Yard someday.

Like Holmes, I didn't care much for him, mostly because he employed two oversized goons, whom he launched at Holmes occasionally. Today Gwilym was alone though, his Praetorian guards having gone home for the holidays. But without them at either side, he could rub shoulders, literally, with Christa, much to his pleasure and her annoyance. She gave him a slight shove, which he appeared not to notice.

"The name's *Gwilym*," he pronounced hotly to Holmes. "It's *not* Willie. I've told you this time and again."

"And I've told you many times that *Gwilym* is just the Welsh version of *William*," Holmes drawled, "so it is hardly erroneous to call you Willie. *William* glides far more smoothly off the tongue, don't you think? Why must the Welsh complicate such a simple name?"

Although his ears had turned a bright shade of pink, Gwilym only huffed at Holmes. He then turned expectantly to Arthur, ready to unleash his displaced wrath. Sensing this, Arthur quickly mumbled that he hadn't signed anything. That appeared to satisfy Gwilym, and he prompted Arthur to go on with his story.

"Drebber was — his body — it was so strange … There was very little blood, but his body had been s-split open, from throat to abdomen, and there was a gaping hole in the middle. Someone had removed most of his internal organs, washed them, and placed them around the b-body." Arthur shook his head, trying to rid himself of the vivid recollection. "There were also splotches of red in the snow, as though someone meant to draw something. They could've been symbols."

"How interesting," Holmes murmured. "Did you recognize any of these symbols? Were they perhaps letters instead?"

"It was all very messy by the time we found the body. The ink — or whatever it was that was — got mixed in with the snow. I couldn't make out anything specific."

Christa looked horror-struck. "Oh, gosh, do you think the dog's blood was used to draw the symbols?" The question, which remained unanswered, made those of us more human and less mechanical shudder. In fact, so shaken was Marieta Charr that she stood abruptly and exited the room, wanting to hear no more of the tale. Holmes, falling into the latter category, barely stirred.

"What happened after the discovery?" he asked.

"We cancelled all the bookings for the day and called the police," Arthur said. "They didn't show up until about three hours later. I don't blame them. The roads were bad and we're more or less in the middle of nowhere, just acres of forest all around. We were all questioned, but nobody saw anything or anyone strange. None of the locks to the dogs' areas had been tampered with. As far as we know, the investigation's gone nowhere. The company opened its doors two days later, told us to be quiet about what had happened, and managed to keep it out of the papers." This appeared to annoy him very much.

"Did you observe any other clues?" Holmes asked. "Perhaps footprints in the snow near the body? That could at least tell you if the perpetrator was a man or woman and the number of people involved."

Arthur shook his head. "By the time I got to the scene, there were footprints everywhere. Word had gotten out and much of the staff had gone to have a look." He added the last bit sounding guilty since he too had muddied the crime scene.

"Troubling, very troubling," Gwilym murmured. "The crime clearly indicates a lack of conscience, maybe someone with antisocial personality disord—"

"You mean like a psychopath?" Christa asked.

"That's not a preferred nor scientific term," Gwilym said matter-of-factly. "I'm worried that what's begun as an animal killing may someday escalate to human killings. If Crooked Forest Adventures is as isolated as you say, Arthur, then someone at the company must've done it. A stranger would've been spotted. Wouldn't you agree, Sherlock?" He didn't wait for Holmes to add his two cents though before turning back to Arthur.

"Arthur, would you describe any of your colleagues as irresponsible, aggressive, perhaps a liar or a thief? Does anyone show uncontrolled sexual behaviour? Was anyone fired recently? That could be indicative of someone unable to keep a job. These are all traits of someone with antisocial personality disorder."

Gwilym said all this with such excitement and speed that Arthur blinked helplessly before finally responding, "Um, I don't think so."

Holmes, I noticed, looked amused as he watched the exchange.

"But you said some of the mushers enjoy horseplay," Gwilym insisted. "I assume you're referring to workplace harassment? That qualifies as aggression. Is there someone in particular who's a bigger rowdy than the rest?"

Arthur didn't seem happy about naming names. "Well, um, there's D—" He stopped abruptly, glancing at Christa, whose eyes, to my surprise, had become threatening slits. "There's, er, Jibril. He's not a nice guy, but he wouldn't hurt the dogs. Actually, he treats the dogs better than he does people."

This obviously hampered Gwilym's theory and compelled him to spew some more psychological discourse, parts of which I missed as I contemplated the name Arthur had been about to divulge. Why on earth had he stopped at the sight of Christa? And why had she looked so enraged? I looked over at Holmes, but there was a faraway look on his face, only traces of his initial amusement lingering.

"Sometimes you just can't tell," Gwilym was saying. "Then something traumatic happens and the other identity surfaces. This new person can be completely different—violent, cruel to those he once cared about, murderous even—*what*?"

The cause of his abrupt stop was Holmes: he had snapped out of his reverie and was mumbling something. All heads turned to him, even those that had been pretending to do something else.

"'*Though this be madness, yet there is method in 't,*'" Holmes repeated more coherently this time.

"What's that supposed to mean?" Gwilym demanded.

I knew Holmes had recited a passage from *Hamlet*, which was surprising in itself since he considered works of fiction to be "a good-for-nothing waste of time" and often ridiculed my mandate to never touch nonfiction, which he preached was more useful in life. What was more puzzling was *why* he had quoted Shakespeare. Instead of answering, his steely grey eyes glided from face to face. Finally, he spoke.

"In case some of you were not following the conversation from the beginning, Gastrell here approached Watson and I as we were discussing the unfortunate stabbings at The Augury. Unless you abstain from newspapers, like Watson here, you will know that the perpetrator justified his crime by declaring that he was ridding the city of devil worshippers. *That* is what reminded Gastrell of the strange event that had occurred in his workplace." Holmes' wandering gaze fell on Arthur. "It is obvious that you have some ideas quite different from the far-fetched ones Lestrade proposed."

Arthur blinked. "I do?"

Holmes nodded. "Oh, yes, you do, but I understand your hesitation." He smiled, but there was more relish than mirth in it. "I too would think twice if I were to perhaps explain away troublesome happenings with witchcraft and devilry."

CHAPTER 3

Invitation into the Wilderness

"Now and again a case turns up which is a little more complex. Then I have to bustle about and see things with my own eyes."

—Sir Arthur Conan Doyle, *A Study in Scarlet*

PAUSING A MOMENT TO TAKE IN THE BEFUDDLED LOOKS ON the faces of his audience, Sherlock Holmes grinned wryly. "Of course, only a fool would believe witches were responsible for mutilating our canine friend," he went on, chuckling.

It was indeed a chuckle; it would be misleading to describe it as laughter because such a description would make it lose its most defining feature—its ability to irritate the person it was being directed at. This particular chuckle usually made an appearance when Holmes dismissed something—or someone—as ridiculous. I had been on the receiving end of that chuckle many times, and now it was Arthur's turn.

Arthur blinked rapidly in embarrassment. "I don't actually believe witches sacrificed Drebber," he said. "It's just that … well, it's all so strange. I-I don't understand any of it. And then there were those symbols …"

"And that's where psychological science can help," Gwilym declared, "to shed light on the complex workings of the human mind. The victim may have been a dog, but the crime reeks of a human element. Psychology can help us understand the *why*, which will lead us to the *who*."

"That's a load of hogwash!" Holmes interjected. "What we need is evidence, tangible clues that point to someone's culpability. In other words, the situation calls for a detective, not a psychologist." He eyed with disdain the large textbook Gwilym had left behind in his seat.

Gwilym sneered. "I don't see one of those in the room."

"I am rather competent in the science of detection," Holmes countered haughtily, "but it is of little surprise that you have failed to notice. Observation is not your strong suit, likely one of the hazards of sticking your nose in a textbook all day long."

Like the rest of Baker House, Gwilym had on occasion witnessed Holmes' talent for crafting narratives from details none had noticed. When Holmes was in one of his more sociable moods, he made a grand display of it, which often stirred incredulity and wonder, but also great irritation. The latter didn't make him think twice about opening his mouth to reveal someone's silly secret or something truly ugly—like a crime. So far, he had exposed a kleptomaniac and a peddler of what my peers referred to as "street pharmacy," among other paltry offenders. There was also the chilling case we had undertaken only a few months before, which had left Baker House's former housekeeper, Mrs. Martha Hudson, out of commission.

Hence, my faith in Sherlock Holmes was unwavering. Gwilym, on the other hand, had been on the verge of disgorging a mouthful of rude words when a large shadow darted past the doorway to the parlour. I nearly yelped, but could one blame me after all this talk of the occult? Luckily, I clamped my lips shut before any sound could escape, although I did stiffen, rather noticeably it seemed.

"Do compose yourself, Watson," Holmes said. "It is only Mrs. Kerrigan."

That did little to ease the tension that immediately filled the room. In fact, the name only inspired fresh fretfulness; even those who had been sitting facing away from the doorway now froze. Such was the effect our new housekeeper, Mrs. Agnes Kerrigan, had on us. Holmes was oddly impervious to her perpetually scowling face or her tendency to snarl at the residents for no proper reason. Still, even he thought she was "mad as a bag of ferrets."

It was not surprising that Mrs. Kerrigan was working on a holiday. The woman kept strange hours, sometimes diligently sweeping and cleaning at dawn, other times disappearing for ages before turning up when she was least expected. But the house looked pristine under her management, and perhaps that was why the university ignored the numerous complaints against her.

In the kitchen, some pots clanged. I desperately hoped she wasn't making one of those awful soups she indulged in sometimes; the stinking smell lingered in the house for hours afterwards. It was our great misfortune that Mrs. Kerrigan had replaced the strict but motherly Mrs. Hudson, but luckily, our new housekeeper wasn't in charge of the cooking.

Gwilym tried to look nonchalant about the lady's sudden appearance although he straightened almost automatically. I was wondering whether she had scolded him for slouching when he spoke in a noticeably lower voice. "Where there's crime, there's psychology. You need the second to understand the first. I bet a psychologist could solve the crime. After all, the police have gotten nowhere with their investigation."

Holmes smirked. "I hope you are not offering yourself as a proxy for a psychologist." He laughed heartily but coldly. "Do *you* intend to investigate this crime, Gwilym Lestrade?"

The answer Holmes wanted to hear was obviously in the negative; that much was evident from his belittling tone. But Gwilym's bravado only grew. His chest swelled and he thrust his chin up as though he were having his portrait done. His small frame loomed over Holmes' seated one.

"Why not?" he asked. "I can bring a fresh perspective to the case."

Holmes chuckled yet again. "With your absurd theory that we are dealing with a psychopath with multiple personalities?"

"Stop distorting what I said. I can play detective just as well as you, if not better, because I actually understand people."

The conversation was spiralling into a preposterous argument. The last of the calm my chamomile tea had instilled in me slowly ebbed away.

"Need I remind you both that you're college students, not detectives or psychologists?" I broke in.

Neither Holmes nor Gwilym even looked in my direction. In fact, no one seemed inclined to lend a voice of support. Everyone was far too engrossed by the tirade of insults being exchanged, pleased that their quiet evening had mutated into something provocative. *Barbarians*, I thought. In all fairness, Elodie and the twins looked on with disinterest, but there was a ruthless shine in Christa's eyes. Even Arthur looked amused, although it was he who brought an end to the verbal tug-of-war.

"Why don't you *both* investigate?" he suggested. "You can come as customers and poke around. I could get you some free passes."

I hadn't thought a face could express both satisfaction and severe irritation, but seeing the mirrored expressions on Holmes' and Gwilym's faces, I now knew this was quite possible. Both their eyes crinkled with delight, but their lips were pursed in contempt like two unruly children forced to share a toy. Both did, however, offer a curt nod of acceptance, doing their best to appear indifferent. It was Christa who now looked unsatisfied.

"What about me and Elodie? We want to poke around too," she exclaimed.

I nearly laughed. The others smiled faintly. We were all undoubtedly picturing Christa waddling through a field of snow in her large fur coat, searching for clues. The notion was ridiculous, and I suspected she simply wanted to ride on a sled pulled by sled dogs. I could already hear her whine through the whole investigation.

Somehow, Arthur managed to remain composed and nodded charitably. "You can both come too. It's a good thing there are lots of spots left for this Saturday. There's supposed to be a storm in the morning, so there aren't too many bookings. Actually, I can probably get passes for all of you." He looked over at me and the twins.

Kofi and Kwame declined the invitation, declaring that dogsledding was a cruel sport they wished to take no part in. They were so soft-spoken and their words so polite that we all instantly agreed, although none withdrew their invitation. Holmes and Gwilym's thirst for the chase and their competition with one another wouldn't allow them to even consider it. Christa, on the other hand, often showed off her costly furs without grievance, so I wagered she cared little about sled dogs. Elodie glanced out the window vacantly; she would go where her best friend went.

Everyone's attention fell on me. I had no intention of spending my precious Saturday in the wilderness, tormented by the bitter cold and my bickering housemates. Drebber's death was mysterious to be sure, but something about the whole affair stirred a sense of foreboding in me. It was perhaps intuition that warned me to stay far away from this mess. I politely refused. The light in Holmes' eyes dimmed, or so I thought.

"All right then," Arthur said. "I'll get four passes for snowshoeing and dogsledding. You'll have to figure out a way to get there though. It's over an hour's drive away. Gwilym, you have a car, right?"

Gwilym nodded. Then, glancing at Holmes, he said, "It's such a tiny old thing though. I can fit the ladies comfortably in the back, but the front seat is out of commission unfortunately." He didn't specify why this was the case. "Sorry, Sherlock, old boy. Looks like there's no room for you."

Holmes stared at him furiously, but then his expression softened. Wearing the faintest of smiles, his shrewd eyes settled on me.

*

Winter is my least favourite season. My aversion probably stems from the long, stormy winters that ravaged the town I grew up in, where no amount of sun melted the icy snow that persisted for months and months. Much to my relief, winters in Toronto were nearly nonexistent, save for the brief spells of bitterly cold days that accompanied January and February. Once, long ago, snow had blanketed the streets all season long, a classmate had told me. Now, the snowflakes melted even before they hit downtown, and the clumps that managed to accumulate were promptly salted and obliterated. However, thanks to Arthur's strange story and Holmes' inability to drive, I was cruelly dragged away from the comforts of Baker House to a place where winter thrived.

Holmes and I left that Saturday morning in our rental car, Arthur having (unfortunately) secured a last-minute pass for me. A wave of flurries bombarded us as we progressed north, turning rapidly into thick, corpulent snowflakes—although even that was too unsuitable a description for the white chunks hitting the windshield. By the time we were halfway through the journey, a blizzard had swept over us. Visibility became so poor

27

that the few unlucky souls on the highway, namely us, had to pull over. The snow came pelting down, completely obscuring what was only two feet in front of us, and the wind howled as we stayed locked in the car.

I was rather comfortable buried inside my thermal jacket, with the heater turned up, but Holmes stared sulkily out the window and complained about not making the one o'clock rendezvous. In truth, he hardly cared about being punctual; I knew he was furiously wondering whether Gwilym had made it through the storm. The idea of someone else trampling all over the crime scene—though I was certain it hadn't remained intact more than two weeks later—or worse, Gwilym making some grand discovery, was more than Holmes could endure. Secretly, I was hoping we would miss the grand excursion.

However, even the weather seemed to cower under Holmes' mumbled rant. Much to my chagrin, the snow began falling more gently, and although the road was now covered with a thick white layer, we managed to meander along until we finally reached Crooked Forest Adventures a little after one o'clock.

As Arthur had said, the place was literally in the middle of nowhere, marked by a brightly lit sign and accessible by only a single, snow-covered road—Brixton Road—lined by frosted forest on both sides. There was no parking lot; we simply parked on the side of the road, copying the two dozen or so vehicles that looked like ice-age relics. A small clearing marked the entrance to the grounds, but it was devoid of both people and further instructions on where to go. Only footsteps remained, and those we followed silently.

The pathless walk lasted about five minutes. Even if I had bothered Holmes with mundane conversation, it wouldn't have been enough to stir the eerie reticence of the acres of land that surrounded us. It felt as though I could hear everything and nothing at all, which was alarming even for someone who had grown up in a small bucolic town. Holmes though, judging by the expression on his face, seemed enticed by it. It did seem rather peaceful, but little did we know that somewhere within the vast expanse of forest, something unnatural sullied the snow.

The small clearing led to a large open area enclosed by gigantic evergreen trees. I spotted two outbuildings to my right and about twenty people loosely gathered around a bonfire to my left. One person turned and broke into a sluggish run toward us.

"Hi, guys! So glad you made it." Arthur panted through the blue scarf draped around his face. In fact, little of him was visible. An oversized parka and puffy snow pants amplified his petite form. The visible bits of his face were a startling shade of red, which complemented the ginger hair poking out of his hat. He had evidently been in the cold for a long time.

"Hello, you two!" boomed a deep voice. "I see you've met one of our junior guides." Another man had manifested like a spectre, a man who in all respects was Arthur's opposite. He gave Arthur what was supposed to be a playful push but that sent him staggering instead. Taking Arthur's place and facing us with a large grin, the man introduced himself as Dimitri Komarov. Even as we followed him to the others, I remained a bit mesmerized by Dimitri's shoulder-length mahogany hair, which was exposed to the elements and danced freely in the wind, and the way his unzipped dark blue coat flapped around, almost supernaturally careful not to block his perfectly curated abs. It seemed as if the cold couldn't penetrate his skin.

"Now that the whole group is here, let's get started!" Dimitri exclaimed once we joined the crowd.

As he began talking about the company and the thrilling experience the staff had in store for us, I saw that Holmes' wandering eyes were at work. I decided, almost competitively, to do the same. If I was to spend the next few hours in the wilderness, I might as well play detective.

It was easy to differentiate between the twenty "adventurers" and the half dozen or so guides and instructors. The latter, apart from Arthur, wore the same blue jacket with the company's logo—a snow-covered evergreen tree that appeared to be enduring heavy winds—stitched on the back. With Gwilym's theory that Drebber's killer worked at Crooked Forest still on my mind, I studied each person, attempting to sniff out something sinister. But my eyes glided over their faces, and nearly none captured my attention.

The plump older woman with the rosy cheeks caught my eye only because her dark eyebrows contrasted so sharply with her white, heavily freckled face that they looked as though they had been painted on. Her unruly curly hair, which she had managed to tame into a low bun, was also blacker than black. And a handsome man grabbed my attention with his perfectly aligned moustache and beard. He oddly resembled Holmes with his pallor, dark hair, and great height, although Holmes was clean-shaven and a stick figure compared to the breadth of this man. However, none of these people looked as though they could mutilate a dog.

The adventurers, who were already getting jittery from the cold, stood close to the fire, which looked pathetic with its small, feeble flames. Those folks had no bearing on the case though, plus there were far too many of them for me to study, so I didn't bother. Instead, I moved closer to them, unable to bear the chill that had invaded my boots. Holmes stood apart stoically; I simply didn't understand how his wool coat—the same one he had worn in the fall—kept him warm. He wore no hat, scarf, or gloves, whereas I had one of everything and was wishing I had brought more.

Preoccupied as I was with staying warm and wondering how I would endure the next couple hours outdoors, I failed to notice that Arthur had come around and divided us into groups. He had purposely kept the Baker House crew together. The first group departed for dogsledding; the rest of us were to wait at the campsite until the snowshoes arrived. Again, I saw Holmes watching the remaining adventurers and staff carefully, as though he were stalking prey.

Quite unexpectedly, our eyes met, and I nearly toppled off the haystack I was sitting on. He glared at me for a moment as though to question why I was sitting around when there was work to be done. He then meandered across the campsite to the only adventurer in our group who had come without a companion, a shivering young blonde woman who looked a few years older than us, and started talking to her. I watched them for a few minutes; for someone who could spend days without uttering a word, Sherlock Holmes was conversing with gusto.

Having received no invitation to join, I overheard bits of their chitchat only when the wind decided not to howl. Their discussion began with commonplace topics like the weather and moved on to more frivolous things like smartphone apps. I grew puzzled; Holmes seldom engaged in featherbrained chatter. What was his game?

Perhaps he tolerated it because, like him, his new friend was British. Had he somehow divined she was from his homeland and approached her for that reason? Since our last case, I hadn't seen any evidence of homesickness; Holmes seemed to be adjusting well to his new home here, but perhaps not as well as I had thought. *Ah, let him mingle then*, I thought. He seemed so engrossed by the woman that he hadn't even noticed that Gwilym had already started to poke around; he, Christa, and Elodie were standing by one of the outbuildings, peering in through a window. I watched them for a few minutes before my attention settled once again on the chilly air and the surrounding forest. Despite the openness, the thicket of trees made one feel trapped.

When I looked around again, I saw that Holmes' circle now consisted of a pretty woman wearing a lilac hijab in addition to the blonde. The women had their phones out and were chatting animatedly about a trivia app called Triviatrix. Holmes hadn't pulled out his phone; it was probably accumulating dust in some neglected corner of his room in Baker House. Oddly, he preferred to consult his old pocket watch for the time, which I suspected had sentimental value although he hotly refuted this. The ornate trinket complemented his character better than a smartphone ever could. That didn't stop him from occasionally borrowing mine, of course.

I tuned out Holmes and his posse to check on Gwilym. He and the ladies were bent over something in the snow. A minute later, high-pitched voices drew me back to Holmes, and I saw that his companions had launched a trivia competition. Holmes played for both sides, providing correct answers for questions that would baffle most people. It didn't seem like he was investigating anything. Meanwhile, Gwilym had abandoned all discretion and was studying the salted path leading to the outbuilding. The staff seemed not to notice.

Despite his efforts, I didn't believe Gwilym could solve this case, nor would Holmes since he didn't even seem to be trying. At the same time, I felt there was something sinister about this crime, a complex sort of evil. I couldn't help but think that Holmes' deductions and Gwilym's psychology were no match for the forces at play here.

CHAPTER 4

A Woman's Intuition

"I have seen too much not to know that the impression of a woman may be more valuable than the conclusion of an analytical reasoner."

—Sir Arthur Conan Doyle, *The Man with the Twisted Lip*

"OKAY, FOLKS, OFF WE GO!" DECLARED OUR SNOWSHOEING instructor once we had put on our snowshoes sometime later.

I didn't move right away though, and it wasn't because my snowshoes were hanging awkwardly off my boots. It was the instructor herself who had turned me to stone. I hadn't seen her among the staff earlier; she had appeared by the fire only moments before. I shot a questioning glance at Holmes, who looked intrigued. Gwilym and the others were as puzzled as I was; we were all wondering why Arthur hadn't told us our housemate, Marieta Charr, also worked at Crooked Forest. I remembered her abrupt departure from the parlour the evening Arthur had told us about Drebber's death; perhaps she hadn't wanted us to know.

Marieta's sylphlike figure hovered by the fire, and she smiled radiantly as she scanned the adventurers. Then her dark eyes fell on Holmes, then me, and then Gwilym and the ladies. Her expression froze.

Despite sharing a home, I didn't know Marieta very well. She studied visual arts, was an expert painter, and generally kept to herself; that was it. The consensus was that she was odd—very odd—and more so even than Holmes. I had always thought there was something otherworldly about her, although not in a bad way. She simply had an abundance of grace that made it seem as though she were floating whenever she moved. Her raven-black hair, flowing dresses, and divergent choice of jewellery, which often featured crescent moons and stars, only added to her eclectic elegance—and mystery. When she spoke, her words flowed slowly, like pouring honey, yet they were compelling. In my opinion, she was tranquility personified, but the rest of Baker House preferred to focus on the macabre rumours that had drifted about since the start of the school year. For a moment, I contemplated those strange stories, and the terrible image of a mutilated dog inevitably popped into my head.

"She doesn't look happy to see us," I muttered to Holmes.

"'Happy' would definitely not be the correct word," he whispered back, looking thoughtful. "Dear Marieta seems worried, Watson. Very worried."

I too was worried. Not to mention, this was my first time wearing snowshoes, so tripping and falling flat on my face was bound to happen.

Regardless, we trudged across the clearing and entered the forest in single file. Holmes installed himself right behind Marieta, and I behind him. Behind me came a Japanese couple and their little daughter, then the blonde woman Holmes had been talking to earlier, followed by Christa, Elodie, and Gwilym. The line was flanked by the other woman Holmes had been conversing with and what appeared to be her scowling preteen daughter.

It turned out snowshoeing in the woods was light exercise for the legs—once one learned to stop tripping over one's snowshoes—and overwhelming exercise for the eyes. The chatter resumed once every step stopped requiring concentrated effort. Christa was giggling like a child as she began photographing everything: trees, muddy snow, stray twigs. "Photographing evidence," she mouthed with a wink when I turned around to give her an incredulous look.

But I could no longer demean her for taking pictures of the scenery, even if her justification was ridiculous. It was impossible to grow bored of looking at tree after snow-covered tree. Even I pulled out my phone to snap a few shots; so preoccupied was I that I even forgot how cold it was.

Marieta, who was as unperturbed by the chill as Dimitri had been, seemed slightly cheerier in the calming wilderness. Hatless as she was, her dark hair thrashed about in the wind, exposing star-shaped gold earrings. Her high cheekbones glistened in the sunlight, and her unzipped jacket flapped around, revealing a heavyweight, chartreuse jumpsuit of wool. The colour went quite well with her tawny skin; she would have been the picture of sunnier times had she just smiled. Her mood improved further as we went deeper into the woods though, and she occasionally regaled the group with an interesting nature fact in that honeyed voice of hers. The forest remained as silent as ever as we cut a fresh path across the snow, always watching, and perhaps frowning at us for talking too loudly.

I overheard the names of some of our companions thanks to all the chitchat. The hijabed woman Holmes had been talking to was Zara Atallah, and her sulking daughter was Amira; Zara snapped angrily at the girl when she loudly proclaimed dogsledding to be a "cruel abomination." The Japanese couple, Kenji and Anna

Sato, were quiet for the most part, but that was because they were constantly preoccupied with their three-year-old daughter, Misaki, who liked to fling snow at people's backs and giggle wildly when they turned around, bemused. When the child wasn't causing mischief or brooding, she was the most adorable thing I had ever seen with her spiky black hair that shot in all directions — and that her mother was always furiously attempting to tame — large coffee eyes, and rosy cheeks, the glow of which Christa's costly makeup could never match.

Twenty minutes into the hike, we stopped at a small clearing for a break. I started snapping photos with my phone again — until the word "dead" flitted into my ears. Holmes and the blonde woman were engaged in deep conversation.

"A dead dog? That's messed up, Leslie," came Holmes' loud, startled voice. The tone and wording of this reply grabbed my attention before the meaning sunk in. Holmes *never* spoke so colloquially. Ever. He was formal, everywhere and to everyone, and his speech was antiquated to say the least. It was one of his eccentricities; he sounded as though someone had plucked him out of Victorian-era London and dumped him unceremoniously in modern times. However, he was bizarre enough in other ways too that even people from a century ago would have thought him unusual.

The blonde, whose name I now gathered to be Leslie, nodded vigorously. "A friend told me. I wanted to check this place out before I left."

"What dead dog? Where?" cried Amira, pushing past her mother.

"Er," Holmes started. "Perhaps it's best if you don't hear—"

"Here, of course," Leslie interjected tactlessly. She shot a curious glance at Marieta, who was taking a photograph of the Sato family. Even though her back was turned, I could tell Marieta was aware of the conversation; her shoulders had stiffened.

Perhaps Holmes had sensed this as well, for he called out innocently, "Hey, Marieta! Is it true that a dog was found murdered in these woods recently?"

"Have the people in this stupid place been killing dogs?!" screamed Amira. "Isn't it bad enough that you all enslave them for sport?" She looked as though she had another mouthful to spurt out, but her mother, rushing to her side, quickly interjected and dragged her away. The wind blew angry words in Arabic to our ears.

Poor Marieta looked about for a moment, paralyzed, before stammering a reply. "We love our d-dogs, and there haven't been any dead animals. Let's continue, please." She threw Holmes a dirty look; she, of course, didn't know why were really here.

We resumed our hike, but an ominous silence hung over us. Again, I found myself behind Holmes and he behind Marieta, who walked faster than before — as if to distance herself from the group. Naturally, Holmes would have none of that. He skipped ahead despite the snowshoes and asked bluntly, "Marieta, if I may ask, are you a witch?"

Marieta stopped abruptly and whisked around. Consequently, the whole group came to a confused stop.

"What are you saying?" she asked quietly. To the adventurers, she hollered a distraction, "Can anyone tell me which way is north?" As the group immersed itself in mumbled discussion, I inched closer to the agitated instructor and her inquisitor.

"You're wearing pentagram earrings," Holmes pointed out, and immediately I realized that what I had initially thought were stars were indeed pentagrams.

"That doesn't make her a *witch*," I scoffed, careful to keep my voice hushed. It was clear Marieta wanted the conversation to be exclusive to us. In fact, she looked as though she wanted to disappear, but she nodded encouragingly at me and cast Holmes a frosty glare.

But my friend was hardly the type to give up. "The tattoo on the side of your neck: *that* is the Triple Loon."

I had no idea what that meant, but apparently Marieta did. I had barely gotten a glimpse of the waxing moon on her neck when her hand whipped through the air and pulled the collar of her jacket up, completely obscuring the symbol.

"The Triple *Moon*," she corrected in an annoyed voice. "It represents the divine feminine—the maiden, the mother, and—" She stopped abruptly, sighed, and then released her hold on her collar. Holmes had purposely mistaken the tattoo to get her to talk; he was shrewd like that. "Lots of people have this tattoo."

"Is that so?" Holmes smiled pleasantly. "Do a lot of people wear jewellery for protection?"

I nearly laughed. Witchcraft didn't exist and protection charms didn't work; Holmes was being infuriating on purpose, although to what end I didn't know. My smile faltered, however, when Marieta's eyes shifted involuntarily to the necklace that hung around her neck. The pendant, an opaque green stone with an odd drop of red at the centre, caught my eye, and I looked from Marieta to Holmes; both wore the most sombre of expressions.

"What do you need protection from?" Holmes asked.

In response, Marieta hastily zipped up her coat. "North is straight ahead, folks. It's time we head back to the campsite." Her voice trembled. Perhaps she was susceptible to the effects of winter after all, although I suspected something else had made her shiver.

*

Precisely twenty-five minutes later, we exited the woods and returned to the campsite. Marieta had practically sprinted toward the outbuilding, leaving a dogsled instructor—the one with the neat moustache and beard—to watch the group. He introduced himself as Jibril Özdemir. I recognized the name right away although Jibril didn't seem as mean-spirited as Arthur had described him.

"But there's no such thing as witches or magic," I whispered to Holmes as we seated ourselves on a large haystack. "You ridiculed Arthur for just thinking it, and now you're acting as though, as though protection necklaces are real."

Holmes merely shrugged. For once, his reticence didn't bother me much; my attention was divided between him and Jibril, who, much to my chagrin, was standing by the fire talking heartily with Christa and Elodie. Even the subdued Elodie wore a grin so enormous, her face looked distorted. Their torturous chitchat finally ended when a voice buzzed out of Jibril's radio, informing him that the dogsleds were ready.

As Christa passed us, she murmured smugly, "See? We're investigating." I couldn't help but roll my eyes.

We were dragged away from the fire then, with mixed feelings of excitement and displeasure, and given a mush lesson, from which I retained very little; I had been far too occupied by Jibril's angular jaws. Christa and Elodie looked hopelessly lost too, and I secretly hoped that the two would be paired together. It would have warmed me just a bit if they drove their sled off course because they didn't know how to apply the brakes. Of course, I could easily find myself in that pitiful situation. All I knew was that "hike up" meant go.

"Not the right bloke for you, Watson, if you want my advice," Holmes whispered as we made our way across the field to the sleds.

"What are you talking about?" I hissed.

"Özdemir, of course," he replied. My cheeks reddened while his puffed into a grin. "I can't say I applaud your choice in men. First, that footballer, now this one. I assure you, he is *not* a keeper. I would recommend you return your affections to the brunette from the bookstore. She is quite charming."

"Alex is captain of the *soccer* team," I said, teeth gritting. "And he's very nice. What did you find wrong with him?"

"Oh, don't get me started! I have a slew of charges against that one. Isn't it wonderful that he won't be returning to Baker House after the holidays?"

I frowned, wondering what Holmes had done to ensure this. Had he exposed yet another illicit affair at Baker House? I sighed. "And what's wrong with Jibril?"

Holmes cast a deprecating look in Jibril's direction. "He has managed to collect the mobile numbers of both Christa and Elodie, without the knowledge of either party. Rather skilled of him, I daresay, since those two are inseparable. He is trouble nonetheless, so—"

"That's impossible! He seems very nice," I insisted.

Holmes' face darkened. "He is *hardly* nice."

A cacophony of wild barking cut our conversation short. Our sluggish walk in the snow to the sled area finally came to a halt, and we found ourselves by the mouth of a snow-clad, well-travelled path lined with forest on both sides, much like the one we had entered earlier but wider. Nearby was a haphazard arrangement of six sleds. They had perhaps once been organized in an orderly line, but the four dogs harnessed to each sled had run askew, unable to contain their excitement. The dogs continued to whirl around tempestuously. Some panted heavily and drooled; others howled, whimpered, barked, or stamped a paw. The chill hardly affected them; they were ready to sprint through the woods and had little patience for their indolent riders.

The first dogsledding group loitered about, some still on the sleds, legs pressing the brakes as they waited for a new musher to relieve them. I had no doubt the dogs would charge into the wilderness if the pressure on the brakes lessened even slightly. The plump, black-haired lady from earlier introduced herself as Alberta den Nomot and took the first sled while Jibril and another instructor jumped on the middle and fifth sleds, both of which looked far newer than the timeworn one Alberta had hopped aboard.

Another staff member, whose name I hadn't caught, came around, assigning us to a sled. I was paired with Holmes in the second sled, sandwiched between those of Alberta and Jibril. Holmes readily accepted the task of driving, and I jumped into the cargo bed. Although I would no longer suffer the consequences of my sled being driven off course, I was still brooding over what Holmes had said about Jibril. It was also unfortunate that my view was filled with too much of Alberta's rather voluptuous back.

We soon set off down the path. Putting aside the treachery that I hadn't been paired with Jibril—Zara got that prime spot—I thought the pairing worked out well. Leslie had been paired with Alberta; the former yapped endlessly although she didn't bring up Drebber the dog again, and the latter listened politely. Jibril and Zara undertook a serious conversation in Arabic. Perhaps Zara was complaining about Amira, who had refused to come dogsledding and chosen to sulk by the bonfire instead.

Kenji and Anna's sled screamed "family fun"; Anna drove while Kenji and Misaki snuggled comfortably in the cargo bed. Thankfully for the rest of us, fascinated as she was by the dogs, the child had temporarily paused her squealing. Gwilym had been paired with the other instructor, a model of a girl with a rich chocolate complexion who belonged on a magazine cover but had oddly chosen a life in the wilderness. He busily chatted with her, his cheeks bright pink, but perhaps that was only due to the cold.

Just as I had hoped, Christa and Elodie got the last sled. I could almost imagine their dogs taking a wrong turn, unnoticed by all until the end of the trip. Their pleas for help would be masked by an opportunely timed howl of wind. Although I reprimanded myself for these thoughts, especially since Elodie had always been cordial to me, I stopped my imaginings only after a vivid envisioning of the scene.

We didn't get stuck or lose control of our dogs —and sadly, neither did Christa and Elodie—but the dogs did stop on occasion to sniff all the curiosities the forest had to offer. For the most part, we travelled at a moderate pace, not fast enough to make the wind feel icier but slow enough to catch an eyeful of the idyllic haven around us.

Still, I felt wretched; I was simply too cold to enjoy the ride or the scenery. My toes had turned into icy lumps because of an accursed hole in one boot, and my bottom was stiff against the hard wood of the sled; in fact, I was almost certain the blood had stopped flowing into the lower half of my poor, shivering body.

It also didn't help that the dogs stank terribly. During one of the lead dogs' unpredictable stops, which consequently halted the entire pack, Alberta had merrily informed us that they didn't give the dogs baths.

With most of my senses drenched in unpleasantness, I soon became quite miserable. Until a disturbing sight shook my core harder than the cold ever could.

CHAPTER 5

Stangers Slaughtered

"His death was an absolute mystery and likely to remain so."

—Sir Arthur Conan Doyle, *The Adventure of the Second Stain*

THE TROUBLE STARTED AT THE FORK.

Initially, the trail had been one continuous path, but about twenty-five minutes into the ride, it split into two. I thought nothing of it when Alberta signalled the dogs to pursue the path on the right, but I soon realized that something was wrong when Jibril hollered for all the sleds to stop.

Since neither Jibril nor Alberta could lift their feet off the brakes and leave their sleds—the dogs would take this as a sign to go—they shouted at one another instead, or at least Jibril did.

"Alberta! What are you doing?" he cried.

Alberta whisked around, looking worried. "What's wrong?"

"We were supposed to go left! We didn't do a safety check on the right one today."

The flustered woman's face resembled a round beet; her nose and cheeks had turned purple. Her mouth opened several times, but words failed her, and in her apprehension, she stepped off the brakes and her dogs began ambling down the path.

"Brakes, brakes!" Jibril yelled, and Alberta jumped back on the brakes, her entire face now a violent shade of red.

"Newbies," Jibril muttered, shaking his head. Although his voice was low, I was sure Alberta had heard. Her eyes glistened and became nearly perfect circles, as though she were doing her best to keep them open. Shutting them might have released a tear, something she must have dreaded doing in front of Jibril. Unfortunately, the longer she refrained from blinking, the brighter the watery glint in her eyes became.

I felt Holmes' hot breath on my ear. "I told you he was an unpleasant fellow," he murmured.

At last, Alberta's voice emerged feebly. "We used this path y-yesterday. I'm sure it's safe, but I'll drive slowly just in case."

And so, on we went. I thought the discomfort would end there, and for me it did—for a few blissful minutes. The interruption had somehow improved my blood circulation and I felt a bit warmer. Also, I was no longer too concerned that Jibril didn't occupy my view; he had been a bit too rude to Alberta for my liking.

Alberta's prediction of a safe path ahead was correct. True to her word, she led the group slowly. Perhaps if the ride had been faster and the details of the woods had simply whisked by us, we wouldn't have spotted the horror in the snow some minutes later.

But before that came to pass, I became a victim of the cold again, my eyelids drooping heavily and the fatigue that accompanies icy weather making my body sink into the sled, which was far from the ideal bed. Even the smallest of protrusions on the ground felt like jumps, and I was constantly being tossed up and down and side to side, so sleep was an impossibility. Even if I had managed to doze off, the maddening howls that suddenly violated the hush of the forest would have jolted me awake. Our sled slowed once again.

"What the deuce …" Holmes sounded stunned, but his voice quickly became urgent. "Watson, get up and hold down the brakes!"

"I don't want to drive," I protested as I attempted to wiggle my toes without luck.

The response to this was a growl, which I would have assumed came from the dogs had I not been looking up at Holmes. "You are not driving," he said impatiently. "You will simply stand on the brakes and be still. It requires very little brainwork."

Flushed, I rose, ready to utter a retaliatory insult, when I saw his gaze fixed on something ahead. Just off the path to our left was a strangely circular snowless patch of frozen ground. At its centre lay a patch of ash-coloured fur.

"What is that?" I whispered. "A squir — no, it's too big. A wolf? No, wait … that's a dog — and it's not moving." I gulped. "Uh, Holmes, I think it's dead."

My friend looked at me grimly.

It is strange how people are drawn to the macabre, and I was no exception. Without a moment's hesitation, I sprinted behind Alberta and Jibril to see the dead animal. Perhaps Gwilym had tried to follow too because I heard his partner order him sharply to stay put. Christa and Elodie remained on their sled by choice; apparently, what lay ahead wasn't worthy of an investigation.

The first thing I saw was the head, the fur of which contrasted the ground. My prediction had been correct; the body belonged to a dog, small and bony but adult-sized. Its long snout hung open, grimacing, and its eyes, black and button-like, stared blankly at the forest. No face could have portrayed anguish as vividly as this one. But that wasn't the worst of it.

I lowered my gaze and let out an involuntary cry, falling back into Holmes, who also evidently felt that curiosity was a good enough excuse to neglect the responsibility of manning our dogs. Naturally, I was far too anxious about the dead dog to care whether our live ones had strayed into the woods with our sled.

As I recovered, I glanced at Holmes as he stepped around me. Even he looked disturbed by the deep cut that ran down the dog's abdomen—and the pink organs that had been placed neatly around the body. My curiosity overpowered my horror for a moment, and I peered into the cavity the slit had created, only to immediately withdraw my gaze. Suppressing the urge to vomit, I scanned the ground. The entire circle, including the dog, had been heavily salted. Thick lines of pink salt criss-crossed the circle. Still, the earlier storm had managed to sprinkle snow on the patches of unsalted ground and fur.

"Oh, no, it's Stangers!" Alberta moaned, looking as though she too were going to throw up. I noted a faint accent then, where the *r* was neglected and all the vowels sounded like "ah"; a trivial observation it was, but it distracted me from the grisly site for a moment. "How did he escape his pen? Oh, poor Stangers! Was he attacked by an animal? And in the same spot as Dreb—"

"Are you an idiot?!" Jibril cried belligerently. "Of course, it wasn't an animal attack! Unless animals know how to salt the ground and use a knife." Alberta looked as though she might burst into tears, but that didn't soften the man's attitude in the least. He rubbed his forehead furiously, unsure of what to do.

"Here lies the original crime scene, Watson, with a fresh crime," Holmes whispered as he traipsed forward with great energy. His nimble fingers, now clad in blue nitrile gloves, began to poke, prod, and press the mutilated creature, his examination aided by a small magnifying glass. He then knelt next to the body and sniffed the snout. So profound was his concentration that he heard none of Jibril's commands for him to stop. Holmes finally stood, and still ignoring the raving instructor, walked around Stangers, examining every inch of the bare ground. When that was done, his grey eyes travelled from the curious onlookers bound to their sleds to the path itself. He frowned.

"A damned clever perpetrator! No footprints and no sled marks. All obliterated by salt and that bloody snowstorm." But then he brightened somewhat. "Not all is lost though. The salt and the snow tell us the incident took place this morning before the storm; otherwise, traces of the perpetrator's arrival would be here."

I added, "There's no blood here, so this animal, Stangers, was killed elsewhere. Its organs were removed and cleaned there as well, and then someone brought the remains here and laid them out."

Holmes beamed. "Excellent, Watson! If I may add, the poor creature was most likely subdued with poison. There is a very strong odour coming from the snout." To me, he asked, "Might I borrow your mobile phone? I appear to have forgotten mine in the car ... or possibly in Baker House or, er, somewhere else." He snatched my phone before it had barely left my pocket and started jabbing at it eagerly.

"Careful!" Alberta suddenly cried. I froze; the remark had been meant for me. "You were about to step on–on—"

I looked down. My boots lingered near one of the lines of pink salt. Though I was puzzled, I stepped away, but Alberta continued to look petrified. Her mouth opened a moment later, but she clamped it shut when Jibril threw her a hostile look. This didn't slip past Holmes' attention.

"Do speak, Ms. den Nomot," he said. "I am afraid Özdemir here will always think you are incompetent no matter what you say, so kindly share whatever it was that came to your mind just now."

As expected, this was followed by an awkward pause that drove Alberta to blink, her eyes watery, and Jibril to turn away violently. I stared straight ahead, feeling embarrassed for Holmes.

"I, uh, witches ..." Alberta's voice trailed off.

"Absolutely," Holmes agreed, much to my bewilderment. He pointed a finger at the line of pink salt closest to my feet and started tracing it up, then down, then up again, then to the right ... on he went until I realized the familiar shape the lines formed: a five-pointed star.

"It's a pentagram ... Is that why you said witches?" I asked Alberta.

"It's an *inverted* pentacle actually—a pentagram enclosed in a circle," she replied timidly.

Holmes gave the woman a curious look. "Exactly. The internet tells me that while the pentagram is associated with positivity and protection, the inverted version represents evil, specifically the devil."

I shuddered, though I convinced myself that the icy weather, rather than the stiff corpse and the ill-boding symbol, was to blame.

"You seem to know more about this than the average dogsled instructor," Holmes said to Alberta.

"She's been here less than six months. That hardly makes her a qualified—" Jibril barked, but Holmes' scowl subdued him.

"I, uh, read a lot," Alberta began hesitantly, looking as though she were admitting to a sinful passion. "I was a history major, and it's just a habit of mine to get acquainted with a place's history. I researched Toronto and the surrounding areas a bit when I moved here, and that's how I came across a theory—a completely ridiculous one, of course, but not everyone thought so. A professor in the city even pursued it so seriously that he got fired."

And just like that, Alberta's diffidence vanished and her Boston accent, which had been barely perceptible before, shone through. I felt as though I had been transported to a lecture hall. The topic, of course, was not English literature. It was the history of witchcraft.

"In 1687," she began, "when the French military passed through what is now Toronto, it was deserted. The Seneca, the Indigenous people who had once lived there, had abandoned it long before. Five years later in 1692, it remained that way.

"That was an interesting year in American history because the Salem Witch Trials were going on. The theory is that a small group of so-called witches migrated north from Salem and ended up in Toronto for a few years. In the latter part of the seventeenth century, the Algonkian Mississaugas drove them further north." She cast a meaningful look at the white forest that surrounded us.

"So you're saying the witches ended up living here, in what is now Crooked Forest?" I asked incredulously.

"It's all complete nonsense," Alberta insisted. "There's no evidence of the settlements, here or in Toronto. It's just that when I saw Stangers and the inverted pentacle, it was the first thing that came to my mind."

"So," Holmes drawled, "do you suppose these witches continue to live in these lands more than three hundred years later?"

Alberta shook her head vigorously, making her bun bounce. "No, no, it must've been their descendants who—" She stopped abruptly, her features contorting with embarrassment as Holmes cast her a wry look and Jibril let out an exasperated growl. I, however, pressed her to go on. Though she stammered, Alberta acquiesced, looking somewhat reassured.

"I–I just thought, well, if there's truth to the theory, it wouldn't have been real w-witches who'd left Salem because, of course, witches don't exist. They would've just been ordinary people who feared persecution. Maybe they practised a pagan faith and made sacrifices to their gods—"

"You mean the devil," Holmes interrupted.

Alberta shrugged and shot the pentacle another look. "It's a strong possibility ... Anyway, I think eventually the community—"

"You mean the coven." This interruption too came from Holmes, accompanied by a faint but sardonic smile.

Alberta looked at him with a searching expression, as though she was unsure whether he was encouraging her or mocking her. Had she known my friend better, there would have been no uncertainty. Holmes was, without doubt, demeaning her, although with more subtlety than he would have granted those he gave "idiot" status to, namely Gwilym Lestrade and his friends.

"Yes, I suppose we can call them that," Alberta said. "Eventually, as the surrounding areas became more populated, the coven disbanded, and the descendants of the original settlers reintegrated into society. That's what I think anyway. I also think that they never forgot their faith—and the prejudice that drove their ancestors away from their homeland ..."

"Ah, so you propose the descendants have slain Stangers for revenge? But why now?" Holmes asked, although his facetious grin made it evident that he didn't expect an answer, nor would he have considered any that Alberta provided. "You are quite the storyteller, Ms. den Nomot, but your tale belongs in the rubbish."

Alberta's gaze dropped to the ground, eyes glistening once again, as Jibril nodded his agreement. He too had heard enough prattle about witchcraft.

"We have to report this," he declared, looking agitated as he eyed the remaining adventurers craning their necks for a better look. I saw that Gwilym's face was still pink but this time out of fury that his rival got to nose around when he couldn't. Christa, on the other hand, was preoccupied with her phone. Only Elodie looked bothered by the unmoving patch of fur.

Alberta pulled out her walkie-talkie. "Arthur, come in." As soon as he replied, she started telling him what had happened.

It was clearly time to go. My gaze fell back to the path and searched for our sled. Our dogs were now voraciously sniffing the snow off the path. One of them, Summer if my recollection was correct, lay atop a snowbank on her belly, legs sprawled, as though she were tanning on the beach. Consequently, our sled lay at an odd angle, half off the path and partly submerged in the snowbank. I was only too glad that the dogs hadn't run off into the woods, taking our quickest way back to the campsite with them. The terror of waiting in the middle of a forest with a mutilated animal for company may have made a shivering, bawling mess out of me — something Holmes would have laughed about for months to come.

We left the crime scene as it was. It took a few minutes to straighten our sled and persuade the dogs to leave the woods for the path. The ride back took about twenty minutes, but our progress was halted once again at the precise spot the trees gave way to the clearing.

I believe the dogs saw it first. Panicked howling penetrated the icy air and started echoing. Our sled slowed, as did the one in front of us.

The campsite lay about a hundred yards ahead of us to the right. To the far left were the two outbuildings I had spotted earlier. My gaze immediately fell on the only part of the view that was neither wood nor snow: the bonfire.

The fire, which had flickered feebly not long ago, was now soaring toward the sky, almost ten feet high. The strangest part was the startling shade of blue it had turned.

CHAPTER 6

Hounded by Cursed Flames

*"But I have seen more than that," said he, "for Hugo
Baskerville passed me upon his black mare, and there ran
mute behind him such a hound of hell as God forbid should
ever be at my heels."*

—Sir Arthur Conan Doyle, *The Hound of the Baskervilles*

ARTHUR WAS FEVERISHLY THROWING A PAIL OF WATER AT
the flames, but the effort was a fruitless one. The fire
climbed even higher and towered over him; he made one
last attempt, but the pail slipped out of his gloved hands
and flew into the flames. He fell back helplessly and
crashed into a haystack.

The adventurers, myself included, gaped, spellbound.
Only Holmes seemed impervious to the dance of the blue
flames. He darted forward, and by the time I found my
voice to protest, he had already reached the haystacks
and was pulling Arthur to his feet. I jumped onto the
footboard of our sled and clutched the handlebar, ready
to drive, as Holmes began dragging our dazed
housemate to one of the outbuildings, hastily waving at
us to follow.

"Hike up!" bellowed Alberta, and the dogs took off, still barking turbulently. As we drove, a new colour as out of place as the blue flames in a landscape so monochromatic came into view. On a patch of snow that sat too far away to be melted by the flames was a splash of bright red. The sled drove away too quickly for me to make out exactly what lay on the snow, but I had a hunch.

By the time we were safely inside the outbuilding, our noses pressed against the windows, Dimitri, Jibril, Alberta, and a handful of additional staff had reduced the fire to half its height. I craned my neck, trying to get a glimpse of the red snow, but it was mostly obscured by the haystacks. Holmes stood hunched over it; he had somehow managed to slip past the staff stationed by the exit to keep us inside.

Minutes later when the snowshoeing group had joined us, the volume of chitchat became monumental, and I was gradually nudged away from the window by the curious newcomers. Of the instructors who had remained inside, one was trying in vain to get the group to settle down. The front door opened once again, and I saw Holmes' slender form snake through the crowd.

We were sheltering in what was called the Great Room, although I couldn't see why the room deserved so grand a title. It was large, rustic, and mostly devoid of furniture. Opposite the door was a dark corridor that led to the rest of the outbuilding.

I slipped away from the masses to the far end of the room, which housed a lit fireplace and several couches. I arrived just as Holmes was taking a seat next to Arthur. The latter did not look well at all. He was mumbling incoherently between heaving breaths and torrents of vomit, which gave off a putrid smell. Thankfully, someone had found him a plastic bag. I sat down opposite them, feeling squeamish at the sight of Arthur's sweaty face and the bits of grey that oozed from the corners of his mouth.

"I shouldn't have—" Arthur sputtered. His speech became mumbled again. I knelt closer as he stammered the words, "cursed fire."

"Cursed fire?!" I exclaimed.

Arthur shook uncontrollably. "Those symbols in the snow … I-I shouldn't have–have tried to put out their fire—something b-bad's going to happen to me now." He fell back against the sofa, only a sliver of white visible between his drooping eyelids. The plastic bag slipped out of his hand and hit the floor, and its contents began to slowly stream out.

Their fire? I wondered. Had Arthur been referring to the clan of descendants Alberta had mentioned? So, he knew the tale of the fleeing witches too. Perhaps Alberta had told him; she had possibly repeated the story to everyone at Crooked Forest Adventures, earning herself the reputation of a fool. Jibril hadn't looked like he was hearing the story for the first time.

"He isn't dead," Holmes declared a moment later after checking Arthur's pulse. "Just unconscious. Clean that up, will you, Watson?"

I shot him a look of disgust before disposing of the bag. A small pool of thick liquid remained, but no amount of glaring was going to persuade me to scrub the carpet clean.

"Is he going to be okay?" I asked.

Holmes nodded, but his grey eyes were slightly unfocused. His nostrils flared and he sniffed the air. I thought he murmured, "interesting," although I didn't know what was so interesting about the stench of Arthur's vomit.

Now watching the crowd that loitered about the Great Room, he said, "He was lucid enough to tell me that he was here in the outbuilding when Alberta's distress call came in. He had just gotten off the phone with the police when he saw the flames through the window. He swears the grounds had been empty."

"When are the police coming?" I asked.

"It will take them about an hour and a half to reach here, that is, if they dispatched someone immediately after the call. However, I reckon animal slaughter is not a top priority."

"But it's not just animal slaughter. There's something weird going on here. The symbol by the fire—was it another inverted pentagram?"

Holmes looked impressed. "You noticed that, eh?"

"Of course, I did," I huffed indignantly, and he nodded in approbation.

"It was a series of symbols actually, all of them associated with witchcraft. The inverted pentagram was there and so was the Triple Moon. They had been drawn in red oil paint. It appears the perpetrator learned from the mistakes of the first slaying. No more botched symbols."

Marieta's tattoo, I thought grimly. A dreadful suspicion was starting to take form in my mind, one that I couldn't admit out loud. "How did you come to know so much about witchcraft?"

"I did much reading in preparation for our visit—while you were indulging in romance novels."

I pretended not to hear him. "How about footprints? Were there any in the snow near the symbols? There must've been."

Holmes scowled. "Oh, yes, there were. It was as though a herd of buffaloes had passed through. The villain picked the spot strategically since, being near the fire pit, there was already a lot of foot traffic. Damned clever bugger!"

It seemed we were stuck with a case that had left even Holmes perplexed.

I searched for Marieta, but she was nowhere to be seen. I then glanced at Arthur again and thought of the mutilated dog. Was it a coincidence that Marieta's tattoo was among the symbols by the blue fire? Although it was far from an answer to my questions, a cry rang out. It was

Zara Atallah. Two instructors were wrestling her away from the door.

Zara screamed, "Let me go! I need to go look for her!"

"It's not a good idea for you to go out there right now," one of the instructors, a short, blue-eyed man, managed to say between strained huffs of breath.

Though I had witnessed Holmes' uncanny ability to vanish from one place and materialize in another many times, that day because I was feeling particularly anxious, I almost yelped when he suddenly appeared by Zara's side.

"What's wrong, Zara?" he asked, his equanimity undisturbed by the vehement woman next to him.

She ceased her fruitless struggle and looked up at him with large, tear-filled eyes. "It's Amira. I can't find her anywhere. She was sitting by the bonfire when we left for dogsledding and now th-that terrible fire—and I don't see her out there. I need to go find her."

"I would advise you against that," Holmes said quietly. "There is a dangerous person out there somewhere, someone who enjoys mutilating innocent animals. We are safer in here."

"But what about my daughter?" Zara moaned.

Holmes smiled, watching the window. "She will be arriving … now."

The door flung open, and there stood Amira, distraught and shivering. The front of her coat was wet, and her gloves were dripping profusely.

"So this is where everyone went!" she exclaimed grumpily. She didn't have the opportunity to say anything more though; her mother enveloped her in a lengthy embrace, one Amira tried furiously to wriggle out of.

"*Alhamdullilah!*" Zara cried. "What happened? Where were you?"

"Playing with the puppies around the back of the other outbuilding," Amira responded, as though it was

the most obvious answer in the world. "One of the staff —
um, Arthur — knew where I was. Why didn't he tell you?"

We all turned to the still-unconscious Arthur in
response. That, of course, only begged more questions,
but before she could ask them, Holmes intervened, "How
did you get wet?"

That seemed to remind the girl that she was drenched.
She threw off her jacket hastily, explaining that she had
fallen into a puddle. Now that was puzzling. Where on
earth had Amira found a puddle that hadn't frozen over?
Apparently, Holmes didn't quite believe her story either.
Though it went unnoticed by everyone else, I saw him
stealthily pick up the gloves Amira had tossed aside and
sniff them. As soon as he had discarded them, I followed
suit, mustering as much stealth as I could, although I was
enormously unmatched by Holmes.

As soon as I brought a glove to my nose, I cringed at
the foul smell that drifted from it — and caught Zara's eye.
Thankfully, she didn't call attention to the absurdity of
what she had seen, but she stared at me with a raised
eyebrow, looking very much like my grandmother when
I had misbehaved as a child. I dropped the glove and
turned away.

Amira's arrival was followed by that of the staff who
had been battling the fire outside. Although they had
been victorious, they returned looking fatigued, as
though the wilderness had drained them of something
precious. The silence following Zara's outburst fell away,
and a downpour of questions erupted as Dimitri and
Jibril tried to calm the adventurers, to no avail. I spotted
Alberta, pink-faced and sweaty and looking worried,
make her way over to the collapsed Arthur. Marieta was
suddenly there too, hovering in a corner, intentionally
standing apart from the swarm.

I went over to the fireplace where Alberta sat with
Arthur. Seeing her puzzled expression, I told her about
Arthur's sudden sickness.

"Poor guy," she mumbled. "The others already don't treat him well and now this. They'll be laughing about his passing out for ages."

Before I could comfort her, Dimitri marched over, gave me a flattering smile and smirked at Arthur before ordering Alberta to help Jibril prepare snacks for the adventurers. They left, leaving me with a warm fire and a tacit companion, not to mention the smell. I sat in silence for many long minutes, frequently glancing at my phone for the time and wondering when the police would arrive.

Alberta soon returned with two platters of mini tuna salad sandwiches, informing any vegetarians in the crowd that Jibril would come along shortly with alternatives.

As there were no vegetarians in the room—even Amira was willing to put aside animal rights in the face of a grumbling stomach—we didn't miss Jibril's presence at first. I only started looking for him because my appetite remained unquenched by the sandwiches. Hopeful for a plate of something more, I began my search for the food-filled platter that was yet to come. In fact, my protesting stomach propelled my exit from the Great Room and down the corridor I had seen Jibril and Alberta disappear down.

The outbuilding wasn't large, and accordingly, the corridor didn't extend far. There were a few doors, but nearly all were locked. In addition to the bathroom, only one other door, at the end of the hallway, was open, and much to my delight, it led to the kitchen. Upon entering, the first thing I saw was the platter of tortilla chips and bowl of salsa on the counter.

The kitchen was small and rectangular, arranged so that the counter jutted out of the wall to my left and ran along the width of the room, dividing it into two. Beyond the counter, the walls were lined with white cabinets, and in the far right corner, a pair of sliding doors stood open, letting in a gust of chilly air.

From my angle, I couldn't see the twitching legs sprawled behind the counter, but when I went to close the sliding doors, cursing the idiot who had left them open, there was no escaping the predicament that had befallen Jibril.

I screamed involuntarily, and even as I write this, I feel a fresh burst of surprise that I had called out Holmes' name, as though he could somehow cure the red-faced, perspiring young man who was foaming at the mouth and choking on his own vomit.

"Jibril!" I cried, kneeling.

He grabbed my hand and began mumbling, "Z-Zebani ..."

"What? Jibril, what happened?" My cries did nothing to make his ramblings coherent.

His eyes kept darting to the sliding doors and he grew panicked. "It's out there somewhere," he whispered. "The Zebani." His grip on my fingers loosened.

I gaped at him, unable to respond. Quite suddenly, we weren't the only people in the room. The others surged in, led by Holmes, and as he nudged around the counter and knelt next to me, Jibril repeated what he had said. Holmes, with his customary calmness, wiped the vomit off the shivering man's face with some tissue that someone handed him. He felt Jibril's forehead and then his pulse before wiping the streams of sweat rolling down his temple.

"You're going to be fine, mate," he said at last, but Jibril was shaking frenetically and started shouting again. Again, his words were nonsensical. He hardly looked like he would beam with health anytime soon, but Holmes seemed unworried. As a matter of fact, he was staring at the spasming man as though he were examining a specimen under a microscope.

Jibril suddenly pointed to the counter. "The witch went that way!" It seemed he had mustered whatever feeble strength was still left in him to proclaim this because soon afterwards he sunk deeper into the floor, nearly lifeless, except for his hands and feet, which twitched intermittently.

"Does the witch have a name?" Holmes asked gently, sparking new life in Jibril. His speech came out unintelligibly, but I managed to make out a name. I turned to Holmes in disbelief.

"Did he just say 'Dimitri'?" I whispered.

Holmes looked grim; however, it wasn't Jibril's accusation but something behind me that had deepened his frown. I spun around to face the interior of the counter, which was lined with drawers. On the white wood was a messy scrawl in red: *The next will be sacrificed.* Beneath this was a series of arcane symbols.

"Photograph the message, will you, Watson?" Holmes asked quietly.

Swallowing my mounting apprehension, I pulled out my phone and did as he bid. When I turned back to face him, he had fixed his attention on the tiled floor beneath the sabotaged drawers. There lay a long black hair, about the length of a finger. It looked like Jibril's hair. Nonetheless, I picked it up since it had sparked my friend's interest. Holmes immediately plucked it out of my fingers and brought it up to one eye.

"Too thick to be human," he murmured.

Jibril nodded during a brief, lucid moment, then added, "Zebani," before falling unconscious.

Holmes pulled out a small zippered bag from inside his coat and deposited the hair into it. One flick of the wrist and the bag disappeared back into his coat.

It wasn't long before we were ushered out of the kitchen and back into the Great Room. Although I would have preferred to sink into one of the couches by the fireplace, Holmes began weaving through the adventurers with a renewed sense of purpose. I naturally followed. I needed a distraction after all; the scene in the kitchen refused to fade from my mind. Unfortunately, Holmes headed straight for the last person I wanted to confront.

CHAPTER 7

A Supernatural Solution

"Depend upon it, there is nothing so unnatural as the commonplace."

—Sir Arthur Conan Doyle, *A Case of Identity*

THE TOWERING FORM OF DIMITRI KOMAROV STOOD AT THE centre of a group of nervous-looking staff. Holmes offered no greeting; his hard stare already seemed to beg the question: *Did you harm Jibril?* But that wasn't what he asked.

"Mr. Komarov, what sort of dogs are employed here?"

The question elicited a look of surprise; Dimitri had been anticipating a question about the dead dog, the mysterious symbols in the snow, the blue fire, or an outraged demand for a refund. Looking somewhat relieved, he answered, "We've got some Siberian huskies and Alaskan Malamutes. Most are Alaskan huskies, the best dogs on the market for racing and hauling. We enter a couple of them in racing competitions every year." There was unmistakeable pride in his voice. I hoped Amira wasn't nearby. *Had he forgotten that one of his colleagues lay in a delirious state only a few rooms away?* I wondered, feeling repulsed.

"Do any of your dogs have long black fur—say, approximately seven centimetres long?" Holmes inquired. The answer was negative, which incited him to walk away and me to follow. "I suppose the hair belonged to the Zebani after all," he added, but he said this quietly and for my ears only.

"What the heck is a Zebani?" I asked.

Holmes shrugged. "I haven't the faintest idea." His pace quickened and he pushed passed some of the adventurers, who looked back at him with the vague annoyance one feels when someone else's child is misbehaving. Holmes didn't notice, however, as he sprinted across the Great Room. I trailed him, mouthing apologies. At last, we reached a lone figure standing by a window.

Zara Atallah glanced up at us, looking only slightly puzzled as my friend skidded to a stop. I didn't need to be Sherlock Holmes to perceive that she looked dreadfully disturbed. Her golden complexion had lost some of its colour, and her eyelids and shoulders drooped in fatigue. Deep furrows marked the corners of her mouth—she was evidently contemplating thoughts so burdensome even Holmes' eccentricity couldn't dissolve her unease.

"My dear Mrs. Atallah, you must be terribly shocked," Holmes said gently. Only his voice was sympathetic though; the rest of him, from the sheen in his eyes to his twitching fingers, radiated a nervous, impatient energy.

Zara nodded vaguely, her dark eyes returning to the snow-capped field beyond, and murmured, "God help us."

"Mr. Özdemir is going to be fine," Holmes said. "You needn't worry."

But Zara shook her head. "Something feels wrong about this place, very wrong. I'm afraid of what will happen next." Her eyes searched the crowd, relaxing only when they landed on Amira, who loitered some distance away, scowling at a large smartphone.

"Mr. Özdemir said something back there—a word I am not familiar with. I believe it was Arabic. Do you know what it means?" Holmes asked.

Zara's face hardened. She knew exactly which word he was referring to.

"Zebani or Zabaniyah," she began slowly. "The definition varies depending on who you ask. In my homeland, they are thought of as fire-breathing demons. Jibril comes from Turkey, where they believe the Zebani are hellhounds or hellhound demons that torment souls in the underworld."

*

"Isn't it curious, Watson?" Holmes said once we had left Zara to her sombre thoughts. "Özdemir sees a hellhound in a place full of dogs."

"But he couldn't have mistaken one of the sled dogs for a hellhound," I said. "I'd think a hellhound, if it were real, would look noticeably different."

"Quite true. There is also the witch to consider. If it wasn't a hallucination, then Özdemir saw a person exit the kitchen. Perhaps he or she is responsible for his compromised state."

I shuddered thinking exactly *how* this individual had "compromised" Jibril. A guttural incantation uttered from the snarling lips of Dimitri Komarov came to mind, but I shook it aside. *No such thing as witches*, I reminded myself. It helped that Dimitri hardly looked like the witches featured in the fairy tales I had grown up with.

"The sliding doors were open when I went into the kitchen. Maybe there are footprints in the snow?" I suggested. I had almost said "pawprints."

But Holmes shook his head. "You must learn to pay attention, Watson. The path is salted. Come, let us hear what all the chatter is about. Perhaps we can glean something useful."

He glided toward a middle-aged couple from the snowshoeing group and inserted himself into their conversation, oblivious to their puzzled scrutiny of him. They soon took a liking to him though, and a spirited discussion ensued. I lingered for a moment and tried to socialize by politely nodding here and there, but the atmosphere felt poisonous, and it was starting to take a toll on me. I slipped away, unnoticed.

Settling into a couch by the fireplace, I watched the slumbering Arthur for a moment, relieved to see his chest move up and down rhythmically, then turned my attention to the room.

If the crowd had been in a frenzied state before, it was completely volatile now. Every conversation centred on words like "devilry," "witches," or "hexed." I glanced about in agitation. For about half the faces, I could attach no name. The others, those who belonged to my group, wore expressions as solemn as mine — for the most part.

Christa's and Gwilym's loud voices overtook the others. Encircled by a group of petrified admirers, the duo spoke with a touch of schadenfreude; they were relaying the grisly details of the mutilated dog as though it were a spectacle. The investigation entirely forgotten, they were basking in the fame brought by something terrible they had witnessed at a distance. Elodie lingered next to them, looking uncomfortable. Kenji and Anna Sato sat on some chairs in a corner, consoling a weeping Misaki, who seemed especially sensitive to all the noise. To my surprise, the chatty Leslie stood alone, not far from me, staring at the flames in the fireplace as though entranced.

I must have dozed off although I wasn't sure how I had managed to do that in the midst of such intense chatter. When I awoke, it was to find Holmes sitting next to Arthur. But he wasn't just sitting; his pale, spider-like fingers disappeared into each pocket of Arthur's coat methodically and with deliberate slowness. When Arthur let out a moan, Holmes froze, but when it became clear that our housemate would not awake, my friend continued his efforts.

I carried on with my feint of dozing as he looked around furtively. Satisfied, he brought one sleeve up to his nose and sniffed. The next sleeve underwent the same treatment before it was gently placed down. Arthur's gloves, which lay discarded by his legs near the vomit puddle, underwent the sniff test a moment later. The hat and scarf weren't touched. Holmes' expression remained as obscure as ever as he straightened.

"Did you have a pleasant nap, Watson?"

My eyes sprang open and I stiffened.

"You were probably wondering why I just did that," he continued in a honey-like voice.

"No point in asking," I responded. "It's not like you're going to tell me."

Holmes smirked, but then he opened his mouth as though he would break his taciturnity just to prove me wrong. It was most unfortunate that Leslie appeared at that exact moment, looking flushed.

"Um, Sherlock, can I have a word with you?"

Holmes smiled graciously. "Of course." When she hesitated, he added, "You can speak freely in front of my friend, Watson."

But her discomfort remained. "I'd prefer to speak to you alone," she insisted.

Holmes stood instantly and they disappeared into the crowd. I slumped back into the couch, feeling very much offended. What did she have to tell Holmes that she couldn't reveal in front of me? Part of me wanted to follow them, but what if she was professing her love for him? Although I couldn't imagine any woman accepting the eccentricities of Sherlock Holmes, I didn't want to risk stumbling across Holmes with his arms wrapped around someone. It would be nearly as perturbing as the eerie message on the kitchen drawers.

The recollection was enough to make me forget about Leslie for a moment. What on earth did the message mean? Did it refer to another dog? But two dogs had already been sacrificed … I shivered; I was certain the threat was directed at people this time, perhaps even someone in the Great Room. Although I denied it adamantly, there was a supernatural ring to all that had happened. I thought of Alberta's story about the migrating witches. Could it be true? *But wand-waving witches on flying broomsticks don't exist*, I reminded myself once again.

Nevertheless, dying flames didn't reach twice the height of a grown man and turn blue unaided. I wondered if the symbols by the fire had somehow cursed the fire. Had poor Arthur suffered the consequences of trying to put it out? He certainly believed that to be the case. Jibril had also battled the fire, and his state too was pitiful now, very much unlike the domineering man who had made Alberta tear up. My eyes scanned the room, picking out Dimitri, Alberta, and the others who had helped put out the fire. They all seemed fine, somewhat rouged and fatigued in Alberta's case, but hearty, nonetheless. The supposedly cursed fire hadn't caused them any suffering.

"Yet," Holmes said.

I looked up, startled, and there he hovered, watching me with those penetrating eyes of his. "Excuse me?"

"Komarov and the others haven't suffered the wrath of the cursed fire *yet*," he clarified, inciting a quiver that shook my body. His words unnerved me far more than his unsettling abilities.

"You don't seriously believe in all this, do you?" I asked, forcing a laugh. "Witches and hellhounds? It's all ridiculous!"

He looked at me fondly. "You were contemplating the existence of phantoms only months ago during that odd business with the Richardson family." He paused as though he were savouring a flavour. "Look at you now. I have been an excellent influence on your logical faculties."

I snorted, then stopped myself. "That day when Gwilym asked Arthur to name someone with, er, psychopathic tendencies, Arthur started to say a name that began with the letter D. I think he meant to say Dimitri. Even Jibril said Dimitri's name before he passed out."

"Oh, did he now?" Holmes said slyly.

I looked at him, exasperated. "Don't play dumb. You heard him. I think Dimitri has something to do with what's going on."

"*We are each our own devil, and we make this world our hell,*" he said. The words were enunciated with deliberate slowness, as though something had entranced the man behind the voice.

Quoting fiction again, I thought. There was a pause during which time I contemplated whether I should show Holmes that my brain attic, at least the part devoted to English literature, was just as vast as, if not superior to, his by naming Oscar Wilde as the author of that quote. I resisted the temptation; doing so would make me as childish as Holmes.

"Why must we make this world our hell, Watson?" he went on with a distracted air. "What drives us to do so? Or perhaps … we are simply trying to fix the hell others have created around us. But either way, we only dig a deeper grave for ourselves, I think."

I could think of no response, partly because I had no idea why Holmes was suddenly spewing philosophy, which I had previously believed was a subject he knew next to nothing of.

"This fire is making my head hurt," he complained a moment later. "Shall we move to the window for some air?"

Although I didn't want to leave the warmth, I followed him wordlessly. I waited until we had found an isolated spot by a window before asking, "If it's not Dimitri, then do you suspect Arthur? Why were you sniffing him?"

"A good detective investigates everything and everyone, my friend."

Although I wanted to inquire about Leslie as well, an embarrassed heat in my cheeks stopped me. Instead, I asked, "Then you're also investigating the supernatural angle? Do you think—is there something supernatural going on here?"

He said thoughtfully, "The mutilations, the symbols, the blue fire, the sudden bout of illness—there *is* something unnatural about this whole business." His voice dropped to a murmur; I only managed to catch the word "commonplace" as he mumbled to himself.

His solemn tone only added to my bewilderment. I simply couldn't accept that the most logical person I knew was considering a paranormal solution; that kind of thinking was usually characteristic of me. I had learned a thing or two about myself during our first case when we had investigated a haunting. As Holmes said, I had entertained the possibility of ghosts—with much relish. Now my thoughts drifted down that path again despite protests from the more reasonable side of my brain. Unfortunately, the last traces of healthy skepticism vanished with a violent screech not much later.

"Alberta?" I called out, recognizing the voice immediately. I reached her, with Holmes at my heel, expecting a calamity—blood-red symbols of witchcraft smeared across the wall, another dead dog, or worse— but I only saw Alberta standing by the fireplace, hands shaking.

"He's gone!" she exclaimed, and I immediately realized who she was referring to. Arthur had disappeared from the couch. "I've checked the whole building. He's not here."

CHAPTER 8

The Witch of Crooked Forest

*"I sat in silence wondering what on earth could be his reason
for kidnapping me in this extraordinary fashion."*

—Sir Arthur Conan Doyle, *The Greek Interpreter*

AN EXCITED PRATTLE OF VOICES BOMBARDED THE BRIEF
silence. Alberta stumbled over and slumped on the
couch, crestfallen. Dimitri strutted about and hollered
something about doing a head count. I saw his face
pucker with frustration amid the swarming crowd; no
one would stand still enough to be counted. Marieta
stood apart like before, but this time she was nervously
clutching the pendant of her necklace. Dimitri's voice
boomed over the panicked chatter, "Everyone, shut up!"
effectively silencing all but the wailing Misaki.

Dimitri made his way to the centre of the room,
holding a clipboard in his hand. Wearily, he glanced at
the crowd and called out a name. A voice answered. Then
he called out another; again, there was a response. But
when he called Leslie Alfredsson-Maine, there was a
synchronized wave of turning heads and whispered
inquiries, but no one spotted Leslie. Someone helpfully

suggested that perhaps she had gone to the bathroom, but it only took a moment to disprove that theory. To say that the atmosphere in the room became tense is an understatement; it was angst-ridden. The staff stood murmuring to one another, unsure of what to do. Dimitri was shouting something incoherent. My anxiety turned into nerve-wrecking fright, egged on by an uncontrollable imagination and the ghastly images it produced.

"Two people have been taken," I said fretfully to Holmes, clutching my hands to stop them from trembling. "How could two people be taken from a room full of people!"

"Yes, it is most mysterious," he replied quietly. "Poor woman. A bit loquacious, but delightful nonetheless, and a sweet reminder of home. We ought to find her *before* she is sacrificed."

Dimitri's voice erupted again, audibly this time. "This has gone on long enough!"

I didn't like the tone of his voice; there was a dangerous ring to it, as though anyone who dared challenge him would face the sharp edge of a sword. I certainly didn't want to be on the receiving end of his glare, and thankfully I wasn't. But someone else was.

"Marieta Charr!" he hollered. He and his faithful followers marched across the room to where Marieta stood. The group's resemblance to a band of townspeople bearing pitchforks and torches was striking. Marieta stared at them defiantly, but I could tell she was afraid.

"We've got a pagan here—the damned Witch of Crooked Forest—and now strange things have been happening. Who thinks there's a connection?" Dimitri sneered. The very thing had occurred to me when Holmes had mentioned the Triple Moon in the snow. I had cast the idea aside quickly, although not before wondering if our housemate was a descendant of the Salem migrants. Marieta was odd, but in my books, she was as unlikely a suspect as Arthur. Dimitri, on the other hand, was entertaining this notion so avidly that his face contorted with hatred; it was incredibly easy to picture him ready to burn a witch.

"I'm not going to answer to your ignorance," Marieta said, gritting her teeth.

That obviously did little to calm Dimitri, who bared his teeth very much like the dogs he trained. His pack of colleagues, who hovered around him, didn't look welcoming either.

"Listen, freak, I don't know what kind of game you're playing. You killed two of my dogs, you made Jibril sick, and now you've kidnapped people. I want them both back here in five minutes, or things will turn ugly."

Marieta didn't bulge. "I have to give you kudos, you know. You're doing a great job deflecting the attention away from you. I heard what Jibril said before he passed out. He said *your* name. You're the one who did something to him."

Things were turning ugly far more quickly than Dimitri had predicted. I reached out for Holmes with the intention of beckoning him to do something. Wiry though he was, he had a knack for disentangling sticky situations. But Holmes was no longer standing behind me. He lingered by Zara, speaking in hushed tones. Zara then passed her cellphone to him, which he stuffed into his coat pocket hastily before disappearing into the folds of the crowd. I wasn't surprised that he had borrowed someone else's phone, but why he needed it at the precise moment Dimitri and his mob were on the verge of murdering Marieta was a mystery.

I wanted to follow Holmes, but Dimitri's thunderous voice and the quivering yet defiant Marieta kept me rooted to the spot. Dimitri stepped menacingly close to Marieta and waved his fist, and I stared apprehensively, already anticipating the blood that would stream down her soon-to-be-injured nose. The other adventurers watched with a mix of horror and avidness. A barbaric scuffle would break out any minute.

The Salem Witch Trials suddenly didn't seem so unbelievable. After all, it was happening again before my very own eyes, and I felt helpless, unable to oppose or rebel against the perpetrators. Did Dimitri really believe a witch was the cause of everything that had happened? Or was he throwing around accusations to divert attention from his own involvement, just as Marieta had said?

Please hurry, I thought. I knew Holmes' disappearance had something to do with the events that had unfolded, yet I couldn't begin to speculate what he was up to. Perhaps thinking about Holmes is what propelled me to think like him … because when my gaze fell on the fireplace, I didn't just see Alberta or the tattered couches or the crackling fire. Something bothered me about the scene; something was missing. The obvious answer was Arthur's slouched figure, but I was sure something else was missing.

I pulled my coat tightly around my body; neither the heat from the fireplace nor the hot agitation that accompanies arguments kept me warm. That was when I realized it.

"The gloves are gone," I pondered out loud. In fact, the hat and scarf, which Holmes had flung off to make Arthur as comfortable as possible, had disappeared too. Had the kidnapper been that concerned with keeping Arthur warm or had he simply left on his own accord?

I wasn't in the habit of talking to myself, but that day, the words just popped out of my mouth. Unfortunately, it happened at a most inopportune time. At that precise moment, Dimitri paused his shouting and the whole room became virtually silent. Even Misaki's screeches had tapered; she was sniffling, red-eyed and exhausted now. Everyone had heard me perfectly, and more than two dozen pairs of eyes suddenly fixed on me.

It was Dimitri who broke the silence. "What are you talking about?"

A familiar voice answered on my behalf.

"A most excellent observation, Watson," said Holmes. "Why indeed would a *witch* care to ensure Gastrell's hands did not freeze? And his head and neck too! As you can see, all his winter accessories are gone. What an awfully considerate *kidnapper*!" He emphasized "witch" and "kidnapper" as though he were putting on a performance for children.

Alberta sprang up, looking hopeful. "So he wasn't taken? Did he go outside? But I checked—"

"It is very probable he is somewhere in the woods," Holmes said, "which is why you couldn't see him from a cursory examination of the vicinity of the outbuilding. Perhaps Ms. Alfredsson-Maine is with him." Gone was the "cool" Holmes; he referred to Leslie with his customary formality. "Why they ventured out there is beyond me, but we ought to conduct a search." Hardly pausing for breath, he declared, "I volunteer Watson and myself."

Although I felt a bit irritated that Holmes hadn't asked if I minded venturing into the unforgiving cold, I offered no rebuttal. I would never forgive myself if Arthur froze to death, which was still a possibility even with his hat, scarf, and gloves.

Some of the adventurers nodded eagerly. Gwilym, unable to contain his enthusiasm, waved one hand frantically, tiptoeing over the crowd like a child crying, "Pick me! Pick me!"

"Absolutely not," Dimitri said firmly. "The staff will carry out a search. You will all stay here." There was a murmur of disapproval. In fact, some of the adventurers looked downright unhappy at the idea of being sheltered under a solid roof with an abundance of warmth and food. But the protests, silent or otherwise, did nothing to deter Dimitri. He promptly assembled a small search party and ordered the rest of the staff to safeguard the flock. I was relieved to see that Dimitri himself was part of the departing pack; the apprehension in the Great

Room would not have cooled had he remained shaking his fist at Marieta.

"Come, Watson, we don't have all day," Holmes said, once the main door to the outbuilding slammed shut. I glanced at him questioningly as disconcerted chatter enveloped the room. But rather than explaining, he pulled my arm and steered me stealthily to the corridor that led to the kitchen.

"Are we going outside? But we're not supposed to—"

He grunted impatiently. "The search party is heading towards the dogsledding trail. It is highly probable that is the wrong direction. If you would rather not recover Leslie and Gastrell alive, then by all means, return to the Great Room."

"Well, of course, I'll come, but why do you think Dimitri and the others are going the wrong way?"

Holmes released my arm, confident now that I wouldn't run back and tattle. "If Leslie or Gastrell had opened the front door, someone would have noticed. The gust of cold air alone would have been enough to turn heads. There is only one other exit: through the kitchen. That is how they left. If there are any clues as to what happened and where they went, that is where we will find them."

He sprinted forward and I followed, passing several doors. One of these doors, which had been locked before, now stood ajar. I slowed and peeked inside.

What I saw was a spacious room, though not nearly as large as the Great Room, its walls and floor lined with an assortment of boxes partly obscured by the poor lighting. There was little room for standing, but someone had hastily pushed aside some of the boxes to create a bit of floor space under the single flickering lightbulb that dangled from the low ceiling. In this space, looking out of place, was a cot and a chair.

Jibril's sweating form lay on the cot. His eyes were shut tight, and his socked feet hung off the edge—the bed was too tiny to contain his sizable height—and this made him look all the more pitiable. If he looked out of place, then Marieta, who occupied the chair, looked more so with her raven-black hair and stiff back. Somehow, she had managed to slip away and hide out in here. Yet, she didn't appear to be hiding—she sat with purpose, eyes closed, no longer tense and distraught. She held Jibril's hand tenderly.

What a transformation, I thought, staring at her transfixed. Had this really been the shaking girl from just moments before? I would have thought of her as a woman sitting devotedly by her lover's side had her lips not been moving noiselessly. Was she praying? No, I decided, unable to explain how I knew this.

"Please close the door, Janah. I need to concentrate," Marieta said softly. Her eyes had suddenly opened, and she was staring at me.

At a loss for words, I did as she asked, then sprinted down the corridor in wonder. Holmes was standing just beyond the sliding doors, eagerly whirling this way and that to examine anything that caught his attention. An icy chill hit my face the second I stepped outside, then released its grip on me and blew in the opposite direction, pushing me down the narrow, salted path to where Holmes now knelt, his nose only inches away from where the snowy field met the cemented walkway.

"Ah, good of you to join, Watson," he said, distractedly climbing to his feet. "You can help me with a little experiment. Come along." He propelled me back to the rear entrance. "Kindly lie down on the path, on your back, feet toward the building."

I eyed the salt crystals and wet cement in disgust. "Not a chance. Why don't *you* lie down?"

My friend looked genuinely disappointed. "But you wouldn't be able to pull my body along this path."

"You think Leslie or Arthur was dragged along this path?" I exclaimed.

Holmes nodded. "I shall show you."

We jogged to a spot a few feet ahead, and Holmes pointed to where he had knelt. The snow had been disturbed; in fact, it had been disturbed all along the walkway-field boundary. The same could be seen on the other side. I reflected back to what Holmes had asked me to do. A disturbing image of a pair of limp legs creating a furrow in the snow as strong hands pulled materialized in my head.

"Our feet tend to splay open when we are in a relaxed supine position—or unconscious," Holmes said. "Either Leslie or Gastrell was first incapacitated, possibly near the back door. You see where the drag marks in the snow start? That is where the perpetrator started dragging the victim. Note how there is much less salt on the path all along here. The body acted like a broom, sweeping the salt along. Let's see where they went." He scampered down the path, which extended for about thirty feet before veering left in an L-shape toward the rear of the other outbuilding. We had reached the spot where the legs of this L joined when Holmes came to an abrupt stop.

I noted there were no drag marks in the snow along the path heading to the second outbuilding, and the salt looked undisturbed. Holmes, having already seen this, was gazing ahead at the blanket of snow between the path and a thicket of evergreens. Someone had been dragged off the path and onto the snow; a trail of disturbed snow led into the forest.

Had it been Leslie? Had Arthur dragged Leslie into the woods? But this was unthinkable. My mild-mannered, guileless housemate wasn't capable of such a thing. Leslie as the perpetrator was just as ridiculous. Although I didn't know her well enough to judge her character, I didn't think she was strong enough to incapacitate and drag Arthur; he was small, but she was much smaller.

"The perpetrator's footprints have been completely obliterated by the drag marks," Holmes murmured, but he appeared hopeful. "Let's see what clues lie among the trees."

We walked alongside the makeshift footpath, Holmes, stoic as always, and I with a tremor to every step taken in the knee-deep snow. I breathed in the icy air, puffed out a white cloud, and then entered the forest.

CHAPTER 9

Commanded by Voices

*"The puckered eyelids had begun to quiver, and now a pair of
vacant gray eyes looked up at us."*

—Sir Arthur Conan Doyle, *The Adventure of the Priory
School*

UNLIKE THE WOODS WE HAD TREKKED THROUGH IN OUR
snowshoes, the trees here grew in dense formation, the
needles of one pine interlocking with those of its
neighbour and creating a nearly impermeable net that let
in little sun or snow. We no longer had to navigate
through a thick layer of snow, but between the sudden
obscurity and the frozen ground, there was no way to tell
in which direction the perpetrator and their helpless
mark had gone.

Perhaps my imagination was being overzealous, but
an inability to walk on one's own two feet implied only
unconsciousness or death in my books, and neither
prospect left me particularly cheerful. Every passing
second felt crucial; Arthur or Leslie, or perhaps both, may
have already been dumped somewhere in this vast
stretch of trees, left to painfully freeze to death, or worse,

they were already dead. I craned my neck and swivelled around, gaze jumping from the ground to the trees to the darkness beyond.

"Watson, stop fidgeting so much," Holmes ordered, his tone acerbic.

Unlike me, he had turned corpse-like: he was unnaturally still, much like everything surrounding us. If puffs of breath didn't escape from his nostrils, his breathing would have hardly been detectable. Only his eyes moved, scanning the landscape. Apparently, nothing of interest caught his attention, for he shook his head crossly. There was no clue hiding on the frosted grounds or in the snow-dusted trees.

"It's hopeless. They could be anywhere," I said. "We should go tell Dimitri what we found, and he could bring the search party here. We'll find Arthur and Leslie sooner with more of us searching."

"Watson, if possible, please stop talking and moving, and perhaps, breathe only when absolutely necessary. I am trying to think, and you are disturbing my process."

I huffed indignantly—and loudly—on purpose, which didn't please Holmes. I expected a fresh torrent of ridiculous commands, but none came since he, mouth open, was staring at something in the distance: a speck of orange that contrasted sharply against the monochromatic landscape, although it was growing smaller and smaller.

"Is that—" I began.

"Yes!" Holmes broke off into a run and I followed suit, jumping with no grace at all over the snake-like roots that seemed to have been purposely stationed to slow down anyone who dared to hurry in a place like this. The slippery ground didn't help either. Holmes somehow managed to skate past each of nature's impediments. I had only tripped twice by the time we slowed to a trot … and the orange speck had metamorphosed into a headful of hair. The odd thing was that Arthur Gastrell appeared not to have heard neither our thudding steps nor our panting breath. He carried on walking through the trees, but there was something unusual in the way he moved. As we crept up behind him, I noticed how taut his arms were. The stiffness seemed to infect his whole body. His legs hardly bent at the knees and his head seemed incapable of turning. His vacant eyes looked straight ahead as though enchanted by something in the distance, but I saw nothing ahead but an endless stretch of evergreens.

"Arthur?" I called out softly.

Arthur stopped mid-motion, one rigid leg in front of the other. Slowly, very slowly, he turned and looked at us. He wore no coat and looked deathly pale. It was difficult to imagine what he saw, but it was apparent that he didn't process the presence of two people—at least not right away. He stared at us vaguely as though we were just another feature of the dreary landscape—a tall pine and a shrub perhaps, Holmes being the pine, of course; I barely passed his shoulder.

"Arthur," I began again. "What are you doing out here? Where's your coat?"

Arthur blinked, and for a moment, he hardly stirred. Then his eyes widened in recognition.

"Janah," he said, then looked at Holmes. "Sherlock." It was only then he appeared to notice the forest. "I-It's so cold." He shivered uncontrollably and hugged himself, looking puzzled. Somehow, he had lost his parka but couldn't recall where. I hoped his sweater and snow pants would keep him warm enough until we returned to the outbuilding. Mine wouldn't fit him, and Holmes ... well, I didn't think he would offer his coat any time soon; his pale face had contorted with hostility for some odd reason.

"Where is Leslie?" Holmes demanded. His accusatory tone caught me offguard; Arthur too blinked at us, forehead scrunched in confusion.

"Who's that?" he asked.

"Leslie Alfredsson-Maine, the blonde woman with the English accent," Holmes huffed. "What did you do with her?"

I hadn't the faintest idea why Holmes had gone from searching for Arthur to suspecting him of something so nefarious. Although I too had briefly contemplated the idea, it was plain from the expression on Arthur's face that he had no idea who Leslie was or that she had disappeared from the Great Room around the same time as he.

Arthur asked shakily, "Is she one of the guests? She should be in the outbuilding with the others. Wait … is that why you're out here?"

Holmes ignored the questions. "Why are *you* out here?" It was unclear whether it was the mistrustful glare or the pointedness of the question that made Arthur look—well, it was difficult to describe his expression exactly. There was a rapid succession of blinking and swallowing, but his mouth remained firmly shut.

Holmes grew impatient. "There is snow in the creases of your snow pants. You walked through snow that was at least to the knee. We have noted only one trail of disturbed snow, created by the transport of an unconscious person. As you are very much conscious, that person is not you. Perhaps you took some other path we are not aware of?" He evidently didn't care for an answer because he went on without pause. "You accosted Leslie, rendered her unconscious, and dragged her through the snow and into the woods. Where is she, Gastrell?" This question was enunciated so forcefully that even I would have relented and given a proper answer.

But Arthur shook his head vehemently and started blubbering in panic. "No, no—I wouldn't—I couldn't—" The rapid blinking returned and I, anticipating tears, quickly intervened in gentler tones.

"Why did you leave the outbuilding?"

Arthur stiffened. It was evident that he wanted to explain; his face was contorting as though there was a wrestling match within him, but something—fear, embarrassment perhaps?—prevented him from speaking. Holmes' penetrating, suspicious stare only worsened matters. I placed a hand reassuringly on Arthur's shoulder and gave it a squeeze. It had the intended effect. Arthur sighed as though relieved of a burden, but uncertainty lingered in his voice when he spoke, and I wondered how certain he was of the account he gave.

"I woke up on the couch, feeling disoriented. I'd forgotten about the dog and the blue fire, and I had no idea why everyone was in the Great Room. Then it all came back. I sat for a bit, but there was so much noise— it was starting to make my head hurt. S-so I got up—I needed air and wanted to see the dogs, to check on them—though I knew someone would've done that already. I just wanted to be near them; it helps me calm down."

"So you exited the building through the back," Holmes filled in, once again impatient. I frowned at him, and catching my look, he let Arthur continue, uninterrupted.

"Yes, I remember doing that. I was standing just outside the door and then—there was a voice—" His coherence faltered at this point and the panic, though somewhat diminished, returned. "A man's voice— deep—a whisper at first, then louder. I thought some of the guys were fooling around, but I didn't recognize the voice, and it didn't sound like someone was trying to d-disguise their voice."

He shook his head as though to rid himself of this mysterious voice. It turned out this presumption wasn't far from the truth, for after a pause, he added, "I d-didn't even know where it was coming from. It almost seemed as though, as though it was coming from inside my h-head." His childlike, watery eyes met our own speculative ones nervously; he was expecting a belittling laugh or, at the very least, a smirk. Seeing how serious and scared he looked, I managed to stifle both reactions. Even Holmes glanced at Arthur mildly.

"What did the voice say?" I asked.

Arthur's stutter worsened. "He s-said I should s-serve him."

"Another ridiculous tale!" Holmes exclaimed. "I can think of only one entity who would make such a demand. I suppose you are under the belief that the devil spoke to you?" He laughed scornfully. "I suppose we shall have to find Leslie the old-fashioned way."

By this, I didn't think he meant to wander aimlessly, but that was what we did. Perhaps there was a method to the way Holmes shepherded us around the woods, occasionally stopping to fiddle with Zara's phone or to peer at something microscopic on the frozen ground. Other times, the object of interest was not so minuscule but banal nonetheless, like a twig or an irregular impression in the mud. Then he would tap away on the phone and freeze, staring at nothing in particular.

Although my friend's odd behaviour was difficult to ignore, my mind lingered on the mysterious voice for much of the search. My feelings of foreboding worsened.

"Stop and listen," Holmes said suddenly.

I heard nothing at first, but then a tune played faintly in the distance. Holmes jabbed at the phone again, and the tune sounded once more, though it was difficult to tell exactly where it was coming from. It sounded oddly familiar. Although Holmes' acute hearing would put some animals to shame, it was I, purely by chance, who spotted a splotch of mustard yellow about two hundred metres ahead. Similar to how Arthur's carrot-coloured hair had contrasted vividly against the forest backdrop, the bright hue caught my eye straightaway. Was it—I squinted—hair? Although I was tempted to scoot forward and leave Holmes to ponder my unexpected departure, I hollered his name, pointed ahead, and beckoned the men to follow before sprinting. Somehow, I managed to avoid tripping, slipping, or falling and reached the site before the other two.

Leslie's hatless head with its flaxen mop of hair was the first thing I saw. I took in the rest of her still body, my icy breath caught in my throat. The first thing that struck me was how dishevelled she looked lying there on the ground, her hair jutting out at odd angles and her coat rumpled as though someone had unceremoniously dumped her. But no, that was not the case. Some invisible hand had arranged her body, hastily though, so that her arms and feet were extended, much like the Vitruvian Man. Luckily, there was no grisly cut running along her chest and belly like Stangers or Drebber, but odd symbols just like those by the blue fire had been painted all around her in that hideous red paint.

Please don't be dead, I thought desperately, and took a step forward when Arthur grabbed my arm.

"Maybe we shouldn't touch anything," he whispered.

I knew he was thinking about the effect the blue fire had had on him, but I wasn't going to wait around for an ambulance to arrive. As expected, Holmes agreed with my sentiments and bounded toward Leslie. He was shaking her gently as I reached his side. Arthur continued to stand from a distance, watching us with a pained expression, but he had his cellphone out at my instruction and was calling for help.

"She's breathing, but she's not waking," Holmes reported. Then he sniffed the symbol closest to where he crouched and touched the paint. "Same paint as before." He added quietly, "Remind me to examine Gastrell's hands for red paint, will you?"

"You still think Arthur was behind this?" I whispered back. "Look at him: he's shaking in his boots."

"That is because he has no coat," Holmes answered coldly.

I would have questioned him further if Leslie hadn't stirred at that moment. She squinted as though even the faint light was too much for her eyes to bear and looked utterly confused. It was evident she had little idea how she had ended up in this desolate patch of Crooked Forest. With our help, she managed to sit up, although her movements continued to be sluggish. It wasn't until she noticed the crimson symbols around her that she gasped, ignited with fresh energy—and fear. She seized Holmes by the coat and clung to him, face buried in the wool, shoulders shaking. My friend, suddenly forced to comfort, turned a bit pink—which he attributed to the chill when I teased him later—and started to pet Leslie's head awkwardly. But heartfelt sympathy from Holmes tended to be short-lived, and he stopped, peeled Leslie's face off his coat, and shook her, which promptly ended her sobbing.

"What happened?" he asked.

"There was a voice," Leslie said. "I remember it clearly. A man's voice. He was calling me."

Holmes and I stared at each other, silent, for a long moment.

CHAPTER 10

A Human Hand

"…a savage blow dealt by a vigorous arm."

—Sir Arthur Conan Doyle, *The Adventure of the Priory School*

THE SILENCE WAS BROKEN WITH A CRY. "YOU HEARD IT too?" Arthur put away his phone and inched closer, his angst momentarily forgotten. "I knew it! I knew it! We couldn't have both imagined it." He looked triumphantly at Holmes, who returned a wary glance.

"Start at the beginning, if you please," Holmes instructed Leslie.

"All right, but there's not much to tell. I remember leaving the Great Room to use the toilet. I wasn't sure where it was, so I walked down the corridor, and that's when I heard someone calling me. It seemed to be coming from the end of the corridor—where the kitchen is—so I went to check it out, but there was no one there. The back door was open, so I stepped outside and started walking down the path and then—" Her hand instantly shot up to her head. "Ow!" She pressed on a spot near the back of her head gingerly. "I think someone hit me with something hard."

"Excellent," Holmes murmured. Luckily, Leslie was too preoccupied with her wound to hear. "We ought to return to the outbuilding. The others will be relieved to discover that nothing gruesome happened to either of you." I supposed hearing strange voices and being struck in the head didn't qualify as "gruesome" in his books.

He helped Leslie to her feet, but if she expected him to serve as her aide, lending an arm and a shoulder—and perhaps words of commiseration—she was sadly mistaken. Holmes sprinted ahead without her. Arthur, though, offered an arm, which she brushed aside. Reassured that she was more than capable of walking without help, I hurried to catch up to Holmes.

"Why is it 'excellent' that Leslie was hit over the head?" I whispered, already starting to gasp for breath as I tried to match his pace.

"Isn't it obvious?"

"Not even slightly."

"Tsk, tsk." He shot a look behind him, then continued softly, "Ever since Gastrell told us about Drebber's death, the possibility of supernatural interference has been contemplated far too often and too seriously for my taste. Here at Crooked Forest, the evidence for it has been piling up—the ritualistic slaying of the second dog, the symbols in the snow, the blue fire, Jibril's sightings of a witch and hellhound, and then, finally, two disappearances." A grim smile punctuated his words. "However, a supernatural being hardly needs to render a person unconscious with a pot or whatever. A human hand struck Leslie, my dear Watson, and that makes my job much easier, for humans are sloppier than unearthly creatures."

The relief I felt exposed me as one of the many who had considered the supernatural with more conviction than skepticism. Hiding my embarrassment as best as I could, I said, "So you were sending Leslie's phone a

Triviatrix request from Zara's phone, and that notification prompts a tune. You kept sending it to her until we were near enough to hear her phone."

Holmes nodded, then frowned when I failed to compliment his simple genius. I didn't want to be responsible for inflating his ego, which was already grandiloquent.

The march back to the outbuilding was a quiet one, each of us weighed down by cumbersome thoughts that left little desire for chatter. The outbuilding was a welcoming site; it had warmth, a roof, and lockable doors, and that was enough for me to feel somewhat safe, even if I had to share the space with unsavoury characters like Dimitri Komarov.

It was fairly easy to picture someone like him clobbering Leslie and dragging her away like an enraged Frankenstein's monster. *But did he need to drag her through the snow?* I wondered. His powerful bulk could have easily swiped Leslie off her feet. Perhaps the attacker was a woman then … or perhaps it was a man after all, a man clever enough to obscure his footprints by dragging his victim in the snow. However desperate I was to paint Dimitri as the perpetrator, the fact was that he had been in the Great Room the whole time.

Holmes stopped us just outside the back door, much to our chagrin. Arthur especially looked crestfallen that warmth was an arm's length away, yet unreachable; he shivered miserably.

"Gastrell," Holmes said, "you may want to omit the bit about hearing voices when you speak to the authorities. No one will believe you, and if your colleagues get wind of it, they will have a fresh new reason to ridicule you. You as well, Leslie."

Leslie nodded and Arthur coloured.

"But how do I explain why I left?" he asked.

"The explanation you provided was unsatisfactory at best," Holmes said haughtily. "Even just staring daftly will serve you better than what you claim to be the truth."

"It *is* the truth," Arthur protested.

"Ah, that reminds me! I would like to inspect your hands, if you don't mind. Well, actually, even if you do mind."

Although I would have reacted indignantly, Arthur held out his hands, looking immensely tired and chilled. It was clear he just wanted the cold scrutiny to be over. I instantly sympathized with him. Holmes shared no such feelings, however; before him was a clue that would either confirm or disprove a theory, and he hardly cared about the mind within the body. He whisked out his magnifying glass and conducted a thorough inspection of the fingers and fingernails. The examination didn't appear to satisfy him though; he extended it to Arthur's sweater, snow pants, and shoes, including the soles. I was happy to see his scowl deepen with each passing minute — he was evidently finding nothing incriminating. His accusing tone didn't diminish though when he straightened.

"Why did you not inform us that Marieta Charr is a colleague of yours?" he asked.

Arthur shrugged. "Well, I d-didn't think that mattered."

Holmes raised a brow. "She is a practitioner of the old religion. It didn't cross your mind even for a moment that she may be involved in what happened to the dogs?"

"Absolutely not," he replied in a quivering voice, but I knew he was lying.

"He wanted to avoid a witch hunt," I said. I knew he had suspected her and then had shamefully admonished the thought just as I had. And he hadn't thought Holmes and Gwilym Lestrade would be as quick to follow suit. Perhaps he wasn't the only bullied staff member at Crooked Forest; perhaps Marieta had also been mistreated.

Arthur nodded. "She would never hurt the dogs."

Holmes' suspicious glare flickered. "One last question: the water you used to put out the fire, where did it come from?"

Arthur thought for a moment. "I filled a bucket using the kitchen faucet. I had to make multiple trips, not that it helped. Why do you want to know?"

There was no answer. Instead, Holmes walked inside as though he hadn't heard, which happened on occasion when he was deep in thought. More than once, I had knocked on his door at Baker House and received no answer, only to find him immersed in a book or simply lost in his thoughts. It was also possible that he was just being rude.

Arthur glanced at me inquiringly. I shrugged. I had no idea why people thought I could decipher Sherlock Holmes; his mind was as much of an enigma to me as it was to everyone else. Leslie was less curious about the inner workings of my friend; she cast Arthur a dirty look—no doubt stirred by Holmes' interrogation—and disappeared inside.

By the time the police and paramedics arrived nearly forty minutes later, the excitement our return had created had died down, but only after relief, bewilderment, and a deluge of questions had muddled the Great Room in equal parts. Vague explanations were given, accurate for the most part, and eventually we were all left undisturbed. Leslie was resting comfortably, wrapped in blankets, in the same room Jibril was in; the colour was returning to her cheeks under Marieta Charr's watchful eye. Arthur and Holmes had vanished from the room; the former, I pictured hiding in a closet, and as for the latter, he was no doubt sniffing or prodding something—the kitchen faucet perhaps.

I gravitated toward the only source of familiarity in the room: Gwilym, Christa, and Elodie. They managed to contain their curiosity until we found ourselves in a quiet, isolated corner in the Great Room and then forced me to divulge all. This I did, though I had the slightest inkling that Holmes wouldn't approve of me talking to the "enemy." However, he hadn't prohibited dialogue, and there was no way Gwilym would beat him to the finish line by knowing what had come to pass in the woods.

I tactfully left out the disembodied voice Arthur had heard; it would have given Christa one more thing to taunt him about. Explaining away his sudden departure as a need for a walk and fresh air, which was partly true anyway, appeased their curiosity.

Soon thereafter, Christa broke off into a discussion with Elodie on the effectiveness of protective charms. She mentioned Marieta's necklace with a covetous eagerness, which she had caught only a glimpse of before Marieta had hidden it. Christa remarked on how pretty the stone was. Then she pondered whether Marieta would be willing to procure one for her, and for Elodie too. Elodie didn't seem quite as enthusiastic about the topic but nodded along anyway as Christa pointed out the benefits of wearing such a charm. Her main argument was how unfazed—and unscathed—Marieta had been in the aftermath of the blue fire incident, whereas Jibril and Arthur had not been so fortunate. She naturally ignored the fact that the rest of the staff, though still apprehensive, were fine despite some of them also having put out the fire.

When the girls finally departed in search of Marieta, I could only shake my head. Gwilym's face didn't echo the incredulity on mine. Instead, he was deep in thought, and those thoughts were making him scowl.

Just as puzzling—and something I would have missed had I not been watching the girls snake through the Great Room—was a fleeting exchange between Christa and Dimitri. The man's face softened uncharacteristically at the sight of her. It wasn't shallow attraction—there was more depth in that longing expression; it was a reaction beyond Dimitri's control, a thing that just happened at the sight of something he felt passionate about. It was odd seeing it on his face, but I supposed even bullies fell in love. And it wasn't one-sided either. It was Dimitri's name that Christa had stopped Arthur from saying that night at Baker House. Although I couldn't see Christa's face, her head was angled toward him, and I was certain she had met his eyes with a reciprocating expression. Did that mean this wasn't her first time at Crooked Forest Adventures? Had she met Dimitri on a previous visit? That must be the case, I decided, for how else would Arthur know about their relationship? But why all the secrecy? The couple hadn't exchanged a word all day. I supposed there could be a hundred reasons why this was so, but something about the matter unsettled me.

Sometime later, after the arrival of the police, one of the locked rooms was converted into a makeshift interrogation room. Two officers began taking each of our statements. No one spoke as we waited to be called. It seemed that the excitement of the day had finally taken a toll on the adventurers. They took turns sitting around the fire, fatigued and eager to leave.

I told the police the little I knew, omitting the real reason behind our venturing out here. Then, finally, we were permitted to leave. As Holmes and I walked to the car, which suddenly seemed very far away, we ran into Dimitri by the exit, shouting something about a full refund. The rest of the staff watched the departing customers with mournful expressions and handed out free dogsledding vouchers, which I immediately threw into the nearest trash can; I hadn't the slightest inclination of spending another winter day in the wilderness ever again. If the investigation demanded we return, I would let Holmes go alone; I'd had enough of the endless snow and the sinister atmosphere. Curiosity would not draw me back.

It was early evening—but pitch black—when we reached the car. Above us, the inky sky was densely spotted with stars, a sight I would have marvelled at if I hadn't felt so exhausted. Holmes appeared to sense this in the way I had dragged myself through the snow. He volunteered to drive.

"So you–you do know how to drive?" I stammered.

Holmes shrugged. "Never said I didn't know."

I groaned loudly. Admittedly, the risk of driving into a tree would be high if I were to take the wheel, so despite feeling disgruntled at the deception, I slipped into the passenger seat of our rental without further argument.

"Did you find red paint on Arthur?" I asked a little while later as we merged onto the highway.

Holmes frowned, then answered grudgingly, "I did not."

"Do you have another suspect?"

A dissatisfied shake of the head and then, "I need more data. I can't make bricks without clay."

A soft groan escaped me. "Please don't tell me we have to come back here."

"I think not, Watson."

His words didn't fill me with relief. Instead, his quiet tone filled me with a fresh dose of dread.

CHAPTER 11

Hounds in a Cup

*"Alas!" replied our visitor, "the very horror of my situation
lies in the fact that my fears are so vague, and my suspicions
depend so entirely upon small points, which might seem
trivial to another ..."*

—Sir Arthur Conan Doyle, *The Adventure of the Speckled
Band*

THAT NIGHT, FATIGUE COAXED ME INTO SLEEP WITHIN
minutes of getting into bed ... or perhaps credit was due
to the melancholic tunes of Holmes' violin, which was the
last sound I heard before drifting off.

But nightmares—and sometimes the sheer perplexity
of the less morbid dreams—pulled me out. I couldn't
recall any of it, though I remembered the strong scent of
evergreen pines. Somehow the herbaceous aroma had
been stronger in my room during those moments of
wakefulness than it had ever been in the woods that
surrounded Crooked Forest Adventures.

It was nearing eleven o'clock when I awoke the next
morning. I dressed and withdrew from my room in haste,

fuelled by a grumbling stomach, only to meet a curious surprise in the dining room.

Pets weren't permitted at Baker House. That was why I raised a brow at the cat sitting on one of the long wooden cafeteria tables in the dining hall when I entered. The creature was completely white, quite lean, and just two or three years old. Two unblinking silver eyes made up most of its small face. It wore no collar, yet it was well-groomed and looked more impeccable than everyone else in the room.

So not a wild stray that had wandered in by chance, I thought with some relief. There had been an earlier incident with an intrusive squirrel that had sent the ladies screaming and the men on a wild chase around the house.

Gwilym, Christa, and Elodie stood over the cat, although Gwilym's dark eyes hovered on Christa more often than they did on our feline visitor. She took no notice though, a high-pitched "aw" erupting from her puckered glossy lips every time an ear twitched or a paw shifted. Elodie was less vocal, but even she was beaming. Kofi and Kwame Makutsi sat nearby at the same table and occasionally looked up from their books to glance warmly at the newcomer. Arthur, also hunched over a book, was less enamoured.

Much to Christa's irritation, the cat was watching me, although I didn't see any advantage in this. There was something unnerving about being in the gaze of an animal that sat as though it would soon pounce.

"Look how she's taken a liking to me!" Christa exclaimed, rubbing a paw. The cat didn't seem to mind her constant need to touch its fur, but I would hardly call it affection. It continued to stare at me. "We should keep her. We can hide her in my room. Let's call her Snow!"

Strange, I thought as I slipped into the adjoining kitchen and helped myself to coffee. *Did that mean the cat didn't belong to anyone at Baker House? Then who had let it in?*

I returned to the dining hall and walked over to Holmes, who was sitting the furthest from the cat at another table. Preoccupied with a newspaper, he paid the creature no mind.

"Whose cat is that?" I asked him quietly, taking a seat.

He gave an irritated grunt and didn't emerge from behind the newspaper. When he spoke, his voice was hoarse. "Not now, Watson. I am busy." His hands trembled ever so slightly.

I tsked. "You need to stop smoking so much. Look how it's changing your voice. What if it's cancer of the vocal cords?" Smirking, I added, "I can come to the doctor with you, if you'd like."

Holmes growled, moved aside the large mug and messy stack of newspapers, textbooks, loose sheets of paper, and notebooks next to him, and laid his newspaper flat on the table. Then he glared at me. The dark rings around his eyes were a commonplace feature of his face, often coinciding with the chemical fumes drifting from his room late into the night, but today they looked darker than ever, possibly because he looked paler than usual.

"You didn't sleep much, did you?" I asked.

His frown deepened. "Perhaps you ought to diagnose people after you complete medical school." I had no interest in medicine and Holmes knew that, but he had made it his mission to divert my course in life from English literature to "something more practical."

"Experimenting with your chemistry set again?" I teased.

The reply was curt. "I couldn't sleep. It was a good distraction."

I nodded in understanding. So, the death—or more accurately, the murder—we had encountered yesterday had disturbed the stoic Holmes after all. But I didn't want to talk about what had happened at Crooked Forest. I repeated my question about the cat.

"Haven't the foggiest idea," he replied, smoothing the newspaper tenderly. Again, his hands shook. "It was sitting there when I arrived with my coffee at ten o'clock and hasn't moved since, despite Christa's attempts to mollycoddle it."

"Maybe it came in through an open window," I guessed. The immediate vicinity of Baker House was largely residential; the cat could have come from any of the dozens of houses and low-rise apartments that surrounded us.

Holmes shrugged and returned to the news, and I gazed over at the cat. It was now staring at the wallpaper, as though mesmerized by the pale gold fleur-de-lis motif that repeated across the turquoise backdrop.

Nearly an hour later, after I had languidly brunched to my belly's content and flushed the food down with more coffee, I noted an absence. Marieta Charr hadn't come down yet even though it was well past noon. I whispered this to Holmes, but he shrugged and continued to furiously scribble in the notebook that had replaced the newspaper.

The last I had seen of her was at Crooked Forest … had she even returned to Baker House last night? She may have wandered in after I had fallen asleep, or perhaps Dimitri, now free from watchful eyes, had done something to her! I stood abruptly.

"We need to go see if she's okay," I whispered to Holmes as Christa and Elodie looked over at me curiously.

Holmes paused his scribbling. "Sit down, Watson. It is not as you fear. She came in late last night, quite unscathed."

"You saw her?" I asked, taking my seat.

"No, but the sound of one's footsteps can reveal much. Hers are quick, steady, and purposeful—and before you ask, it was certainly her steps I heard." I had indeed opened my mouth to interrupt. "As you are aware, there are presently only three occupants on the second floor:

you, me, and Marieta. I recognize the cadence of your steps, and the others have no reason to walk across the landing." He disregarded my questioning look. People had an identifiable gait, but was it possible to identify someone by the sound of their steps? He carried on, "She was in perfect health last night, although I can't say with certainty that applies now."

"What do you mean by that?"

"Well, she didn't sleep a wink, but one sleepless night never killed anyone."

"How could you possibly know that?" I asked.

"Know what? That one sleepless night never—"

I growled. "You know exactly what I'm referring to." Unfortunately, I was unable to intimidate him into responding, which sometimes worked but only when I was genuinely angry. Before he could ignore me and return to scribbling his odd notations in his notebook, I rose again—this time with determination. "I'm going to go find her."

Holmes sighed. Then, to my surprise, he closed his notebook and straightened his long, lanky frame. "After I get another cup of coffee."

But I grabbed his arm and steered him out of the dining hall before he could veer off into the kitchen. He'd had far too much caffeine since coming downstairs; that much was apparent from his twitching fingers. One more cup would only worsen his mood, and I didn't care to be on the receiving end of that.

Marieta didn't open her door right away. In fact, although our knocking halted the rapid rustling of paper that came from within her room, she only poked her head out some moments later.

The poor girl looked even more terrible than Holmes: her eyes were puffy and red, though not in a teary sort of way. A nervous energy coursed through her; apart from her face only the fingers that gripped the door were visible, and they twitched abnormally fast. There was something terribly wrong with her.

Now that we were standing before Marieta, I hadn't the slightest idea what to say. She had always been pleasant with me, but we had spoken of nothing more than "trifles," as Holmes would say.

"Are you well, Marieta?" Holmes asked placidly. The response was a surprised blink. He went on, "It is past noon, and you hadn't come downstairs, so we came to inquire into your well-being."

"Oh … is it that late already?" she mumbled, then pulled open the door, revealing herself and her room. She was still dressed in the clothes she had worn yesterday.

Beyond her lay what I had been anxious to see since late September when rumours about some of Marieta's nocturnal habits had started to circulate among the residents. I saw no sign of the skulls unearthed from her supposed nighttime strolls in the nearby St. James Cemetery, but there was an easel with a blank canvas. Several paintings hung on the walls, all cheery landscapes that I supposed Marieta had painted herself. The dull grey curtains provided by the university had been exchanged for sheer fabric with crimson flowers. Light streamed through, brightening the space. The room was a pleasant compromise between my Spartan one and Holmes' cluttered one.

Perhaps my eagerness was obvious in the way I stared, but at least I tried to restrain myself. It was Holmes who marched in without invitation. Marieta didn't resist the intrusion, so I followed. There was an earthy scent to the room that I found calming until I realized it was the same one I had smelled when I had awoken in the middle of the night.

"Is that coffee?" Holmes asked with shining eyes, but his grin faltered at the smell that drifted out of the French press he had picked up. It was too faint for me to catch its aroma, but apparently it wasn't to his liking. "Cinnamon …" He sniffed, frown deepening as though some abomination had occurred. "Cardamom —"

"Yes, that's spiced coffee," Marieta said.

I didn't think cinnamon and cardamom could smell so unpleasant, but Holmes took his coffee black, without sugar, and seldom wavered from this default.

"I have fresh black tea if you'd like some." Marieta motioned us to a desk in the corner, which was littered with an electric kettle, a hand-painted porcelain teapot, and, to my irrepressible surprise, numerous little teacups.

Holmes picked up one of the cups and peered at the dregs. "Is that—"

Marieta hastily took the cup away. Her twitch worsened. "Please don't touch anything. I, uh, I think it's best if you leave. I'm perfectly fine and I appreciate you both coming to check on me."

But we didn't leave. Instead, I counted the cups; there were eight in total. There was also an unwashed cup by the French press. They were the single oddity in this otherwise neat room.

"Did you drink all this last night?" I asked.

"Throughout the night and morning," she admitted shamefully.

Ah, I thought, *the caffeine had kept her up*. Holmes had been right about her sleepless night. But why on earth had she done it? Holmes voiced the question before I could, but Marieta seemed reluctant to answer. However, an answer almost always followed when Holmes decided to unnerve people by staring at them with unblinking eyes.

"I've had a bad feeling ever since Drebber was found." She clutched her strange necklace. "And then after what happened yesterday, the feeling became overwhelming. I just needed to understand what was happening, *why* it was happening. So I did a–a reading when I got back last night. To get answers." The expression she wore looked much like Arthur's when he had told us about the voice: like somebody who was bracing for a beating.

Her answer puzzled me at first, but when I glanced at the cups once again and saw the dried brown leaves within each, it clicked. Apparently, Holmes too had connected the dots, for he looked over at me in mild amusement.

"You did a tea-leaf reading?" I blurted out. I hadn't meant to sound so incredulous, but the damage had been done. Marieta nodded, dark eyes filled with fresh apprehension. I was suddenly desperate to ask if her family had hailed from New England, whether her ancestors had any connection to Salem, but I didn't. Motivated by both guilt and curiosity, I asked her what the reading had revealed.

"Dogs," she said. "I did reading after reading, and saw a dog in every cup. See for yourself." She thrust a cup at me, and I peered inside. It could be a dog, I supposed, but it was hard to tell, yet Marieta seemed so convinced. Holmes glanced at the interior nonchalantly, then went over to the desk to examine the other cups.

"I think I see a camel in this one," he declared a moment later, smiling faintly. "Perhaps *you* are seeing dogs because that is what you want to see."

Marieta snatched the cup with surprising ferocity. "What appears in the cup is a reflection of what is happening or will happen in life."

"I see," Holmes said, looking unconvinced.

I asked, "What does it mean to see a dog?"

"Specifically, it's a reference to the bloodshed we've seen, the killings of Drebber and the other dog, Stangers. In general terms, a dog means secret enemies."

"So you're saying a secret enemy killed the two dogs?" I asked, not quite comprehending what she—or I—was saying.

Marieta nodded, then looked uncertain and shook her head, clutching the cup in her hands so tightly I was sure it would crack under pressure. "I need to show these to my aunt. She has years of experience in tasseomancy."

Still surveying the cups airily, Holmes said, "Perhaps you ought to do a, erm, reading for us now." His face puckered at "reading" as though it distressed him to admit it was a word. "Let us see if a dog manifests once again."

I wondered if he suspected that Marieta had staged the supposedly dog-like figures in the cups. Or perhaps he simply thought the idea of reading tea leaves to be preposterous and wanted an opportunity to ridicule it when the dog failed to show itself. Although I had no proof, the teacups didn't look staged to me; the young woman before me was a little eccentric, but she wasn't dishonest. All the same, it would have been inspiriting to take part in a reading, if only for fun, but Marieta shook her head.

"I can't. I just can't. I can't do this again. Please leave. I need to sleep." She ushered us out onto the landing, but just before the door closed, she stuck out her head and said to Holmes, "You're always reading the newspapers, right? Was there anything about Stangers' death in today's papers?"

Holmes looked at her curiously before shaking his head. I wasn't expecting Marieta to let out a deep breath, but that is what she did. For the first time since she had opened the door, her face relaxed.

"We can do a reading tomorrow," she said. "At my aunt's shop. She'll have answers for us. And here, take these." A hand shot out and dropped something into my palm. "Christa asked for these. Can you give them to her?"

She didn't wait for us to respond. The door shut quietly. I glanced at my palm and saw two replicas of the strange necklace she had been wearing yesterday.

CHAPTER 12

Slander and Accusations

*"At the same moment the convict screamed out a curse at us
and hurled a rock which splintered up against the boulder
which had sheltered us."*

—Sir Arthur Conan Doyle, *The Hound of the Baskervilles*

I DIDN'T BROACH THE TOPIC OF TEA LEAVES AS WE
descended to the first floor or mention the protective
charms; doing so would have incited a slew of insults
from Holmes, and I thought Marieta had encountered
enough of that already.

We wandered into the Baker House library, which we
often did after breakfasting on the weekends. I left
Holmes for the bookcases. By happenstance, I plucked
Hawthorne's *The House of the Seven Gables* from a shelf.
Perhaps chance hadn't dictated my selection at all; I had
read the book in high school, and though the plot was
now a blur, I knew it held hints of witchcraft. I was no
longer in the mood for Christmas tales; it seemed the
festive atmosphere had seeped out of the house. Here
was a book that seemed to complement the exceptional
situation we found ourselves in.

When I stepped into the sitting area, I found Holmes settled in an armchair. His eyes were unfocused, and he looked deep in thought, which naturally compelled me to disturb him.

"How did you know Marieta hadn't slept?" I asked.

He grunted. "Isn't it obvious? The fatigue in her face, the clothes from yesterday, the bed that hadn't been slept in."

"But you said that before we went to her room."

"Oh, all right. Those were confirmatory points I used to strengthen my initial deduction." He paused, distracted by a fleeting thought. Then his face cleared. "I heard footsteps last night—incessant, irritating footsteps—downstairs, upstairs, roaming into every unoccupied room in the house it seemed. No one else in the dining hall looked as though they had been awake all night, so by process of elimination, the person I heard was Marieta."

"Or possibly Mrs. Kerrigan," I said. "The lady does keep odd hours."

"No, no, her steps would have been heavier. I'm certain it was Marieta. That foul smell is proof."

"What smell?"

"Don't you smell it? The house was saturated with it last night. I suppose it has faded somewhat. Thank goodness!" He added, crinkling his nose, "Sage, if I am not mistaken."

"Oh, isn't sage used to clear negative energy or something?" I had to sound nonchalant and only vaguely familiar with such things when discussing them with Holmes.

"Hm, seems exactly like the kind of thing Marieta would do, wouldn't you agree?" He leaned into the armchair and muttered to himself, "So she thinks there is negative energy in the house, eh? Now *that* is curious." Then he glanced at me sharply. "Don't you have a delivery to make? Off you go, and don't come back. I need to think."

The next morning began with the shattering of glass. I, however, was too groggy to wonder who had broken what. In fact, I barely had the strength to stir even though it was already half past nine. One could blame either Hawthorne's ability to captivate or my habit of reading late into the night.

When I made my way downstairs half an hour later, the dining hall looked much like it had the day before, although Snow the cat was nowhere in sight. Mrs. Kerrigan had turned up briefly yesterday even though she didn't work weekends, and the cat, perhaps sensing banishment, had made itself scarce ever since. It was probably sleeping off its nocturnal misdoings in some corner of Christa's room.

Apparently, ten o'clock was still too early for the residents of Baker House—Holmes occupied his usual corner in the dining hall, hunched over a book, and Christa and Elodie sat at another table, heads together, speaking in hushed, serious tones. The rest slumbered on.

I helped myself to a generous mugful of coffee and then contemplated where to sit. Holmes hadn't even looked up when I had entered the room, so immersed was he with his reading. It was likely I would get few words out of him; he had been in one of his strange, distant moods most of yesterday and I had a feeling it would bleed into today.

So I veered left toward the girls and took a seat at their table, nodding good morning. Surprisingly, Christa waved me over, and I slid closer out of curiosity. Evidently, there was something she was eager to tell me, something that didn't even warrant a greeting. Even Elodie just stared, unsmiling, whereas her friend's mood was funereal.

"Mrs. Kerrigan stole my protection necklace," Christa moaned loudly.

In my peripherals, I saw Holmes' head jolt up. I too gaped in surprise. Our housekeeper was an odd woman, but this accusation was just silly. However, Christa's neck was devoid of the protective charm I had given her the day before. Elodie's, which she had accepted sheepishly and put on only because Christa had insisted, remained nestled within the bony bumps of her chest.

"You probably just misplaced it. I can give you mine," Elodie said.

"No, I know where I left it." Christa turned to me. "I took it off this morning before my shower and put it on my bedside table, just by the lamp. Mrs. Kerrigan came in to clean up the mug I'd broken. I should've been suspicious then; she never does that sort of thing. She was sweeping up the mess when I left for the bathroom, and when I came back, she was gone and so was the necklace."

Holmes' voice drifted over to us. "Your door had been unlocked the entire time, was it not?"

"Well, yeah. I couldn't lock it with Mrs. Kerrigan inside, and that old bat left the door wide open when she left."

"Hence, anyone could have come in and taken it, although why they would want such rubbish is beyond me."

Christa looked indignant. "It's not rubbish! And that nasty old lady stole it!" Perhaps she had spoken a bit too loudly. Mrs. Kerrigan suddenly appeared at the doorway, her normally powdery-white face flaming.

Everything from Mrs. Kerrigan's thinning salt-and-pepper hair and twitching beady eyes, both of which worsened the severity of her wrinkled face, to her morbidly rotund form, which miraculously flitted like a firefly around Baker House, was unnerving. Today her teeth were exposed in a wild grimace, making her even more terrifying than usual.

"You brat!" she cried. "You overprivileged, spoiled brat!" Spit shot into the air, following each word like bullets. "How dare you!"

We sat in dumbfounded silence for a moment. The housekeeper advanced toward us, a broom in one shaking hand and a corpulent finger on the other pointing menacingly at us. I had never seen her so furious, which was saying something, since she took it upon herself to shout often.

"I clean up your mess and this is the thanks I get? You're a liar—a slanderous—"

Holmes stood up gracefully. "Ah, I fear there has been a misunderstanding, my dear Mrs. Kerrigan. Christa here was narrating the plot of the book she is reading. You see, there is a housekeeper by the name of Mrs. *Berrigan* in it, who is fixated with shiny objects. Ladies, weren't we just about to head upstairs? Come along now."

It was evident the housekeeper didn't believe him. Neither would have I; Christa didn't read books. Neither Holmes' English charm nor his flattering smile had any effect. The lady's scowl deepened as we shot up in unison, steered clear of her broomstick, and scampered toward the exit.

"You'll suffer for spreading lies, girl," the housekeeper muttered as we passed.

We followed Holmes upstairs in awkward silence, unaware of where we were heading until he stopped in front of Christa's door on the third floor. He motioned at her to let us in, which she probably would have refused to do if she hadn't been still recovering from the insults exchanged in the dining hall.

Once inside, Christa and Elodie slumped on the bed, looking dejected. I hovered uncomfortably, dodging Holmes as he poked about the desk and bedside table, pulled open drawers, and peered in the closet.

Christa didn't object to having her fineries touched by the likes of Holmes; in fact, she hardly seemed to notice. She teetered sideways, and her head landed on a large pillow. One hand clutched Elodie's and she looked as though she might cry. *She must've never been reprimanded in her life*, I thought.

"The necklace doesn't appear to be here. Yet your fine jewellery sits untouched," Holmes said at last. "Very curious."

"She's such a weird old lady. Who knows why she took it, I … I just know she did," Christa mumbled.

Holmes nodded thoughtfully. "It's not a completely far-fetched idea, I suppose. Have any of you heard of the Forty Elephants? No? Well, they were an all-female gang of thieves thought to have been in operation as early as the late eighteenth century in the West End of London. Apart from shoplifting in large shops, they also masqueraded as housemaids to rob and blackmail their wealthy employers."

I laughed. "Are you suggesting that Mrs. Kerrigan belongs to a gang?"

Holmes shrugged. "If she were, I daresay she would have pocketed the Tiffany lamp, or at the very least, the smaller precious items in this room." He looked around as though he were taking inventory. His eyes came to rest on the scatter of photographs Christa had pasted on a portion of the wall by her desk.

"Maybe her gang collects mystical objects," Christa said quietly. She was starting to look less like a wounded child and seemed quite unwell.

It was apparent she was still ruminating about the events of yesterday, as were we all, but I wished she hadn't drawn such parallels. I wanted to leave Crooked Forest far behind me. It was a crime to bring it here to Baker House, where life was predictable and safe — unless Holmes decided to play with his chemicals, which always made me nervous, particularly since he had disabled the smoke detector in his room.

"Do you mean like a cult?" I asked stiffly.

"Or a coven," she said. Next to her, Elodie rolled her eyes.

"And here I thought the anachronistic practice of defaming people with accusations of witchcraft was in the past," Holmes muttered. "Perhaps we ought to ask her to recite the Lord's Prayer?" he added with a sardonic smile. "You see, the inability to recite the Lord's Prayer was used to sniff out a witch in the past."

"I'm sure Marieta can give you a new charm," I said kindly to Christa. "Actually, we're going to her aunt's shop today for a tea-leaf reading." I hadn't meant to share this, but Christa looked so unlike her usual self — almost pitiful, in fact — that I felt sorry for her. The admission perked her for a moment, and she glanced at me questioningly. I quickly told her about the dogs in Marieta's many cups and the invitation to the tea shop. Unlike Holmes, Christa regarded me seriously.

"Secret enemies, eh?" she muttered, looking worried.

"Why don't you both come along? Maybe the shop also sells charms," I said. Internally, I kicked myself for being so cordial; apart from Elodie — for reasons unknown — and the Baker House men — who were easily infatuated by glossed lips — few could tolerate Christa's company for long.

"And a reading to find out who took the necklace," Christa added, glancing meaningfully at her friend. Elodie, on the other hand, was staring at me as though I couldn't have said anything more absurd. I didn't point out that it was *her* friend who had conjectured about Mrs. Kerrigan's sorcerous activities. Dabbling in divination after a cup of tea was no more ridiculous than that.

"Don't encourage this nonsense, Watson," Holmes grumbled.

Christa couldn't disagree more. Looking a bit revived, she said, "It's a great idea. Go with them, Elodie. Buy me a charm and do a reading. I need to know what happened to my necklace."

Elodie didn't look pleased at all. "But what about you? Won't you come too?"

But Christa shook her head, her mind made up. "I don't feel so great. My head—I'm going to sleep this off. The sooner you get me that charm, the better." Meek though her voice was, there was a finality to it that left no room for discussion. Elodie's shoulders slumped in resignation, and she glowered at me.

CHAPTER 13

The Ritual

"I have seen too much not to know that the impression of a woman may be more valuable than the conclusion of an analytical reasoner."

—Sir Arthur Conan Doyle, *The Man with the Twisted Lip*

OUR DESTINATION THAT AFTERNOON WAS A TIMEWORN, two-storey, red-bricked building that sat snugly in a corner lot near Trinity Bellwoods Park. It was perfectly symmetrical, with its carved wooden door flanked by small paned windows that projected from under a canopy. The quaint lettering overhead spelled out Tea & Tee in bright gold. It had the look of a nineteenth-century apothecary, fit to sit on the cobbled streets of London, except for the sign, which looked new. Spying leatherbound books and tea things through the window, I rushed inside in anticipation, while Holmes and Elodie dragged their feet, still wearing the matching expressions of disdain they had left Baker House with.

A number of things kept me rooted at the doorway: the strong aroma of frankincense; the chimes that echoed throughout the cluttered space to announce our arrival, then gave way to the soothing tunes of a harp; the high shelves that snaked around the walls, stacked with paraphernalia; and finally, the marigold tapestry that covered the wall behind the cash register at the back of the shop. Here, my eyes lingered, and one hundred black-and-white eyes—splattered across the body of an enormous, bearded man—stared back. I turned away— one could only look at the many eyes of the mythological Argus for so long before discomfort took hold—and stumbled into a woman. I immediately knew she was no patron; in fact, Holmes, Elodie, and I were the only customers there.

"Welcome," the woman greeted us in a voice that was melodious enough to serenade folks with the harp that was playing.

She was so tall that I had to look up at her and so very thin that her collarbones jutted sharply from beneath the long cornflower-blue dress she wore. Strands of dark hair fell neatly from the pale gold scarf that turbaned her head. One thick strand in particular curled its way down her left cheek, hiding the jagged pink scar that seared her skin. She was no doubt Marieta's aunt; the resemblance, down to the slightly upturned nose, was uncanny.

Once Holmes and Elodie trudged inside, she introduced herself as Tina Stillaway but begged us to call her "Aunt Tee" like her niece. I rather liked the moniker, but I was certain neither Holmes nor Elodie would use it. She then shook each of our hands, and her fingers, which reminded me of the legs of a spider, held ours for a bit longer than was usual. Probing dark eyes accompanied the gesture, but I was too intrigued by the shop and this formidable stranger to care much. Holmes, though, was quick to raise a deprecating brow and shake loose his hand.

Mrs. Stillaway regarded us with a solemn smile. "It's such a pleasure to meet Marieta's friends, although I suppose it could have been under better circumstances." We didn't inform her that Marieta didn't have any friends at Baker House; people either admired her nervously from a distance—the men—or gossiped in hushed voices—the ladies—which I supposed was better than the treatment Holmes sometimes received.

"You will all feel a bit more restored after some tea," Mrs. Stillaway said. Beckoning us to follow, she twirled, her dress making a *swish*, and glided down the aisle, leaving behind a trailing scent of jasmine.

I followed distractedly, taking in the overwhelming number of accoutrements that lined the shelves. We passed bags and bags of loose-leaf tea, the packaging branded with a blackbird; teapots, some of which were housed in glass cases and priced at hundreds of dollars; and teacups whose interiors were decorated with the strangest of symbols. Some I recognized to be signs of the zodiac; other cups had numbers and drawings of playing cards etched onto the white porcelain.

Mrs. Stillaway parted the Argus tapestry, revealing a brick-walled extension of the shop. It was relatively barren, save for the low circular table that sat at the centre. Cushioned stools had been placed neatly around it. It seemed the only thing missing was a scatter of lit candles, and perhaps a crystal ball, to cast the space into mystical duskiness.

"My dearies, I hope you aren't in a hurry." Mrs. Stillaway was staring at Holmes as she said this. "A tea-leaf reading is a ritual, and there is a process to rituals that can't be rushed. Go on inside. I think you will be satisfied with the arrangements I've made."

I wasn't sure how satisfied Holmes and Elodie were, but the delicious scent that drifted from the three tiers of the serving plate on the table was enough to lift my spirits. Like the chairs, there was precision in the neat way the blueberry scones and tea sandwiches had been arranged on the plates. A stack of small plates sat to the left, and white teacups and saucers sat on the right, all arranged purposefully.

Marieta was already seated, her fingers absentmindedly drumming against the spotless wooden surface of the table. Her scone lay untouched. She nodded at us gravely as we stepped in.

I hadn't expected food at a reading, and perhaps my surprise showed, for Mrs. Stillaway smiled, more brightly this time.

"Food is an essential part of a reading. It helps to stir conversation and relaxation," she said.

Holmes nudged me and murmured, "It is during such socializing that these charlatans cleverly extract information from their naïve clients and spit it back at them during the reading." He snickered, and I glanced worriedly at Mrs. Stillaway, but her pleasant expression didn't falter as she laid out the plates. I returned the nudge, a bit forcefully, and took my place at the table.

"Food is also important for grounding—that is, peace in mind and body," Mrs. Stillaway went on. "Worry and agitation are not conducive to a good reading, and I sense some of these emotions in excess in some of you." She cast a peculiar look at Holmes, as though to say: *But you, dearie, are not anxious. You're just a naysayer, here to stir anxiety in others.* I had the vaguest sensation that she had heard Holmes' remark perfectly.

Holmes didn't touch the food. Instead, he drummed his fingers on the table. Elodie pecked at a scone, unable to defy Mrs. Stillaway's insisting gaze. I needed no such encouragement and helped myself, although it was watchful eyes and good manners, rather than the hearty lunch from an hour ago, that stopped me from piling food onto my plate. By the time our plates were whisked away, timed perfectly with the whistling of the kettle on the stove, my belly was content. Holmes looked bored though, and the girls hardly looked any more grounded than they had before their first nibble.

Mrs. Stillaway noticed this too. Looking rather sombre, she handed us each a wide-rimmed, white teacup and placed half a teaspoon of oolong in each.

Holmes pushed his cup away. "No, thank you, Mrs. Stillaway. I will not be participating. I am simply here to observe."

The smile returned to Mrs. Stillaway's face. "Not a tea person, eh? I've got just the thing for you then." She went back into the shop and returned a moment later with a black metal tin, grinning victoriously. "My strongest blend." A faint aroma of coffee penetrated the air as she shook the tin. "I'm going to boil this on the stove so the grounds don't float to the top." With her customary twirl and swish, she set off toward the other end of the room.

A few minutes later, she placed a cup full of coffee in front of Holmes, black and sugarless just as he liked it. Even he didn't have the heart to reject the offering after she had gone out of her way to make it. He took a reluctant sip, then another. His face told me he approved immensely.

As our teas steeped, their aromas drowned by that of the coffee, Mrs. Stillaway sat down and peered at us.

"Does anyone know the origin story of tea drinking?" she asked.

No one replied, although I was certain Marieta at least knew the answer, having likely heard her aunt ask the question many times before. Even I recalled the story had something to do with a happy accident in ancient China.

Mrs. Stillaway went on, "According to Chinese lore, nearly five thousand years ago, the emperor of China was relaxing under a tea tree when a sudden gust of wind blew some of the leaves into his cup of hot water." She brought her cup up to her nose and inhaled the steam. "A most wonderful aroma arose from the cup, and he took a sip, beginning the cherished tradition of tea drinking."

Holmes sniffed and cleared his throat. "I do believe," he began in one of his more pompous tones, "scholars credit our prehistoric ancestors with the discovery of tea."

"Yes, I'm aware—"

"Anthropologists believe early humans in Asia encountered tea leaves while looking for food, and possibly even chewed them at first, imitating their four-legged counterparts. Once fire, and then the practice of boiling water, were discovered—"

"Yes, dearie, I am aware." Mrs. Stillaway enunciated her words slowly, as though she were dealing with a pedantic child who was only capable of hearing his own voice, which Holmes certainly was at times. Yet she also looked mildly amused. It appeared she rather liked Holmes, although I had no idea why. He had been nothing but insolent so far.

"You can all begin to drink your tea. Please stop when only a small amount is left," she said, once she was sure Holmes would speak no more. He had evidently taken offence to the interruption and broadcasted his scowl for all to see; we naturally ignored him. "As you drink, focus your thoughts on a question."

I took a sip and cringed. My usual pick-me-up being a latte brimming with milk and sugar, it was somewhat difficult to digest this floral—specifically "grassy"—taste. It appeared Elodie had even more trouble swallowing the tea. To my surprise, her usual timidity fell away, and she asked for sugar.

"It's best to drink it without sugar, or any other additives for that matter," Mrs. Stillaway said.

Elodie didn't reply, but there was something retaliatory in the way she put her cup down. Again, I was surprised to see her behave this way, as impetuously as Holmes, in fact. Perhaps her inner spunk revealed itself only when Christa wasn't around to stamp it out.

Sighing, Mrs. Stillaway whisked out a ceramic sugar jar and spoon and laid them before Elodie, who eagerly helped herself to a generous amount. I too was tempted, but the lady's look of disappointment as she watched Elodie kept me still.

The raw taste of the tea stuck to my tongue, but the more unpalatable matter was the question. There were too many questions that needed answering—who had killed Drebber and Stangers? Who—or what—had caused the blue fire? What had lured Arthur into the woods? Who had hurt Leslie and laid her out like some diabolic sacrifice? How was I to pick when each seemed as important as the next? I inevitably lingered on all of them as we drank.

I also contemplated the reading itself. On the spectrum of critics like Holmes and Elodie on one side, and believers like Marieta and Christa on the other, I fell somewhere in the middle. The whole affair—the old shop, which I was tempted to spell as *shoppe* to better capture the antiquated atmosphere, and the ominous Mrs. Tina Stillaway, who seemed all-knowing and stirred contradicting feelings in those who met her—provoked a sense of wonder in me. A part of me desperately, and a bit sheepishly, hoped for answers in a cup.

There soon remained only a teaspoon of liquid in my cup. The rest of the group set their cups down shortly after I did, although Holmes continued to slurp noisily, no doubt as retribution for his earlier dismissal. This caught Mrs. Stillaway's attention, just as he had intended; she stared at him, but not in a malign way. Rather, it was as though he were as much of a curio to her as she was to me. At last, the spell broken, Mrs. Stillaway turned to us.

"Do as I do." She picked up her cup, swirled it three times, and covered the cup with the saucer. Then she flipped the cup, letting the remaining drops of tea fall onto the saucer. "Continue thinking about your question—or perhaps a series of questions—as the liquid drains."

Her eyes hovered on me for a moment, then watched us as we repeated the motions.

"Now look into your cup. What's the first thing you see? You don't need to say it out loud. Just make a mental note of it."

There was a simultaneous bending of heads as we stared into our cups. All I saw was a squiggly tangle of deep-brown tea leaves. There was no clear shape or even a vague indication of anything recognizable. I slumped further into my seat—as far as one can in a backless ottoman—feeling disappointed and wondering if the other cups had churned out anything noteworthy.

Holmes' slurping had tapered to sipping, probably because he was nearing the coffee dregs at the bottom of his cup, and not due to a sudden realization of how childish he was being. Elodie looked about nonchalantly and twiddled the spoon. I wondered if she had even glanced in her cup. Marieta, on the other hand, was stooped over hers, nose almost touching the rim. She seemed utterly distressed as she peered at the dregs; she looked away and then peered in again, as though hopeful a few seconds would miraculously alter the contents of the cup.

Mrs. Stillaway regarded her niece solemnly. "Let's start with Marieta's cup as it seems to be inciting quite an emotional response from her. What is it you see, dearie?"

But Marieta's lips remained pursed as though announcing her findings would make them all the more real.

Her aunt smiled at her kindly and then took the cup. "A dog," she told us. "Just like the other readings."

"And some clouds," Marieta added miserably before mumbling, mostly to herself, "How could I have secret enemies?"

Mrs. Stillaway looked surprised. "What secret ene—oh, I see! No, Marieta, you've misinterpreted the message."

I held my breath in anticipation. An unknown foe was nerve-racking, but there were far more terrible things out there: another fiendish slaying, for example.

"The dog is typically a symbol of friendship and fidelity, but its position in the cup can change the meaning," Mrs. Stillaway explained. "A dog at the bottom of the cup symbolizes secret enemies, Marieta, but your dog is near the middle. This means unfaithful friends."

Her tone was grave, but she didn't survey us with suspicion, for which I was grateful. I hadn't done anything to Marieta to deserve such scrutiny anyway, nor had Holmes, and Elodie was one of the demurest girls I knew. But Mrs. Stillaway didn't know that. The new verdict did nothing to put poor Marieta at ease; her forehead creased deeply.

"And the clouds," Mrs. Stillaway went on, "mean trouble is brewing."

Holmes was audacious enough to laugh. "Well, that goes without saying if one's friends are disloyal. All in all, a rather vague prediction, wouldn't you agree, Mrs. Stillaway? It doesn't shed any light on the mystery at hand, which is what I presume Marieta was thinking about."

But Mrs. Stillaway didn't seem to hear; her eyes remained fixed on the dregs for a moment longer until a shiver returned her to us. Her gaze then fell on me. I silently passed her my cup, wondering what she would see. She did indeed see something, and right away too.

"Have you lost a family member in the past couple years?" she asked softly.

Somehow, I managed to keep my voice steady, but I didn't have enough of Holmes' stoicism to stop the surprise that impregnated my face. "My grandmother passed away just before I started university. She raised my brother and me after my parents died."

I thought quickly. Had I ever told this to anyone but Holmes at Baker House? I must have; small talk among young people stuck in a house together often centred on school, the weather, or rants about how vexing one's family is. Had someone mentioned my grandmother to Marieta, who then passed it on to her aunt? Evidently, Holmes was thinking along the same lines; he cocked his head and looked amused.

"Have you a message from the other realm?" he asked, making no attempts to stifle his laughter.

Mrs. Stillaway nodded and lifted the cup so I could see the interior. "You see that symbol?" She was pointing at three shaky lines that joined at a single point and radiated away from one another, forming what looked like a triangle, if one used some imagination. "It's a rudimentary version of the triquetra. In tasseomancy, it signifies communication from those who have passed."

Holmes pitched the question I had been about to ask. "And what is dear old Grandma Watson trying to tell us? Do not delay any longer, Mrs. Stillaway. The suspense is taking a toll on Watson's nerves." His sarcasm escaped no one's notice, and even Mrs. Stillaway frowned, although it was difficult to tell whether her frustration was directed at Holmes or the cup.

It may have been the cup; where I had seen a squiggly string of tea leaf, she saw a snake, and apparently, that wasn't a good thing to see in a cup. "It symbolizes the presence of someone in your life who shouldn't be trusted," she said.

"Ah, I sense a theme to these readings," Holmes interjected. "From what I gather, having friends appears to be a terrible inconvenience, but one hardly needs tasseo—what was the term? Tasseomanology? Well, one doesn't need tassimology to know this."

And that concluded my reading: my grandmother had vaguely told me to be wary of my friends but had failed to name names, and the tea leaves had answered none of my many questions.

Elodie didn't slide her cup over to Mrs. Stillaway, but that was because she was busy looking at it herself. Hers was an expression of disbelief; she even gave a subtle shake of her head, as though she were silently protesting what her eyes relayed to her brain. She must have felt our gaze, for she straightened. Then, holding her cup with only two fingers as though it were contaminated, she passed it to our host.

Even Mrs. Stillaway turned a shade paler after peering into the cup. She then glanced at Elodie with those unnerving, probing eyes of hers. It was a dissection of sorts, one that did not involve a blade, yet extracted so much. I wondered what Mrs. Stillaway saw in Elodie, who seemed to shrink under her scrutiny. Finally, she set down the cup.

"The devil is in your cup," she announced.

CHAPTER 14

A Formidable Enemy

"It sounds incredible, for I have not, as far as I know, an enemy in the world."

—Sir Arthur Conan Doyle, *The Naval Treaty*

"WELL, THAT IS RATHER STARTLING," HOLMES SAID AFTER the silence had stretched on too long. He reached across, snatched Elodie's cup, and brought it up to his nose. "What an excellent likeness! Does it foretell death and destruction for poor Elodie here?"

Elodie grinned sheepishly, but there was something superficial about it. She was solemn by nature, but she looked even graver now. Naturally, I wanted to take a peek at the cup, which I did when Holmes set it down. Sure enough, the tea leaves took a deliberate shape—the two horns caught my attention first, followed by the face of … of an animal? No … it was a man, and with some imagination, I could even describe it as a furry-faced man.

"It's nothing to be startled about," Mrs. Stillaway said reassuringly. "What startles me is *why* anyone would want to see the devil in their cup."

"What do you mean by that?" I asked.

Here, Mrs. Stillaway gazed at Elodie strangely. "The leaves provide us with warnings or news of things to happen, but that's a superficial view of *tasseomancy*." She stressed "tasseomancy" for Holmes' benefit, although I was certain he hadn't forgotten the term since he had the memory of an elephant; he had simply indulged in an opportunity to further disparage Mrs. Stillaway's craft. "Essentially, what we see is what we manifest."

"I didn't ask for the devil to appear in my cup!" Elodie protested. "I don't even believe ..." Her voice faltered. "I was just thinking about who took my friend's necklace. This cup doesn't answer that question—unless the devil took it." She tried to sneer but didn't quite manage. In fact, she was starting to look a bit worried.

Mrs. Stillaway took the cup, and her fingers absentmindedly stroked the porcelain. She appeared to be contemplating something.

"The devil is not a positive symbol," she finally said. "It can represent negative feelings or concepts, like dishonesty, difficulty, embarrassment, insecurity, or a harmful person in your life—a person with power over you."

Holmes coughed, although the cough didn't quite mask the name he expelled: "Christa Bretti." Elodie cast him a dirty look, but he was having too diverting a time to stop now.

"This is far more believable than obscure messages from Watson's grandmother," he said jovially. "Do go on, Mrs. Stillaway."

We all scowled at him in unison, although that didn't dampen his spirits. He waved impatiently at Mrs. Stillaway to continue, which she did, but only after a sigh. "You may reach out to this powerful influence for aid, but know that there is a price to be paid." As an afterthought, she added, "I'm referring to a flesh-and-blood person, not the devil figure from Christianity and other religions."

Elodie didn't seem very reassured for someone who didn't believe in the fallen angel.

Mrs. Stillaway went on, "Alternatively, the symbol may refer to you—that is, *you* may be a devil."

Apparently, I wasn't the only one to think how absurd this statement was; both Holmes and Marieta looked mildly surprised. Elodie looked outright offended.

"By this I mean that you may be the kingmaker yourself, influencing those around you, essentially making you the powerhouse."

Our surprised expressions softened into grins now, and downright sniggering on Holmes' part. Mrs. Stillaway's predictions were becoming more and more droll. Marieta and I didn't contradict her though, she out of embarrassment and I out of politeness. Elodie was too demure to protest even though she had shown herself quite capable of being bold that day. *Perhaps the devil in the cup was nothing nefarious at all*, I thought; it was simply telling her to rid herself of Christa. I didn't think that was likely to happen though; in Elodie's view, she wasn't enslaved to her friend, she was devoted.

Holmes rose and clapped his hands. "Well, I think that brings the reading to a conclusion. I feel no one's question was answered though, and no light has been shed on the problem at hand. Nonetheless, thank you for such an entertaining afternoon, Mrs. Stillaway."

But it seemed our host wasn't quite finished with us.

Perhaps it was her stillness that alerted me of this. Ignoring Holmes, she went on surveying us. Only her eyes moved, and her composure remained intact as though she hadn't noticed the traces of mockery and jest around her. I attempted to look as unprejudiced as possible, but Holmes became belligerent when she asked him to sit back down.

"You are a special young man, Mr. Holmes," Mrs. Stillaway said slowly, her penetrating gaze now fixed on my friend. Although he would never admit it, I thought he looked a little unnerved by those staring eyes.

"That is very kind of you to say, but—" he began, scowling.

"I would like to do a reading for you."

Mrs. Stillaway didn't wait for him to object, which he surely would have if she hadn't spirited away his cup and carried out the swirling and saucer motions. All this was done so quickly, and with such a practised hand, that Holmes had no time to protest. He certainly couldn't leave now that she had peered into the cup and uttered a soft "Interesting."

One brow raised, he pried the cup from her hand and inspected the coffee dregs.

"I see nothing interesting," he huffed and slid the cup to me.

He was right; there was nothing of interest per se, but I did spot something that looked like the sun almost immediately—an oval with wavy rays streaming out, at least from the top half. I paused, taking a closer look. No … it wasn't the sun.

"It's a woman," I announced.

Mrs. Stillaway nodded. Suddenly, the image became clearer: there was a larger oval under the head—the abdomen—and smaller shapes to represent the arms and legs. Each piece of her was disjoined, as though she were just an assembly of parts that had never been put together properly.

I asked Mrs. Stillaway what it meant since Holmes would certainly not.

She didn't look at me when she answered; her gaze was still fixed on Holmes. "You will face a formidable enemy," she declared.

Here was the drollest prediction yet; even Holmes wasn't theatrical enough to appoint himself an archnemesis. Still, no one but him laughed. Mrs. Stillaway was unusual, and she graced us in a way that made one wonder, against their better judgement, if she was composed mostly of air. In fact, she had stirred in me ideas that would have seemed preposterous had I been sitting anywhere but here. Yet nothing about her seemed staged, and that was why the rest of us looked at her sombrely.

Her face lightened and she smiled. "Don't be alarmed, Mr. Holmes." Is that what she had sensed behind his scornful guffaw? "There is also an *awen* in your cup." She turned to me. "See those three lines there that shoot out from a single point of origin but do not touch one another?"

Indeed, the dregs had assembled themselves in such a way. The surrounding dregs nearly engulfed the symbol though; if it hadn't been pointed out, I wouldn't have noticed it. I also hadn't known it was a symbol to begin with.

"It symbolizes inspiration," she explained. "There's knowledge coming your way, Mr. Holmes, and some luck too."

He scoffed in response. I thought he would sprint toward the exit now that our host had finished with him, but he remained sitting. It was now his turn to watch Mrs. Stillaway. She didn't look away in discomfort though like most others. She stared back benignly.

"What's on your mind, young man?"

"I was wondering," Holmes drawled, "if your tea leaves forewarned you about the man who gave you that scar?"

For the first time that afternoon, Mrs. Stillaway turned stiff like waxwork, her eyes widening to a degree I didn't think was possible. Her customary complacency disappeared altogether. Those spidery fingers of hers twitched and one hand jerked up but stopped midway. She had been about to touch the scar on her face. Instead, her hand fell on the table, and she closed her eyes. A long, deep breath followed. By the time she met our gaze a moment later, her shoulders had relaxed, but her face looked mournful.

"I was warned," she said quietly, "but I didn't take it seriously. I lost Rosalie because of that. A good, kind woman. She'd been working at the shop for nearly nine years when she died—when she was killed." The sorrow transformed into bitterness as she said the last word, and I suddenly realized where we were: The Augury.

Mrs. Stillaway looked at Holmes sharply. "The newspapers never reported the exact address and there were no pictures of the shop in the papers. This isn't even the only tea shop in the vicinity, and I've changed the shop name. So how did you know?"

"I did think it was strange that none of the articles mentioned the owner by name," Holmes said. "I underestimated you, Mrs. Stillaway. It appears you have friends in the press. You wanted to sweep the whole thing under the rug, didn't you? You like being invisible."

"Invisibility aids survival." There was that bitterness again. "I didn't want history to repeat itself."

"Do you mean the Salem Witch Trials?" asked Holmes.

Mrs. Stillaway laughed, but there was no mirth in it. "People accused of witchcraft were condemned long before Salem, and in much more terrible ways. Between 1520 and 1700 alone, eighty thousand people in Europe were tried for witchcraft and half were executed."

The words had spewed out heatedly, which was perhaps why she forced herself to stop. When she began again, there was less emotion, but the acrimony hadn't wholly disappeared. "I suppose for my ancestors it may have begun in Salem. My father's side of the family was originally from Boston. They migrated north during the Civil War and settled in southern Ontario, which was part of the Province of Canada then and under British rule. Before Boston, their ancestors lived in a village nearby. The name's lost to history, and all I know is that they were forced to leave their home. I'd always wondered if they had lived in Salem during the trials and fled when the persecution got out of hand."

"Were they practitioners?" Holmes asked delicately.

Mrs. Stillaway said, "They practised whatever the art looked like back then. It has evolved considerably throughout the centuries."

It was an opportune time to pitch the question I had been contemplating since I had learned of the Salem witches' northward migration. "Were there *real* witches in Salem then?" I felt somewhat ridiculous having voiced it, and wished I hadn't emphasized "real," but our host only shrugged unhappily.

"Some historians believe that to be the case, but I think the answer depends on what definition of 'witch' you follow. More than three centuries ago in Salem, a witch was usually a woman, often without children of her own, who was rude, outspoken, and didn't get along with the community. All in all, an ugly old misfit.

"I'm sure there were quite a few people who fit this description, but could they make your children sick and die? Curdle milk and cripple livestock? A wicked, lustful creature who stirs up mayhem in the name of the devil, that's what people believed to be a witch. The truth is that there were women and men with a divine connection to the earth and an understanding of nature's gifts. They knew about herbs and brewed concoctions to heal and cure. These people have existed throughout history, and they would've been present in Salem too. They may or may not have practised an alternative pagan faith."

When no one said anything, including Holmes, who looked at her with unwarranted suspicion, she went on, "There was also English folk magic, like divining the occupation of one's future husband based on the shapes that appear when an egg white is dropped in water, little things the settlers of Salem would have frowned upon but inevitably brought along when they migrated from England to the Massachusetts Bay area."

"Apparently, this may have been what sparked the witch hunt in Salem," Holmes said, and Mrs. Stillaway nodded. As if to excuse why he had infused his brain attic with such trifles, he added in an explanatory tone, "I've been reading about the trials because of their possible connection to what happened at Crooked Forest Adventures."

Mrs. Stillaway looked astonished; it was evident that the theory Alberta den Nomot had mentioned had been so fatally crushed by academia that it had had no life left to make itself known to the public. Holmes summed up the idea in two curt sentences. Marieta didn't look surprised; the story had evidently reached her ears. Her aunt, however, now looked thoughtful.

"No, I've never heard of a northbound migration of real witches. You think the descendants of that coven are causing havoc more than three centuries later? But why?"

"I believe no such thing," Holmes said haughtily. "Someone is stirring trouble, although I have yet to uncover the motive."

Mrs. Stillaway's face grew tense. "Be very careful, Mr. Holmes. You will face—"

"Yes, yes, a formidable enemy, as you said before." He snickered, but then his expression hardened. There was something accusatory in the way he said, "So you are a *witch*, I presume?"

Mrs. Stillaway shook her head. "I don't identify with that term. I'm a practitioner of Wicca: magic that heals, guides, and supports those in need." It was then that she seemed to realize the intent behind the question. Her tone turned acerbic. "I—and Marieta as well—would never hurt anyone."

Holmes cocked his head. "Even if they hurt you?"

There was a deep sigh, followed by a long silence, before Mrs. Stillaway found her voice once again.

"In 1916, my great-grandmother, Edith, opened a tearoom, exclusive to women, just a few blocks west of here. Her husband went to war and never came back, but her shop, and the seances and tea-leaf readings she started doing, put food on the table for her five children.

"Business boomed as the war came to a close; women wanted answers—to know what had happened to their sons, husbands, lovers, fathers — to speak with them one last time. Not everyone was appreciative though. Edith's shop burned to the ground in 1921. It was written off as an accident. Luckily, no one was hurt. She rebuilt her shop and went on with her life. She told her children that revenge is not the way."

Mrs. Stillaway sighed again. "People have always treated me differently, but I'd always thought cold-blooded brutality was a thing of the past … until my shop was ravaged, and my employee was killed."

It wasn't easy to move Holmes. I sometimes wondered if he had even an ounce of the softer emotions. He did, of course, but they just rarely surfaced. That day, however, a simple story managed to do away with his derision. One long arm reached past me, and Holmes patted Mrs. Stillaway's hand.

"The world is not as unkind as you think, my dear woman. The trial of Mr. Edward Kerfoot will reveal that soon enough."

Mrs. Stillaway regarded him curiously. She didn't demand an explanation, as I would have done if he hadn't already theorized out loud about Mr. Kerfoot's real intentions. Instead, she nodded. A strange understanding had passed between them, and just like that, the mood lightened.

Holmes stood, less abruptly this time, mumbled something about perusing the shelves to no one in particular, and bounded out of the room. It had taken all his strength to muster some comforting words, and he was now done talking. When we all entered the shop a moment later, he was standing by the cash register, drumming his fingers impatiently on the wooden counter on which sat a dozen black tins.

"I am afraid I have cleaned out your shelf, Mrs. Stillaway. Hope you don't mind terribly," he said, flashing a set of teeth that somehow remained white despite the copious amounts of coffee he drank every day, not to mention his indulgence in those foul-smelling cigarettes.

Mrs. Stillaway returned the smile, once again her graceful, serene self. She picked up one of the tins and thumbed the blackbird silhouette on the gold label. "This was how you knew. I didn't have the heart to change the logo."

"Indeed," Holmes said.

Even Elodie seemed to understand this exchange, so I nodded along as well, although I still hadn't the slightest clue how Holmes had figured out Tea & Tee and The Augury were one and the same. Once we were outside, I inquired, of course, but Holmes, transfixed by the sleepy street, didn't seem to hear me.

He did, however, suggest a walk. "For just a quarter of an hour or so," he added, seeing my aghast expression. I enjoyed walks, but not in the wintertime. "It is a lovely day after all, and we can use some fresh air after that stifling warmth."

The street did look picturesque. Fresh snow had fallen while we had sipped our tea, throwing a thin veil over the city. The streetlamps twinkled and cast a yellow glow as the sky darkened. If, like Holmes, I could see only this beauty and not feel the December chill seep through my coat and throttle my bones, I may have contemplated a walk. Elodie, mittened hands clasped around the paper bag that held the charm she had bought for Christa, wisely hopped on the streetcar, which left before I could decide who to follow.

Holmes took my arm, extinguishing the last of my hopes of a warm ride home, and we began walking. I decided to make the most out of the situation.

"Tell me how you knew Mrs. Stillaway's shop was the same one that had been attacked. And what's the bird logo got to do with it?" I asked.

Holmes shrugged nonchalantly. "Oh, a simple matter, that one. First, there are only so many tea shops in Queen Street that specialize in the divinatory arts. I suspected when Marieta gave us the address today. Then there was the brand-new sign, a bit worn by the winter, but still sparkling compared to the rest of the store façade and the neighbouring shops. I wondered why only the sign had been replaced when the entire shop could do with some renovation—did you notice the rot in the timber floors? Someone ought to look at that. There were also cracks in the—"

"You can send Mrs. Stillaway a list," I interrupted. "Now tell me about the bird."

"Come now, you must have realized the significance of the original name. You fancy this sort of nonsense, after all."

I huffed impatiently. His banter became tiresome quickly when he not only zigzagged around the point but was also insulting.

"With your inclination toward the mystical, I would have thought you would be familiar with ancient Roman divination. I myself only read up on the subject after coming across the incident at The Augury. I will do my very best to forget what I learned—as soon as this little problem is cleared up, of course."

"Next time I want to know about something, I'll just search the internet," I grumbled. "It's a lot faster than asking you."

"Oh, all right, all right. Impatient as always!" He muttered something about "the shortcomings of modern youth," failing as he always did to recognize that he too was part of this posse of fledglings. "Roman augurs were individuals trained to interpret the behaviour of birds. Everything from the type of birds in the sky to their cries and flight patterns was used to divine the future and obtain guidance. Satisfied now?"

I shivered. What a fitting name for what Tina Stillaway did with her tea leaves.

*

A well-played violin is a treat for the gods, but the effect is somewhat ruined when one is played at an ungodly hour.

I lay in bed that night fully awake because Sherlock Holmes refused to put his fiddle away. Someone — possibly Gwilym Lestrade — had even taken the liberty of beating at his door, but Holmes' ominous music went on. The slow notes, punctuated with an occasional vibrato trill, captured my mood precisely as I reflected on our visit to Mrs. Stillaway's shop. My thoughts inevitably landed on the Salem Witch Trials.

Although I had heard of the trials, I realized I knew little about the subject. A few hundred years ago, a witch hunt had plagued New England, and some people had been executed, possibly by burning as far as I knew. That was the extent of my knowledge. Some of it was wrong and the story was much more complicated. This I found out that night, nestled under my comforter, as I searched the trials on my phone.

Salem was the first town established in colonial Massachusetts, settled by English Puritans. The grisly events that soiled the town's history had begun the winter of 1692.

The popular origin story tied the witch hunt to two girls: the daughter of Minister Samuel Parris of Salem Village, nine-year-old Betty, and his niece, Abigail, who was a few years older. As Mrs. Stillaway had hinted, the story went that the girls, and possibly others, had played with folk magic in secret. A coffin had surfaced in their bowl of egg white and water, which had flooded their minds with fear — and guilt for meddling with unnatural forces.

Before long, there was talk of the devil, and possession, which manifested in the young girls in the form of some terrible symptoms: they purred and barked, complained of being pinched and bitten, and saw spectres. They soon started naming women from the Salem community as their tormentors. The finger-pointing went on until over two hundred people had been accused. Although the New England courts didn't use the same *methods* as continental Europe to detect witches or evidence obtained under torture, fifty-five people confessed, possibly under duress. In the end, fourteen women and five men—and two dogs—were executed, most by hanging; one man had been pressed to death by stones.

It was tragic to say the least, which was what made it an unwise bedtime story. Consequently, my mind delved on it, and I turned this way and that long after I had put my phone away.

Until a faint sound stilled me.

CHAPTER 15

Descent into Madness

*"Through the gloom one could dimly catch a glimpse of bodies
lying in strange fantastic poses, bowed shoulders, bent knees,
heads thrown back ..."*

—Sir Arthur Conan Doyle, *The Man with the Twisted Lip*

I LAY FROZEN FOR MANY MINUTES, TRYING DESPERATELY TO
discern what I had heard. Finally, a low hiss seeped into
my awareness. My first thought was there was a snake in
the room. I stopped breathing altogether for a moment
before realizing how ridiculous the idea was.
Admittedly, wildlife was not foreign to Toronto; we
shared the city with pigeons that made the streets their
litterbox, loud-mouthed seagulls that bullied the smaller
birds, squirrels who drew near if you clicked your
tongue, and raccoons that ravaged trash cans in the night.
But snakes were not commonplace, and there was no way
one would have slithered into my room by chance.

Had one been left in my room then—with murderous
intentions? My imagination was running wild again,
borrowing ideas from a detective story I had read long

ago. Unlike the young woman in that story, I had neither a fortune nor a greedy, ruthless stepfather.

Perhaps the sound had been a figment of my imagination. I had heard a snake because my mind had wandered from the trials to Mrs. Stillaway before settling on the contents of my cup and the message that had supposedly come from my grandmother. *Someone around me doesn't deserve my trust.* It had been a puzzling, even frightful, message at the time. Hours later, those feelings had dissipated, replaced with longing and a bit of melancholy; I missed my grandmother. Of course, that was when I had heard the hissing.

Holmes would have been proud of the way I explained away the sound. Even I would have convinced myself if it hadn't sounded again.

I nearly panicked, but then I heard Holmes' voice in my head: *Be logical, Watson!* So, I dissected the facts as he would have. Listening closely, I couldn't tell where it had come from, but it sounded distant. The window was shut tight, so it wasn't one of the many sounds that trickled in from the street. Neither did it come from beyond the wall I shared with Holmes, nor the opposite wall, on the other side of which was a bathroom. Perhaps it had come through the crevice of my door? Praying I wouldn't be greeted by a coil of scales on the landing, I inched toward my door and opened it.

There on the dimly lit landing was a glimmer of white—that shuddersome cat! Its pale head swivelled around to look at me before resuming its statuesque pose, silver eyes stalking the staircase that led to the third floor. Sighing with relief, but also annoyed that I had been spooked by a silly cat, I returned to my bed.

I had been about to dive under the comforter when I heard the growl. *That* certainly didn't sound like a cat. It was also not coming from the landing. I glanced up at the ceiling, trying to remember who lived in the room above. Was there another pet loose in Baker House? I didn't think it was possible for two furry creatures to avoid the clutches of Mrs. Kerrigan; she had a knack for uncovering such breaches.

My suspicions were confirmed when the growl suddenly morphed into a bark. Yet there was something odd about the bark, and it bothered me enough that I left my bed once again. I put on my fleece robe and slippers and exited the room.

Luckily, something had drawn the cat away from its post, and I found myself quite alone on the landing. I turned in time to see a pearly tail slink up the staircase to the third floor. The cat had gone to investigate, and I followed suit, although I halted my progress as I approached the bottom step. If I hadn't looked up, I would have missed the shadow that had appeared at the top of the staircase.

Someone else was out of bed and prowling about … or perhaps it wasn't a resident of Baker House at all. That was hardly a comforting thought, of course; it meant there was an intruder in the house or, considering the recent strange events, something far worse. I considered waking Holmes for the briefest of moments but bounded up the stairs before I could convince myself.

The third-floor landing looked much like the one I had left behind: an open space, dimly lit, its walls lined with wooden doors. One of these doors — the one directly above mine on the second floor, was ajar, and peeking through the crack was a tall, lanky figure.

Sherlock Holmes.

"What are you doing here?" I hissed, approaching.

He turned his head nimbly, unperturbed by my sudden arrival, and said pleasantly, "Oh, hullo, Watson. Good morning to you. Did you hear the dog too? I am rather surprised. You slept through the fire alarm last month."

If we hadn't been out of bed in the middle of the night, hovering by the doorway to someone else's bedroom, I may have reminded him that it had been his nocturnal experimentation, involving a minor explosion, that had caused the alarm. Instead, I ignored the remark and, unable to help myself, peeked inside, instantly recognizing Christa's room.

The lamp's yellow glow created only an illusion of warmth; even though I had stuck just my nose inside, it was enough that I could feel the icy change in temperature. But where had the cold come from? The curtains didn't billow, which meant the window beyond was shut tight.

A thick comforter lay crumpled on the bed, the sheets rumpled and obviously slept in, and a pillow lay neglected on the ground. Christa was nowhere to be seen, but that conniving cat was there, sitting majestically atop the pillow, gaze fixed on me.

By the desk stood—or rather squatted—Elodie. Her cotton nightgown told me she too had been drawn out of bed, but she neither wore the fatigue on my face nor the quivering excitement on Holmes'. She was wide-eyed—and sweaty despite the chill. Whatever she was peering at underneath Christa's desk was making her anxious.

It was making me nervous too. The sounds that had echoed faintly in my room now rang clearly—a procession of whimpers, growls, and barks. Whatever it was that had hidden beneath the desk moved a great deal; it dodged Elodie's hands as though they would electrocute and yelped in a high-pitched whiny voice each time she tried to invade its space.

"Not a Great Dane," Holmes whispered, his hot breath on my ear. He was leaning on me as though I were a pole, his ear angled at the door. "Nor a poodle, though that is the breed I would expect Christa to stow away in her room. That, or a Papillon." There was another frantic eruption of barks. "Certainly not a Papillon—"

I pulled out of the crevice and shook loose of him. "You can tell apart dogs by their bark?" I whispered incredulously.

He waved the feat away with nonchalance. "Well, only fifteen or so. Each breed has a distinctive bark. I worked at a dog show one summer and had the great fortune to become intimately acquainted with the contestants—"

Woof, woof!

"Ah, not a beagle either."

"I grew up with dogs myself and there's something weird about this barking," I remarked after a particularly angry yelp. I heard rustling and feet dragging behind some of the doors on the floor. Christa's canine friend was starting to wake the others.

Holmes didn't say anything for a moment, his ear angled so sharply to better discern the bark that his neck muscles bulged from the strain. Then satisfaction settled on his face at the low growling from within. "Really, Watson, you excel yourself! There is no dog under the desk."

"Are you saying that something else … but, but what could bark like a dog but not be a dog?" And that was when it struck me. "Is someone … is *someone* barking like a dog?"

Holmes' head bobbed avidly. "Precisely. It cannot be a real dog for three reasons. One, I have never spotted dog hairs upon Christa's person. Two, she has been unwell and in bed all day, so there is no chance of her having procured one today. Lastly, if someone else had brought the dog into Baker House, we would have surely heard a bark at some point during the evening."

"Then who's under the desk?" The equally pertinent question was *why* they were barking like a dog.

"Isn't it obvious?" He didn't wait for me to answer; he had already seen the answer dawn in my eyes. One long finger pushed the door fully open, and he marched in.

Apparently Elodie had neither heard our whispered conversation nor seen our heads take turns peeking into the room. She looked utterly surprised to see us and straightened so abruptly that she lost her balance and wobbled, having to lean on the desk for support. However, it only took seconds for me to wonder whether she had feigned the whole thing. There was something odd about the way she lingered by the desk, as though to shield us from it … or it from us?

"What are you doing here?" she demanded.

"It appears Christa's illness has taken a turn for the worse," Holmes stated. "Barking like a dog is not a good sign."

It was Elodie's turn to growl. "She wouldn't want people to see her like this. You both need to leave. I'll take care of her."

"On the contrary, you need our help to get your friend out from underneath the desk. Your efforts thus far have been fruitless after all." Holmes turned to me. "Don't just stand there, Watson. Come inside and give me a hand."

By this point, Arthur and the twins, who also had rooms on the floor, had appeared at the door. Elodie glared at them, but she couldn't intimidate them into leaving as her friend could have done. They made no chivalrous move to lend a hand; they appeared too stunned to help, or perhaps the unblinking gaze of the cat kept them back.

I did as I was bid, although it was with some reluctance that I stuck my hand into the dark underside of the desk and felt around for Christa's arm. Perhaps the barking was to blame, but I expected a feral, salivating creature to sink its teeth into my flesh. Fortunately, Christa did nothing of the sort, though she resisted mightily and whimpered like a wounded animal the entire time. It took all my strength, and little of Holmes', to pull her out.

When the lamplight finally hit her lithe figure, I dropped her arm — in astonishment. I took several steps back and stumbled into the pillow on the ground, causing the cat to shriek and shrink away into a dark corner.

This was not the Christa we had said goodbye to that morning. Her face, devoid of the usual rosy blush and lipstick, was as pale as her white sleepshirt. Together with her hair, which seemed to have somehow lost some of its flaxen colour, and her pasty, bare legs, she almost looked spectral. There was a forced stillness to the way she sat on the rug, not meeting our eyes. Suddenly, she stiffened and grabbed at the flesh of her arm.

"Stop it!" she cried.

Elodie, alarmed, knelt and tried to hold her friend. "What's wrong? What is it?"

"She's biting me! Make her stop!" Christa wailed.

For a moment, everyone stared at me, but it was rather silly to suspect that I had bitten Christa. I wasn't even standing within arm's reach of her. But it was clear she wasn't alluding to Elodie, and I was the only other female in the room.

"Make *who* stop, my dear Christa?" Holmes drawled, perhaps in an effort to vindicate me, although he looked too amused to be concerned about that.

Christa understood his question despite her disoriented state, but when she answered, her words were a mumble. Although I couldn't speak for the others, Holmes and I heard her answer, which was why he looked bewildered, and my face mirrored his. If the barking hadn't been a good enough excuse, here was a new reason to admit Christa to a hospital.

But Elodie was appalled by the idea. "No!" she said loudly when I suggested it. Then, taking a breath, she spoke in a carefully controlled voice. "She can sleep it off. If her parents found out, she'd be toast."

"Ah." Holmes nodded in understanding. "Just as I suspected! Under the influence of something nefarious, eh?" Christa's predicament had probably reminded him of his own experimentations with cocaine—a habit that had gotten him expelled from university in London. His grin, I was happy to see, faltered under my deprecating glare.

"Does Christa use drugs?" I asked.

Elodie squirmed uncomfortably. "Sh-she's tried— well, I don't know exactly what she's tried, but she has in the past, just recreationally, you know, like everyone else. It wasn't an addiction, and she's never acted like this before. Maybe she took a bit too much this time …"

I glanced at Christa again, watching her rigid body. Had narcotics triggered her bizarre behaviour, or was there something more sinister at work? The name of her supposed tormentor still rang in my head as I inched closer.

Squatting, I took her face in my hand and stared into her sleepy eyes. She didn't protest; she didn't even look puzzled. The others watched silently as I gently pried her mouth open and sniffed the warm breath that came out. I didn't need to study medicine to recognize the signs of someone who taken the hard stuff; living on campus, surrounded by peers who were of an age where delinquency was fashionable, was enough.

"Well, she's not on drugs," I said. "Her pupils look normal: no constriction, no dilation. Her eyes aren't red either. We can rule out everything from heroin to marijuana to speed. She isn't drunk either."

Elodie opened her mouth as if to protest — what did an English major know about these things anyway? — but no sound emerged. Holmes, on the other hand, looked astonished. Whether this was due to my knowledge of something other than literature, or because I had tossed out the only reasonable theory that could explain Christa's state, I didn't know. Behind me, our housemates spoke in hushed tones.

"We need to get her to bed," Elodie murmured.

She looked expectantly at Holmes, who at once took Christa's arm and pulled her to her feet. Her legs wobbled unsteadily, but there was no chance of falling, thanks to the iron grip that kept her upright. The room was becoming warm again, but Christa hadn't seemed bothered by the chill. Her gaze jumped about furtively, perhaps anticipating the return of her tormentor or some new danger to pounce on her without warning. She clutched Holmes' hand tightly, and I noticed him throw a nonchalant glance at her arm—the same arm she had claimed had been bitten. I too craned my neck for a look.

There was no mistaking what I saw. The lamp light was bright, and I was standing near enough to see the fading remnants of teeth marks on the pink flesh.

Christa climbed into bed willingly, although she didn't release Holmes' hand. He looked uncomfortable at first, but it only took seconds for this to turn into impatience. He pried her hand off, frowned, then stepped back. That unfortunately only worsened her discomposure; she started shaking in fear under her comforter.

"A bed of thorns," she moaned. "You've put me in a bed of thorns."

Holmes smirked. He would have cracked a snide remark about Christa's sudden ascent to poetry if Elodie hadn't murmured, "Everything will be okay in the morning, Christa." The way she hunched over her friend and held her hand was admirable, done with the tenderness of a mother. Or a lover.

Christa shook her head. "No, no, he won't leave me alone until I sign the Red Book." As ominous as the words were, the fidgeting ceased soon after and her eyelids drooped.

"Everyone needs to leave now," Elodie commanded. "She needs to sleep."

"I assume you will watch over her?" Holmes asked, and she nodded. "Excellent. I have just one question before we take our leave: did you shut the window when you got here?"

"The window?" Elodie looked flustered. "Why does that even matter?" But it was apparent Holmes wouldn't leave without an answer. She thought for a moment. "No, the window was already shut."

CHAPTER 16

A Presence from the Past

"It is an old maxim of mine that when you have excluded the impossible, whatever remains, however improbable, must be the truth."

—Sir Arthur Conan Doyle, *The Adventure of the Beryl Coronet*

"THEN WHERE DID THE COLD COME FROM?" HOLMES murmured after we had stepped onto the landing. Once Arthur and the twins had disappeared into their rooms, he said, "Perhaps Christa shut the window, but the timeline doesn't permit it. It was freezing in there when we arrived, as though someone had just closed the window, but Christa wouldn't have been coherent enough to do that, and Elodie confirmed she didn't either."

"Then where did the cold come from?" I repeated his question.

"A sinister presence perhaps." He grinned, seeing my shock. "I ought not to stir your imagination. It is wild as it is."

"If not that, then what?"

"Once you eliminate the impossible, whatever remains, no matter how improbable, must be the truth," he said simply.

"Well, neither Christa nor Elodie closed it, and a supernatural being didn't cause the room to suddenly get cold. I'm not sure what else remains."

"Have you actually eliminated those 'impossibilities'?" He was toying with me again, vaguely hinting at a not-so-commonplace solution yet taunting me if I dared to consider it. "Let's let the matter rest for now, Watson. It is rather late, and even I require sleep occasionally."

I wasn't sure what time it was, but midnight had certainly come and gone, and the late hour was making my eyes ache for rest. I would have gladly crawled into bed, but Holmes didn't look even slightly fatigued despite his claim, and that prompted me to continue the conversation as we descended to the second floor.

"You saw the bite mark on Christa's arm?" I asked.

The answer was a prompt nod, followed by a nonchalant shrug.

"And you don't think it's strange that not only did she say she was bitten but there are actual bite marks to prove it?"

Holmes shrugged again, smiling slightly. "Perhaps she bit herself or ... perhaps Elodie bit her."

"That's ridiculous! Elodie worships the ground Christa walks on. And why would Christa bite herself and then think someone else did it?"

"My dear, do not expect the mind to behave rationally under the influence of narcotics."

"But it wasn't drugs! There were no physical signs. Then there's that unexplainable cold. The bite mark, the barking — this is all starting to sound familiar."

"Oh?"

I decided to spell it out for him. "The Salem Witch Trials."

"Ah!" He smirked. "I thought you had ruled out supernatural influence."

"And you said we hadn't actually eliminated that 'impossibility.'" My cheeks grew hot under his skeptical stare, but I couldn't stop now. "You've been reading up on the trials, so you must've noticed the similarities between what we just witnessed and what the accusers reported during the trials: they were pinched and bitten, they barked like dogs a-and—"

"The accusers were charlatans whose actions condemned innocent people to death," Holmes said frostily.

"I know, I know," I said, then blurted out, "Goody Carrier! That's the name Christa said when you asked who had bitten her."

I had expected a berating reaction, but it stung anyway when he laughed. Even when he was done, amusement lingered in his eyes, and he cocked his head at me as though I was a silly child. For once, I didn't feel indignant. My declaration had been ridiculous at best and nonsensical at worst. After all, how could a woman who had lived more than three hundred years ago, albeit one accused of witchcraft, sink her teeth into Christa's arm?

"Martha Carrier," Holmes said, "accused by Abigail Williams, Elizabeth Hubbard, Susannah Sheldon, Mary Walcott, and Ann Putnam Jr. of hurting them using witchcraft. Carrier apparently also tried to make them sign the devil's book." Smirking, he added, "Oh, then there is that bit about Carrier having killed thirteen people in Andover, the ghosts of whom the girls could see in the courtroom, among other ridiculous charges."

He didn't need to finish the tragic story of Goody Carrier; it was fresh in my memory. A jury had found her guilty in the summer of 1692 and sentenced her to death by hanging two weeks later. She, and the others who had met the noose that day, had declared their innocence even when they had lost all hope.

Holmes continued, "As you say, there are some similarities between what happened in Salem and what just happened in Christa's room—"

"It could be a descendant of the Salem migrants," I said, cheeks growing redder by the minute. I knew I was uttering nonsense, but I had dug a hole that was too deep to climb out of; my theories spewed out before I could stop myself. "Not one descendant, but maybe two. Christa used two pronouns: a 'she' to indicate who was biting her and a 'he' to show who was coercing her into signing the book … unless 'he' refers to th-the devil himself—"

"Watson, please stop!" Holmes ordered. The mirth had left his eyes. "Your preference for a bizarre explanation instead of searching for a more commonplace one worries me."

I turned away. The heat in my cheeks became overwhelming and made my eyes water.

Holmes sighed and said more gently, "You are letting your imagination run wild, my friend. Now, think carefully. Are you certain Christa said 'Goody Carrier'?"

I hesitated. "Yes, that's what I heard."

Holmes nodded. "A precise choice of words. 'Goody Carrier' is what you heard, influenced as you are by all this business with the trials, but that is *not* what she said."

*

The next morning brought with it the last day of December. I didn't ponder about how quickly the year had passed or wonder whether I had squandered the days, or even write down some New Year's resolutions. My mind was too preoccupied for such reflections.

It seemed no time had passed since Holmes had left me on the landing, refusing to reveal what Christa had actually said. Part of me doubted his declaration; I was certain of what I had heard … wasn't I? Had "Goody Carrier" been on my mind because I had been reading about the trials, just as Holmes had said?

And then another idea struck me.

Perhaps my ears — and mind — hadn't played tricks on me at all. What if Christa too had done some research on the trials after Alberta den Nomot had drawn parallels between the Salem "witches" and the inexplicable events that had come to pass at Crooked Forest? Although it was difficult to imagine Christa plunging into anything scholarly, she was capable of curiosity, even if that curiosity was usually limited to the latest lipstick.

Like me, maybe she was worried; she seemed to believe in the supernatural after all. I remembered how upset she had been when her necklace had been taken. Had feeling unprotected sent her into a panic? It was becoming easier and easier to picture a rattled Christa reaching for narcotic comforts. Her fears had manifested anyway — her barking, sensations of being bitten, and being compelled by terrorizing forces to sign over her allegiance — her mind, fuelled by drugs, animating what she had read. Of course, drugs *had* to be at the centre of it. Perhaps I hadn't spotted any signs, but what did I know anyway? I wasn't a professional.

I had no definitive proof, but the theory made perfect sense. It was a logical solution that left no room for anything beyond the ordinary. Perhaps Holmes had been thinking along the same lines.

I had no explanation for what had happened at Crooked Forest Adventures, but that didn't matter; the place suddenly seemed far away. Only my curiosity suffered from not knowing; the rest of me was grateful for the distance, and I headed downstairs with a subtle bounce to my steps.

Holmes wasn't in his usual place in the dining room. Rather, I found him perched on a bar stool in the kitchen, hunched over a newspaper, which he had spread across the kitchen island. The room was saturated with the smell of coffee and something burnt. *So Mrs. Kerrigan was around somewhere*, I thought, eyeing the plate of blackened toast distastefully. She prepared breakfast when it suited her, although the edibility of her preparations didn't score too highly. I opted for just coffee, which I knew Holmes had made since it wasn't burnt.

"Anything interesting in the news?" I asked.

Holmes shrugged vaguely. "Nothing striking, reports of a virus of unknown etiology in China and a series of home invasions in Cabbagetown, but still nothing of what happened in Crooked Forest. I had half expected today's headlines to dub the affair 'the Brixton Road Mystery.'"

I took a seat at the island opposite him, my good mood somewhat spoiled by the mention of that wretched place. A few minutes passed in silence, then Elodie walked in, interrupting my doleful thoughts and Holmes' studious reading. Adding to the scowl from a few hours ago were red-rimmed eyes; she looked tired beyond measure. Had she slept at all? She had probably passed the night uncomfortably in a chair, watching over her friend.

"How is Christa?" I asked as she slumped onto a stool next to Holmes, elbows on the tabletop and head bolstered by her arms, looking wearier still.

"She's sleeping soundly."

I poured her a cup of coffee and slid it across, and she took a grateful sip. After she had taken a few more sips, I gently asked, "Did you happen to make out the name Christa said when Holmes asked who had bitten her?"

Elodie stiffened. She set her cup down with a thud and stared straight ahead for a moment, not meeting my eyes. At last, she let out the breath the question had halted.

"I wanted to talk to you both about that," she began uncertainly. "Maybe Marieta should be here too."

I raised a brow in surprise. The two girls rarely talked, yet Elodie felt inclined to include Marieta all of a sudden. What could it mean? Had Christa named Marieta as her tormentor? *Impossible,* I thought. I couldn't have misheard that badly. Unfortunately, our conversation progressed no further because Mrs. Kerrigan shuffled in, wearing a dress that was fit for springtime, not the winter. She hadn't expected us, and her face, which had looked surprisingly placid, clouded with suspicion. Holmes' cheery "Good morning!" distorted her gnarly features so much that poor Elodie shivered. The lady took no pity on her though.

"Ah, Miss Willis," she grumbled, "don't forget it's your turn to clean the fridge today."

Now here was a cruel punishment, or so Elodie seemed to think since her terror quickly turned into disappointment and annoyance. She had always been diligent with her share of the housework, but it was New Year's Eve; the custom was to sleep past noon, lounge like a sloth all afternoon, then race off to celebrate the coming of the new year. Elodie, and Christa if she were well enough by tonight, would certainly have an entertaining night planned. I myself had gotten an invitation or two to watch the fireworks at city hall and count down to midnight as was tradition. I had declined though; I was itching to find out what Holmes would be up to. So far, he hadn't mentioned any plans.

Elodie's disappointment was short-lived. Her expression turned fearful again as Mrs. Kerrigan drew near, frowning at us. The untouched plate of toast fouled her mood some more, and she muttered the usual "overprivileged brats" and "wasteful rascals." Accustomed though we were to it, today's mumbled insults agitated Elodie more than usual. She stumbled off the stool. Her cup, which she had hastily picked up, spat out a generous splotch of coffee on the island.

For a moment, no one moved. Then Mrs. Kerrigan's eyes blazed, and she bared her teeth. This alone was enough to jolt the girl into action: without thinking, she frantically wiped away the spill with the sleeve of her — white — sweater, stuttered an apology with a departing nod to us, then rushed out of the kitchen.

The old housekeeper huffed, looking even more suspicious than before. She surveyed the kitchen slowly and then peered into the garbage can. It was obvious she was searching for evidence of Elodie's crime—a half-eaten toast, a broken mug—anything that would grant her the right to march upstairs and give the guilty party a mouthful of unpleasant words. She found nothing though.

I was just as surprised by Elodie's abrupt departure. Mrs. Kerrigan was the most intimidating woman I had ever met, but to my knowledge, she had never caused anyone at Baker House to flee in terror before.

Holmes folded his newspaper neatly into a rectangle and put it aside. He was watching Mrs. Kerrigan with an innocent attention that looked odd on his face. "Ah, young people!" he exclaimed. "They're always in a rush, eh, Mrs. Kerrigan?"

All he got was a contemptuous stare, but that didn't stop him from carrying on about how bright and beautiful the morning was. This time, she decided he was worthy of a response.

"No," she barked, "it's not a beautiful morning when the blasted cold makes your arthritis act up." She made a show of limping toward us, her burly figure growing larger and larger until she loomed over us.

Holmes' smile didn't waver. "At least you have the afternoon off to enjoy yourself. Heading to the Christmas market with your son, aren't you?"

Perhaps Mrs. Kerrigan had heard of Holmes' remarkable abilities of deduction, but she had never been on the receiving end of them. Her shock was so great that her ever-present frown disappeared—for about five seconds. Then she glared at him, eyes narrowed and lips puckered, distorting what could have been a grandmotherly face.

"And how did you know that, young man?" she demanded. She spat out "young man" like an insult.

I braced myself for a complicated series of deductions from Holmes, which would inevitably result in a loud reprimand from Mrs. Kerrigan; she didn't take too kindly to smart alecks, particularly if they were less than fifty years old.

But Holmes simply said, "I overheard your telephone call earlier." He obviously anticipated the angry preaching that would follow on good manners and privacy because he went on quickly, "Say, Mrs. Kerrigan, what are your thoughts on the properties of bloodstone?"

Caught offguard yet again, the lady stared blankly for a moment. "Properties of what?"

"Bloodstone, my dear woman!" he chimed. "Oh, perhaps you know it as heliotrope? No? Ah, never mind then." He stood — or rather shot up — with the rigidity of something mechanical. "Good day to you, Mrs. Kerrigan. Come along, Watson."

He ushered me out of the kitchen and up the stairs. It was only after we arrived on the second-floor landing, coffee sloshing about in our cups, that Holmes spoke.

"Ha! Did you see that, Watson?" he cried. "She had no idea what a bloodstone is."

I scowled. "Neither do I. Care to explain?"

He huffed impatiently, sounding much like the housekeeper. "It's a cryptocrystalline quartz, opaque and green in colour, with splashes of red formed by the presence of iron oxide minerals." His tone relaxed and he grinned. "Sound familiar? It is the gemstone in the pendant of Christa's necklace, and Marieta's too. For two thousand years now, people have believed it has protective, as well as healing, properties."

And the housekeeper had known none of this. "Mrs. Kerrigan didn't take the necklace, did she?" I asked.

"I think not, Watson."

"Then who did?"

Holmes shrugged cheerfully. "Another mystery to add to the lot, albeit a trivial one."

"Should we go find Elodie now? She'd been about to tell us something."

"Ah! No need for that, friend Watson. I already know what she was going to say."

Perhaps if I had begged, he might have elaborated, but I was given no chance to do so even if I were willing. In just seconds, Holmes' slender form skirted across the landing and disappeared into his room, with only a curt wave of the hand serving as adieu.

CHAPTER 17

The Devil's Offer

"There is nothing new under the sun. It has all been done before."

—Sir Arthur Conan Doyle, *A Study in Scarlet*

SOMEHOW THE HOURS PASSED THAT DAY EVEN THOUGH I recalled doing little. I had lost some time to *The House of the Seven Gables*, gone out to buy lunch, run into some friends from class, then wandered about campus with them, surviving the cold for as long as I did only because we had armed ourselves with cappuccinos. Again, I was offered an entertaining evening—a house party this time—and again, I declined. At last, our cups drained, I returned to Baker House, grateful for the warmth and quiet.

Holmes didn't answer when I knocked on his door that evening. In fact, his room was unusually silent. Not even the turning of a page or the pacing of restless feet sounded. Had he gone out after all? Though I tried, it was difficult to imagine him draining a red plastic cup and rocking to something that was supposed to be music alongside a houseful of noisy partygoers. Wherever he had disappeared to, I was sure it wouldn't be entertaining in the conventional sense.

Still, it was in a sulky mood that I went downstairs.

Arthur had already stationed himself in the parlour, vigorously tapping away on his phone, when I arrived. We exchanged pleasantries, most of which ridiculed the idea of being sandwiched by a thousand others at city hall yet still managing to freeze, just to look at fireworks. Worse still was a party on campus where the chances of being vomited on was sky-high. We were perfectly happy — so we said — at Baker House, where it was blissfully peaceful and warm. Eventually, the conversation died.

Several interruptions followed though. First, the twins poked their heads in as they headed out. Next came Gwilym, who graced us with a few minutes' conversation about his date with "a gorgeous theatre major," who I presumed wasn't Christa since she hadn't left her room all day, not to mention she favoured hulking men who could survive the extreme cold and were skilled at commanding dogs. He lingered for a moment longer, perhaps hoping Holmes would appear, giving him another opportunity to boast. He too soon shuffled out the front door. Elodie arrived around nine o'clock, looking as though she needed her bed more than a night out. Apparently, though she herself had opted to stay in bed, Christa had compelled her friend to enjoy the night as planned with their other friends. Elodie reassured us that Christa was recovering nicely.

So there remained only four of us in the house that night: Christa, Marieta, Arthur, and me. No sound came from Christa's room, although we couldn't have heard anything on the third floor from the parlour — unless someone were to start howling. I had caught faint piano music from Marieta's room as I had knocked on Holmes' door, but she too failed to make an appearance.

It was a little before ten o'clock when Holmes trudged in, dusting the hall with the snow that had settled on his coat, hat, and violin case. Catching sight of me from the doorway, he stepped into the parlour with gusto. Arthur almost immediately excused himself and hurried off to his room; he obviously still felt resentful over the way Holmes had accused him of hurting Leslie.

Holmes didn't look apologetic in the least. In fact, he looked cheerful as he took off his hat and gloves, followed by his coat, and tossed them aside. Not all found a seat on the couch, but this went unnoticed. The violin case he put down with more care. He then rubbed his hands energetically, not to rid them of the cold but to express his satisfaction with an unknown something.

"What have you been up to?" I asked, setting down my book and eyeing the violin case with more suspicion than it deserved.

Holmes shrugged. "Oh, nothing, really." Perhaps he realized such an answer would only pique my nosiness, so he added, "I passed the evening in a halfway house, the one in Gerald Street."

"You're offering music lessons to the kids living there?" I nodded at the violin case.

"Precisely!" he said with exuberance. "I was rather pleased with the turnout. Who would have guessed?! But they are a rather irregular group: sharp as a needle, street-smart, and very resourceful." There was something deeply suspicious about the way he said this, but I hadn't the slightest clue about how to pry more information out of him.

"Won't you join me in the library, Watson? I could use a strong cuppa and something decent to read." He eyed my book distastefully.

Although drinks were not permitted in the library, Holmes' mug accompanied us as we descended to the basement. The next hour and a half passed with little conversation. Much to my dismay, Holmes refused to discuss the case Arthur had brought to us; he didn't even seem worried that Gwilym would clear up the matter before he did. In fact, he pointed to the return bin nearby, inside which someone—he, of course—had unceremoniously dumped a stack of books on witchcraft, its history, and related persecutions throughout the centuries. There were at least three books on the Salem Witch Trials. So he had finished his research ... I wondered if he had gleaned anything useful to the case.

I was contemplating borrowing a few of the titles myself when a loud bang echoed from upstairs. I nearly jumped in my seat; Holmes, on the other hand, glanced at the ceiling, unperturbed. Even he looked curious when muffled voices followed though. It was difficult to make out what was being said, but one voice, a high-pitched girlish one, sounded frantic. The deeper second voice could barely get a word in.

Holmes smiled sardonically. "That was the fridge door slamming, I believe. A fight over the last sausage, perhaps?" He laughed. Such a scenario wasn't as ludicrous as it sounded; it had happened on several occasions, usually among the men, over meat, orange juice, and contraband that had been poorly hidden and uncovered by persons it hadn't been intended for but devoured by them anyway.

"I hear both male and female voices. Who else is here, Watson?" he asked and I told him. "No doubt Gastrell is quarrelling with one of the ladies then."

I frowned. "I really can't imagine him arguing with anyone, let alone Christa or Marieta."

Holmes didn't care for my character assessment. "Ah, listen. They are going upstairs. The sausage fight has been resolved."

Although I couldn't hear the shuffling feet, the stairs screeched as though in pain. The knocking—that, I heard perfectly. I would have to be deaf not to hear the pounding that reverberated throughout the house. All was quiet for a moment, and then the frantic voice squeaked, answered in turn by a calmer, muffled voice. More loud knocking followed, then silence, then more knocking. The stairs started screeching once again.

Very soon another set of steps began groaning: the ones descending to the basement.

"It appears someone is searching for us," Holmes murmured, and sure enough, only seconds passed before the panting figure of Elodie Willis stumbled into the library. Arthur, and then Marieta, ran in after her.

"Did you do it? It was one of you, right?" Elodie cried.

I jumped to my feet as she ran up to me and grabbed the collar of my shirt. The gesture wasn't violent; rather, I sensed a deep desperation in the way she looked at me, in the way her whole body seemed to crumple at the sight of my bewildered face. She released her hold and stepped back unsteadily.

"It was *him*. It really was him," she whimpered.

For a moment, I thought she was referring to Holmes, but no—that wasn't the case. She didn't even cast him a second look as her legs gave way and her little body landed in a heap on the carpeted floor.

"What on earth is wrong with her?" I exclaimed, kneeling to feel her forehead and then her pulse. "She's very cold, but her pulse is steady."

Holmes gave me a curious glance before looking inquiringly at Arthur and Marieta. Each glanced mutely at one another, silently prompting the other to speak.

"She was saying all sorts of nonsense when I met her in the kitchen," Arthur said at last. "I'm not sure what to make of it."

"Maybe we should call for an ambulance," Marieta added, but at that very moment, Elodie's eyelids flickered open, and she looked up at us vaguely. Holmes and Arthur helped her to one of the couches, and we gave her a moment to gather herself.

At last, she looked up at Holmes and me, and asked meekly, "Did one of you clean the fridge today?"

After such an entrance, this was the last thing I had expected her to say. Mute with surprise, I shook my head. Holmes answered with a raised eyebrow. Our silent responses put Elodie in a remarkable state—the terror from moments ago returned in a flash.

I couldn't think of any way to soothe her, so stunned was I with all that was suddenly disrupting my quiet evening. Holmes, on the other hand, didn't care to console her; he was studying her like a curiosity. Arthur's expression was difficult to read: there was certainly alarm, but there was something else as well. Only Marieta dared to sit at the edge of the couch and take Elodie's hand.

"Tell us what happened," she said in a serene voice that reminded me of her aunt.

Elodie let out a single, suppressed sob before a torrent of rapid words burst out.

"I met up with some friends at a bar a few blocks from here. It was a little past eleven when I started to feel a bit sick. I decided to walk home, thinking the air would do me good—and I did feel better until I turned onto a small side street." Her voice caught in her throat for a moment, but then suddenly she wailed, "That's when—that's, that's when a voice called out to me, b-but there was no one around. The street was empty!" At this point, her stuttering worsened. "B-but I knew it wasn't someone standing nearby—I c-can't explain it, b-but it seemed–it seemed as though—" She was unable to go on.

"As though the voice was coming from inside your head," Arthur finished.

Elodie stared at him with bulging eyes. "Yes! But how did you—" She didn't know about the voice that had lured him into the woods of Crooked Forest Adventures. Arthur had initially agreed to leave that bit out of the narrative; no one, especially not the police, would have believed him, after all. Now, however, he seemed unwilling to hide the incident any longer.

"A deep male voice?" he asked eagerly.

Elodie nodded, eyes growing wider still, no longer afraid of ridicule as Arthur had been when we had found him wandering in the woods. In fact, even Arthur's spine straightened a bit, and a small but self-satisfied smile lurked on his face as he tried to catch Holmes' eye. Here was evidence echoing the truth of what he had experienced, and he took pleasure in seeing my friend's reasoning and logic — and disdain for the supernatural — fracture.

Holmes didn't notice the smirk. He was watching Elodie with interest but in silence.

I asked, "What did the voice say?"

"The fridge — it offered to clean the fridge. I'd forgotten to do it before I'd left, and the voice — it seemed to know that." Elodie shook her head as though she didn't believe her own words. "It even knew about Mrs. Kerrigan. It said she'd be upset if she arrived in the morning to find a messy fridge."

Holmes grinned. "Ah, it appears the voice is not acquainted with labour laws and statutory holidays. Mrs. Kerrigan wouldn't be required to come into work in the morning, although that hasn't stopped her before." He paused, then asked quietly, "Did you accept the offer?"

Elodie shook her head rapidly. "I–I was so shocked. I couldn't believe what I was hearing. I just ran all the way home."

Of course, she had naturally made a beeline for the refrigerator upon her arrival — hence the sound we had heard — and what had she found? A perfectly clean fridge.

"And, of course, good sense stopped you from giving this mysterious voice credit for finishing the chore," Holmes said. "You went around the house, asking who had done it. First, Arthur, then Marieta. You didn't bother going up to Christa's room. I've seen you doing her chores on several occasions. That she would voluntarily take up one of your own, particularly when she is not completely well yet, is unimaginable. So you came in search of Watson and me."

Elodie nodded dejectedly. "What does it all mean?"

Holmes laughed. "Oh, don't look so morose. It is rather convenient to have a voice at your beck and call to do household chores, don't you think? A real-life Cinderella story—" His grin froze, then faded completely as he looked over at the stack of books he had returned—the books on the history of witchcraft and the trials—and there his gaze lingered, accompanied by furrowed eyebrows.

"You didn't hear the voice!" Elodie cried, shivering. "I-it was no fairy godmother. It was evil, that much I could tell. It felt like if I argued with it, it would hurt me."

As if that wasn't a shocking enough exclamation, Arthur decided to puzzle us further. "The devil—that's who's responsible." He spoke with such conviction that had I not been listening, I would have nodded along. It was perhaps Holmes' and my matching expressions of incredulity that made him add, "Elodie told me about the devil in her cup. The reading was a warning."

"Ought we not to rule out suspects of the flesh-and-blood variety first?" Holmes asked coldly, his interest in the books gone as quickly as it had come.

Arthur's manner was just as frosty. "Sure, let's do that. Maybe it was the Makutsi twins or Gwilym Lestrade, although why would they willingly do someone else's chore? Gwilym may have done it if it were Christa's turn to clean the fridge, but he's not infatuated with Elodie. I didn't do it, Marieta didn't either. You two have confirmed that you didn't. You already explained why it wasn't Christa, and Mrs. Kerrigan definitely wouldn't have—she likes putting students put to work." He paused, eyes rolling skyward in mock thought. "Let's see … that leaves only the cat."

And the cat hadn't been sighted all day.

"Your reasoning is excellent, Gastrell," Holmes said, the retaliatory mockery in his voice unmistakable. "You have effectively eliminated all the suspects, provided no one is lying."

"And why would anyone lie about this?" It was Marieta who spoke. She had been quietly watching us all that time, her expression indecipherable.

Holmes shrugged and turned to Elodie. "Let us pursue another line of inquiry: what, and exactly how much, did you drink?"

"One beer," she answered indignantly. "The waiter opened the bottle and poured it into a cup in front of me. There's no chance someone tampered with it, and I obviously didn't drink enough to start imagining things."

Holmes nodded thoughtfully. "I had crafted a scenario where one of our fellow housemates paid off the bartender to give you more than what you paid for and then cleaned the fridge themselves to give you a fright. But how could they control your hallucination?" He shot Arthur a look.

Elodie suddenly sat up, back hunched though. Her head was canted at such a sharp angle that her ear almost touched her shoulder. She was staring at Marieta with bulging, unblinking eyes. Nothing could have sounded more out of place than the low, hoarse voice that emerged from her quivering lips: "You can't make me, witch! I won't do it. I won't, I won't, I won't!" Elodie suddenly thrust her head forward, straining her neck further. She was now staring past Marieta at a corner of the room darkened by a towering bookcase. "Th-there's something—" She squinted until her eyes were slits, trying desperately to see.

I briefly wondered whether she'd had more than just one beer after all. Yet she had seemed coherent until now. Without warning, she jerked back into the couch in a feeble attempt to distance herself from—

"A woman with wings ... and the head of a dog!" The scream that followed blared like a siren, loud enough to bring the neighbours to our door had they not left to party.

And yet, the worst of Elodie's fit didn't happen until after she had stopped screaming, although she didn't stop because she believed our reassurances that no dog-woman creature was lingering in the library.

No, a fresh disturbance overtook her.

First, she clutched her leg, looking agonized; then her hand shot up to her left breast, and she howled in pain. In no time at all, her body started contorting and she fell off the couch. Her dry mouth opened several times, but it seemed she had lost all capacity for speech. Then the barking started, punctuated by roaring and screaming so loud it was difficult to believe they could come from so small a person.

"Call an ambulance!" Marieta shouted as she and Holmes struggled to keep Elodie pinned to the carpet. Arthur had turned to waxwork at Elodie's transformation; he simply stood, gawking, mouth hanging open, as Elodie tried to wriggle free, hollering and growling the entire time like something wild.

I sprinted upstairs to my room to fetch my phone. The next several minutes passed in a haze. Sweet relief only came when Elodie, placated once again, was wheeled out of Baker House. I stood by the window, watching the ambulance drive away, when Holmes glided to my side.

"What do you make of that, Watson?" he asked, his face betraying not the slightest tick of emotion.

My voice shook as I replied, "I've never witnessed anything like it."

"Ah, but there is nothing new under the sun. As with everything, it has all been done before."

CHAPTER 18

A History Lesson

*"These deeds are written in history, and there are records
wherein one may read the details of them."*

—Sir Arthur Conan Doyle, *The Valley of Fear*

I AWOKE THE NEXT MORNING TO FIND A PAIR OF GREY EYES
peering at me. The locked door had evidently not been
enough to bar Sherlock Holmes entry. This was no
surprise though; he had rampaged my room once before
in search of a magnifying glass despite the lock. The truth
was that I wasn't even certain I had locked my door the
night before. My mind had been too disarrayed as I had
climbed into bed. Perhaps I had left the door wide open
because the cat had also snuck inside. Sitting majestically
on my desk, it too leered at me.

"Ah, you're awake! And before nine o'clock too,"
Holmes exclaimed as though he had played no part in
this. "Well, since you're up, perhaps you would like to
accompany me to the hospital to see how Elodie is
doing?"

"Sure," I said, throwing off the comforter and trying
my best not to look at the cat. "When are you leaving?"

"Well, the cab is due to arrive in five minutes. Do you think you can manage?" He blinked innocently.

I couldn't have managed that even if I had gone to bed dressed to go out. Somehow, within the span of ten minutes though, I washed, dressed, and swallowed the lukewarm coffee Holmes had left for me on the desk. Unfortunately, I had a nasty suspicion that the cat had taken a stealthy lick or two while I had been in the bathroom. There was something telling about the way its tongue lashed in and out as it watched me drink. I didn't touch the buttered toast that accompanied the coffee and left the door wide open on my way out. Hopefully, the sinister creature would be gone by the time I returned.

The cabbie was drumming her fingers loudly on the steering wheel when I took my seat next to Holmes. We arrived at our destination about half an hour later after enough jerky turns and sudden stops to make one grateful for seat belts. It didn't take much time to determine Elodie's room, but navigating the maze-like corridors of the hospital took long enough to make me regret having left the toast behind.

Imagine our surprise when we arrived to find Arthur already there. He and Elodie were deep in conversation, which halted at the sight of us. They were just as surprised to see us but beckoned us to enter nonetheless.

How odd, I thought. Elodie and Arthur had always been on friendly terms, but nothing had hinted at a closeness that would propel him to be at her bedside first thing in the morning. Were they perhaps romantically involved? Not under Christa's watch, I decided. It could very well be a friendship that had blossomed because of a bizarre, shared calamity; that tended to bring people together. After all, Holmes and I were here too, and Holmes had barely acknowledged Elodie's existence before the holidays while I had only exchanged complaints about the weather or midterms with her.

If Holmes shared my reasoning, it didn't show on his face. He glared suspiciously at Arthur, but for Elodie, he softened and asked how she was faring.

"So much better, thanks. Actually, it all feels like a dream," she said, smiling. Despite her sprightly manner, there was no mirth in her smile. In fact, some of her anxiety from the night before resurfaced at the sight of us. I noted a jumpiness to her movements, as though she feared the winged woman with the head of a dog would charge through the wall at any moment.

We were interrupted by a plump, red-haired nurse garbed in scarlet scrubs. We watched quietly as she did her routine checks and consulted the clipboard hanging on the wall. Holmes naturally accosted her with questions on how the patient was doing, but she answered to Elodie rather than him, reporting the opposite of what we had expected to hear: Elodie's temperature, pulse, breathing rate, and blood pressure were all normal. The blood work had revealed nothing that could explain what we had witnessed last night. In fact, the nurse cheerily reported that our housemate was in perfect health and would be discharged later that morning.

"Have any brilliant deductions, Sherlock?" Arthur sneered once the nurse left. He shot me an apologetic glance as though to say: *he deserves this treatment.*

"No, but I believe Elodie does," Holmes said, seating himself in a chair by the bed. One long leg crossed the other. He leaned against the cushioned back, fingers steepled, and looked inquiringly at Elodie. "You can start with what you wanted to discuss yesterday morning in the kitchen. You see, Watson misheard what Christa said that night and has consequently formed some erroneous conclusions."

Elodie drew a breath. "Christa said, 'Goody Kerrigan.'" She paused, and I took the moment to process this. "The woman I saw last night, she looked like Mrs. Kerrigan, at least below the neck."

"The woman no one but you could see," Holmes said quietly.

Elodie shrugged helplessly. "Just like Christa saw people in her room we couldn't see. I th-think Mrs. Kerrigan cursed us."

I wasn't sure if I was more shocked by the words themselves or by the fact that Elodie had said them. What had happened to the girl who'd had to be *forced* to wear the charm Marieta had given her, the one who had thought tea-leaf readings were ridiculous?

Holmes appeared amused by Elodie's sudden change of heart. "So, you are saying Mrs. Agnes Kerrigan is a practitioner of witchcraft and has hexed you and Christa," he drawled. "For what purpose I wonder? I reckon she resents everyone in Baker House impartially."

"Because she overheard us accusing her of stealing Christa's necklace." She added shamefully, "We weren't very nice about it."

"Ah, yes, the exact words were 'nasty old lady,'" Holmes recalled with some glee. "Rude and ageist. Tut, tut. And she responded by saying Christa would suffer for spreading lies. Melodramatic, that woman is. I suppose you were hexed for simply associating with Christa, yes? Unfortunately, I am no subject-matter expert on curses."

"That's why I wanted Marieta there," Elodie said. "She knows about these kinds of things."

"Ah, yes, perhaps another tea-leaf reading is in order, you know, for guidance. The last one was *so* informative," Holmes snarled.

Elodie shook her head seriously, missing his sarcasm. "No, no, not that again. I can't risk seeing the devil in my cup again, not after what happened last night in this very room," she said, her voice nearly a whisper.

Arthur appeared unsurprised by this news; they had evidently already discussed it. Holmes tried not to look eager, but his face twitched with fresh excitement, even if he claimed to find the matter silly. I didn't bother hiding my curiosity; I urged Elodie to go on.

She began, "It was very early, maybe four or five o'clock in the morning. Something woke me and I couldn't fall asleep no matter how hard I tried. I'm not sure how much time passed before the man appeared. He just materialized right before my eyes. He was holding a red book and asked me to sign my name. I recognized his voice right away: it was the same one that offered to clean the fridge. He opened the book and kept pushing me to sign, b-but I said n-no. There were already names on the page, but the only one I recognized was Mrs. Kerrigan's."

The mockery in Holmes' voice didn't fade. "And how did the man exit the room? Through those doors?"

Elodie blinked. "I'm not s-sure. One moment he was there, the next, he'd disappeared."

"Sounds awfully like a dream," my friend grunted, vexed that a precious thirty seconds of his life had been wasted by the retelling of a mere dream.

"But it felt so real," she murmured.

"Christa mentioned a book as well," I said.

"Which is most likely what influenced this fantasy." He asked Elodie, "Have you by any chance read Eric Zhang's *A History of Witchcraft in New England*?"

She shook her head.

"But you have researched the topic, haven't you, in light of all the recent chatter? Perhaps Christa too? Did you come across the Salem court documents with Tituba's testimonial?"

Elodie shrugged. "Uh, I don't know … maybe I did."

I recalled from my late-night readings that Tituba was a slave from Barbados who worked in the house of Betty Parris and Abigail Williams. They had accused Tituba of being their tormentor, and she had eventually confessed.

"Well, there you have it!" Holmes exclaimed, clapping his hands. "During her cross-examination, Tituba spoke of a grotesque creature, the familiar of another accused woman, and described it as 'a thing with a head like a woman with two legs and wings.' Sounds awfully similar to what your mind conjured."

Elodie looked indignant. "My mind *conjured* nothing! I know what I saw."

"If you say so," Holmes said resignedly and stood up. "Well, I think we have learned everything there is to learn here. Shall we, Watson?"

But Arthur blocked the exit. "There's more to this than meets the eye. First Christa, now Elodie. And I haven't been feeling myself ever since I saw the blue fire."

Holmes scoffed, "Well, Watson and I are perfectly fine, and we saw the fire too."

I would later wonder if these very words had jinxed us. Considering what followed, I could hardly be blamed for having such preposterous thoughts.

Holmes went on, "What is the significance of this blue fire anyway? I haven't come across any information on it."

"There's a story about it," Arthur answered. "Folklore has it that the group of witches who left Salem followed a ball of blue fire that guided them to a land where they could live free of persecution."

Holmes cringed. "Ugh, more mythos. I shall do my utmost to forget it." He sidestepped Arthur and strode briskly out of the room.

I lingered for a moment and glanced about apologetically, but Arthur and Elodie bore me no animosity. In fact, the entire room relaxed after Holmes' rude departure. Elodie asked me to tell Christa where she was without giving too many specifics; she wanted to explain to her friend in person what had happened. She seemed to be under the impression that Christa would be devastated by the news and begged me to take her treats—specifically, her favourite carrot muffin and oat latte combination—to pacify her. She nodded at Arthur's coffee cup and told me that the bakery on campus was open that day. Stuffing some bills into my palm, she practically ordered me to treat myself—and Holmes too, although this was added out of politeness—and looked happier as I left to catch up to Holmes.

He was loitering by the main entrance to the hospital, puffing at a cigarette, which he hastily put out as I approached. The vile smell clung to him though.

"What do you say to a brisk walk back to Baker House, Watson?"

"So long as we make a pit stop at Monton Hall." I told him about Elodie's request, and he shrugged.

I winced as the snappy January air struck me, and I took a brave step forward. We embarked on a brisk walk as promised. Holmes, unfazed by the grey morning and having apparently forgotten all about the sinister business that had drawn us away from Baker House, chirped cheerily about violins. At least a quarter of an hour had passed with a spiel on the difference between a Stradivarius and an Amati when I interrupted him.

"You don't seem concerned at all about everything that's happened," I complained.

Holmes shrugged. "As I mentioned before, I am collecting data. Emotion of any kind will only muddy the waters."

"Do you think Mrs. Kerrigan is involved in what happened to Christa and Elodie?"

"Absolute rubbish," he scoffed. "In fact, I expected this accusation." When I raised a brow in surprise, he added, "Do you remember Mrs. Stillaway's description of a witch? 'An ugly old misfit.' That is what she said. It is the archetype people tend to pick on, and that is precisely what Christa's and Elodie's imaginations did. Watson, let me repeat this: it has all been done before. That was why I asked Elodie if she had read Zhang's book—oh, but then perhaps she had read about *that* curious incident elsewhere. Her imagination simply borrowed the details—"

"What incident?" I interrupted. "The Salem Witch Trials?"

Holmes shook his head. "No, I am referring to a real-life Cinderella story, one nearly as macabre as the original tale presented by the Grimm brothers. I refer to what happened to Elizabeth Knapp in 1671."

I had read the collection of fairy tales compiled by Jacob and Wilhelm Grimm; the original Cinderella story was indeed gruesome. Each stepsister had either cut off her toe or sliced off her heel to fit into the golden slipper Cinderella had left at the ball. I shuddered, recalling that they also had their eyes pecked out by birds in the end, and hoped the tale of Elizabeth Knapp wouldn't be nearly as terrible.

"Miss Knapp was a young servant girl who worked for a reverend in New England. One day, she heard a voice in her head that she presumed belonged to the devil. It offered to do one of her chores: bringing the wood chips inside. She refused, of course, but when she returned to the house, the chips were there." Holmes smiled grimly. "Sounds familiar, doesn't it? But the similarities do not end there."

I had often thought of Holmes as a walking crime encyclopedia, but apparently that brain attic of his documented anything sensational. I cursed his dramatic pause and pressed him to go on.

"Miss Knapp feared that she had lost her soul, and her agitation started to manifest physically. As a matter of fact, she manifested many of the symptoms Elodie did." He looked at me triumphantly. "Don't you see, Watson? It was all in Elodie's head, provoked first by what happened at Crooked Forest and then to her friend. Seeing by chance what vaguely resembled the devil in her teacup didn't help matters either. There is nothing nefarious at work, just an overtaxed brain struggling to understand some frightening, inexplicable events, events with reasonable explanations, I assure you."

"Which you've yet to uncover," I murmured.

Holmes looked annoyed. "In 1689, Cotton Mather, a Puritan minister in New England, published a book recounting the possession of the Goodwin children in Boston. Three years later, in January of 1692, Betty Parris and Abigail Williams started exhibiting similar symptoms, igniting the Salem Witch Trials." He added conspiratorially, "Some historians theorize that the girls read Mather's work … You see, there was a copy in Samuel Parris' library."

"And they faked their symptoms?"

Holmes shrugged. "Maybe … or perhaps the overwhelming guilt and fear for having taken part in what they believed was sorcery made the symptoms manifest because they expected such things would happen to those who consorted with the devil, as revealed in Mather's book."

I hadn't the slightest clue what to make of this. Perhaps it addressed why Elodie had heard a voice; she expected it after what she had seen in her cup. But it didn't reveal who had cleaned the fridge. Had the flick of an unearthly hand done it, or was the credit due to someone at Baker House, as Holmes believed? Marieta Charr came to mind as I remembered the way Elodie's crazed eyes had bulged as she had called her a "witch." The accusation had hardly stirred Marieta. Had she been responsible for what had happened last night, or had Elodie's frazzled brain jumped from one archetype to another?

CHAPTER 19

Servitude or Death

"She was weak and helpless, shaken in mind and nerve."

—Sir Arthur Conan Doyle, *The Sign of the Four*

I SHOOK THESE DISTURBING THOUGHTS AWAY AS MONTON Hall came into view moments later. The building, which housed our normally bustling student centre, was dead silent when we arrived. A few students lounged on the couches; one had passed out, judging by the way his arm and leg hung off the seat. Every eatery apart from the bakery was closed for New Year's Day. We followed the faint aroma of coffee eagerly and placed our order with the young barista, who oddly reminded me of Mrs. Kerrigan—had she been tall, broad-chested, and smiled occasionally. Evidently, my thoughts still hovered on the devious "Goody Kerrigan" despite Holmes' firm defence of her.

With one gloved hand tasked with holding Christa's treats and a blueberry scone for me, I hastily sipped my latte—sprinkled generously with cinnamon and nutmeg—as we exited the building. Somehow, the cold didn't seem as brutal armed with fresh baked goods.

Holmes didn't seem pleased with his black coffee though; he muttered a dissatisfied "brunt" although he continued sipping. Even he occasionally needed a safeguard against the winter.

Fifteen minutes later, we embraced the warmth of Baker House. Holmes' first order of business was to toss his half-full cup. He then sprinted to the basement without uttering a word. I trudged upstairs slowly, suddenly feeling reluctant to make the climb to Christa's room. In what state would I find her? I hadn't seen her since Monday night, and what I had seen then had disturbed me more than I cared to admit. Even if she was well now, would the news of Elodie being in the hospital hark back her recovery? I wasn't certain I could calm her, and the treats I carried suddenly seemed inadequate.

Taking a deep breath, I knocked. Beyond the door, nothing stirred — and then a faint meow answered. Ah, so the cat had found its way inside again, or at least I hoped the cat had meowed, not Christa. Even as I knocked again, I knew I wouldn't wait for the door to open; a meowing Christa was just as unnerving as a barking one. I placed the treats by the door and nearly broke into a run to my room.

I stayed there only long enough to drop off my coat and winter accessories. Chugging my now-lukewarm latte, I picked up the plate of toast from that morning — a sizeable chunk of which was now missing — and my scone, then tucked *The House with the Seven Gables* under my arm and descended to the dining room. Unlike Holmes, I didn't enjoy being confined to my tiny room when Baker House offered so many charming nooks.

However, I arrived at the dining hall to find Mrs. Kerrigan wiping the tables, furiously mumbling the entire time. Her jerky movements halted when she sensed me in the doorway. She straightened, holding the wet cloth like a whip, and scowled at the toast.

"Can't you see I'm cleaning?" she barked. "Go eat that somewhere else." As an afterthought, she added, "And don't leave any crumbs!"

I didn't need to be told twice. I scurried across the room to the kitchen, threw out the toast, and returned to my room, feeling both disappointed and relieved. Here at least I would be safe from ill-humored housekeepers who didn't understand the concept of not working on a holiday, especially since the dining tables didn't look like they were in desperate need of a wipe-down.

It was with some hesitation that I left my door open; there was a strong possibility that doing so may invite inside Mrs. Kerrigan, or the cat should it decide to leave the third floor. But the heater was working a little too well at the moment, and though I had longed for it while I had been outside, the warmth had reached a suffocating level.

Some time elapsed in silence, which I now and then broke to turn a page or noisily chew, as I sat at my desk reading. Had I been so enraptured by the goings-on in the book's depressing New England mansion that I failed to notice what was happening around me? In fact, I may not have noticed anything had I not felt around distractedly for my scone. Instead of oven-baked dough, my fingers touched the prickly tips of tall grass. Then a cool breeze hit my face.

I was sitting at the base of a low hill near a towering oak tree. Rising, the first thing I noticed was the odd scatter of people who lingered nearby. Had I somehow stumbled upon the cast of a film set in colonial times? How else was I to explain the young men in linen shirts and breeches, older men in doublets and wide-brimmed hats, and women in flowing skirts and aprons, their long hair hidden behind coifs? But the restlessness, fear, and agitation that ran through the crowd made it bewilderingly obvious that this was no film set. There was something oddly real about these people that no actor could capture. There was also the fact that they couldn't see me.

To my right was a large but lacklustre bay, fed by a nearby river, beyond which lay the homesteads and larger structures of a small town cut into squares and rectangles by dirt roads.

Up ahead, a small procession trailed an ox cart. It crossed the bridge that spanned the river, and a sharp turn later, made its way to the oak tree. It was then that I saw the rope tied to one of the branches. Its looped end rocked gently in the breeze, and the crowd watched it as though hypnotized. A wooden ladder leaned against the tree. Some of my confusion lifted, replaced by a horrifying realization.

A woman emerged from the cart when it finally came to a stop, and flanked by two men, she dragged her feet toward the tree, looking forlorn. She was about sixty and had certainly seen better days. A plain brown dress shrouded her thin frame, and a dirty apron hung lopsidedly from her waist. Unruly greying hair poked out of her coif, but she hardly seemed to care about her slipshod state. Her dark eyes were fixed on the noose—until she turned sharply to meet my unblinking gaze, and proclaimed: "Will you stand in the inner circle round about the gallows? Will you be the loudest to applaud the work of blood? Will you be the last to confess yourself miserably deceived?"

I gaped at her. There was something oddly familiar about what she had said. I had heard these words before; of that I was certain. Yet how was that possible when this woman was a stranger?

I wanted to desperately answer her: no, I would *not* watch as the noose tightened around her neck, and I would most certainly not applaud. In fact, I would thrust aside that ladder before she was forced to climb it. I would fling it into the bay and take off with the prisoner.

None of this came to pass though. Even if I hadn't been too frazzled to speak or move, I couldn't have stopped the woman from climbing the ladder or pushed aside the burly, scowling men who bound her hands and legs. The woman fixed her gaze on me the entire time, the struggle gone from her limbs as the noose was placed around her neck.

And then she changed—not her expression, but her entire face. The salt-and-pepper hair turned black and burst out of the coif like snakes. The wrinkles disappeared and scarred pink flesh replaced her pale cheeks. In the place of the old woman stood another, much younger woman. She had the same dark eyes, yet hers burned with mania. Her voice emerged in a threatening whisper. "Sign the book and serve … or die."

One of her captors kicked the ladder aside, and although I had shut my eyes, that didn't save me from hearing the thrashing of legs and skirts.

Suddenly, I realized it was the sensation of falling, rather than the sight of the brutal hanging, that had made me shut my eyes. At first, I thought I was tumbling backwards into the bay, but no, my fall lasted only seconds, broken by a clatter of wood against wood, followed almost simultaneously by a painful collision of skin against wood.

Then there was silence.

Slowly, my eyelids unglued themselves. I could no longer hear the water that coursed through the grey terrain—or the young woman's struggles for breath.

I was lying on the floor of my room in Baker House. My chair lay next to me, toppled. I gradually pieced it together. I had fallen asleep while reading, dreamt a rather chilling vision of the infamous Salem Witch Trials, and then had fallen off my chair. My mind had re-enacted the hanging of Bridget Bishop, the first to be dragged off to the gallows in 1692. Nothing in the dream had indicated the identity of the woman, yet I was certain. But I hadn't the slightest clue who the second woman had been; the scars had rendered her face beyond recognition, although I sensed a vague familiarity. Holmes would no doubt theorize that she was a warped rendering of someone I had seen in the streets or read about in a book, her message obviously influenced by the ones I had heard from Christa and Elodie. Reasonable though the explanation was, I felt no better. Would I soon start barking, hear strange voices, or see a woman-dog chimera?

"Watson, are you all right?" asked the familiar voice of Sherlock Holmes. "You look rather dazed."

Startled, I craned my neck to look up at his towering figure. Somehow, I had been oblivious to his peering gaze or the shadow he cast on me. I immediately decided he would not hear of my dream; he would only laugh or scoff.

"I fell asleep in my chair," I said sheepishly.

He extended a nitrile-gloved hand to help me up, which my clammy one gripped tightly. His other hand, also gloved in the same bright blue, held a palm-sized glass plate that housed a mass of mucky brown.

"Must have been that awfully dull book," he said, gesturing at *The House of the Seven Gables*, which lay abandoned on the desk. "Oh, stop lingering, Gastrell, and come inside."

Arthur emerged from beyond the doorway, looking terribly pale, and mumbled, "Er, sorry, I heard a c-crash."

As soon as our eyes met, I knew something was wrong. He stared with wide, frightened eyes, as though I was a ghastly sight. I was tempted to reach for a mirror, yet Holmes hadn't perceived anything unusual about me or anything else in the room. He also didn't appear to notice Arthur's trembling exterior.

I shot Arthur a questioning glance; it was the only thing I could covertly do without attracting Holmes' attention. The gesture made Arthur realize he had been staring, and his gaze immediately fell to the floor.

Holmes said, "Watson, why don't you lie down for a bit? Rest up and then we can meet for a late lunch, eh? I must return to my experiments." He whirled around. "Come along, Gastrell."

But Arthur refused to move. He was looking intently at me again. "Maybe I should stay—"

"Nonsense! She is perfectly well. Aren't you, Watson? See? Perfectly well!" Holmes ushered a still reluctant Arthur out, adding over his shoulder, "Should you desire a book that will *not* put you to sleep, try Oddfellow's *Physical Chemistry*." The door shut behind them.

I slumped on the bed and stared at the chair for some time. An odd hesitation stopped me from touching it; its toppled frame filled me with foreboding. Conversation would have been a welcomed distraction, but the door had closed with a finality that told me only thoughts of a mutilated face would keep me company for the next little while. The hung woman, the younger one, couldn't have been much older than me, I reflected, recalling her slender figure. Where had my mind summoned her from? She resembled no one I knew; even Mrs. Stillaway had just a single scar running down her cheek. Still, the mention of her name beckoned another one, but the thought scampered as a faint rustling interrupted the silence.

The sound had come from the door. Sure enough, near the gap at the bottom lay a torn-out sheet from a notepad. I practically leapt to it, one hand already flying to the doorknob as I quickly studied the neat handwriting.

The landing beyond was empty, and the house was devoid of sound. I couldn't even hear the footsteps of the person who had slipped the note under the door shuffling away. It almost seemed as though the note had delivered itself. *Don't be silly*, I reprimanded myself. I closed the door and read the note: *Come to the parlour in 30 min. We need to talk. Don't tell Sherlock.*

So Holmes wasn't the author, but that much was evident from the handwriting, which was too neat to be his. He or she was a resident of Baker House though, but one who didn't have my cellphone number and didn't dare knock on my door for fear of being overheard.

I arrived in the parlour ten minutes before noon to find Marieta Charr, the flowing skirt of her long umber dress draping the armchair she occupied. She was studying a small leatherbound book, whose pages she returned to after giving me a curt nod. I took a seat across from her.

All was still for some minutes. Marieta didn't look up or question why I sat staring at the wallpaper, and soon, a panicked doubt overtook me when no one else entered the room. Had there even been a note, or had I imagined it? Something felt wrong. I didn't feel like myself; a dreadful unsteadiness lingered and with it came a feeling of disorientation. Tempted though I was to run upstairs to see the note, to verify its existence, the fear of finding nothing kept me glued to the couch.

Then Arthur walked in, steps hesitant, eyes watchful. There was something telling about the way he looked at me, and I breathed with relief. There *had* been a note and Arthur had been its author. This time the sight of me didn't make him cringe like it had a half hour earlier; instead, I sensed a tense caution as he took a seat beside me. He eyed Marieta and seemed to contemplate something. When he spoke, it was direct and to the point, without his customary meekness.

"What happened to you earlier?" he asked. Marieta straightened in her seat, but Arthur didn't appear to care that we had an audience.

"Did you see something when you came in?" I asked vaguely, although I wasn't sure what he could have seen to frighten him to this degree … perhaps I had worn an odd look on my face or said something peculiar as I woke.

"You tell me first," he insisted. "Tell me everything that happened after you walked into your room." I cast a wary eye at Marieta. Arthur sensed my hesitation. "Marieta might be able to help."

So, he had seen something after all. Something inexplicable ... something strange enough to involve Marieta. The realization reanimated the panic I had felt earlier. Was I now plagued by something malevolent, the way Christa and Elodie had been? There was no point in stalling any further, and so I told him—and Marieta, who was now peering intently at me—everything.

There was no skeptical eye rolling as I mentioned the crisp Salem air, the bridge, the village, the rushing river, or the bay, and not even as I described in detail the dull colonial accoutrement and the nervous, angry presentiment of the crowd. There wasn't a single interruption; Arthur and Marieta hung onto every word. When I finished, neither one ruminated on a plausible explanation. Both remained in thoughtful silence, although Arthur looked unnerved once again. It was he who spoke first.

"I'll tell you what I saw." He drew a quick breath. "I'd just come back from the hospital and was heading to my room. When I reached the second-floor landing, I saw that your door was open. And I saw your chair—it was empty. I didn't think anything of it, of course; I just thought you had left your room. So, I started to head upstairs when I heard the crash. When I looked into your room from where I stood, the chair had fallen over."

"What are you trying to say?" I asked.

Arthur pressed his lips. The hesitation I had seen at Crooked Forest Adventures when we had asked him to explain why he was meandering through the woods returned. This time, perhaps because Holmes wasn't around, he didn't require much compelling, but his voice was careful and slow.

"You weren't sitting in your chair when I first looked into your room. I don't think you were in the room."

I shook my head vigorously. "No, no, maybe I was sleepwalking. There's one corner of my room you couldn't have seen from your vantage point. I could've been standing there."

But Arthur looked skeptical. "Do you have a history of sleepwalking?" He already knew the answer though. Because the Baker Street crowd, and students in general, kept the oddest hours, even happenings late into the night didn't go unnoticed. Holmes himself would have told me if I was a sleepwalker. "So, something compelled you to get off your chair and walk to that corner, somehow not colliding with the bed that stands in your way. Then you dream about Salem and leap over the bed, crashing into your chair and waking up?" He frowned. "That makes no sense to me."

"It doesn't, but it makes more sense than believing I travelled to Salem." My reply came out more haughtily than I had intended, but even as I spoke, a confusing cycle of rejection, then contemplation, of what he was insinuating swelled my anxiety.

"Whatever it was that really happened, it wasn't normal. I think we can agree on that." Turning to Marieta, he asked, "Is there anything you can do to help?"

She thought for a moment and then nodded slowly. "Yes, we can cleanse the room."

"With a spell?" I asked dubiously.

Marieta shook her head. "No, spellwork won't be required. There are other ways. My aunt can tell you more if you like."

CHAPTER 20

Trust No One

"One never knows either who to trust or who not to trust."

—Sir Arthur Conan Doyle, *The Valley of Fear*

WE ARRIVED AT THE FAMILIAR FAÇADE OF TEA & TEE HALF an hour later. The shop was closed for New Year's Day, but forewarned by her niece, Mrs. Tina Stillaway knew to expect us. She beckoned us in with a warm but concerned smile and poured us a cup of tea, which she had brewed and kept warm in advance. We didn't enter the back room this time, standing instead at a small, high table stashed in a corner of the shop. I drank, grateful for the warmth and pleasant scents that worked their magic to calm me as Marieta and her aunt talked.

"Frankincense resin from the *Boswellia sacra* tree along with myrrh should do the trick," Mrs. Stillaway was saying.

Marieta shook her head. "No, Aunt Tee, I think we need something more powerful." Her face looked so urgent that her aunt didn't protest.

Mrs. Stillaway looked over at me thoughtfully, and I did my best to remain still under the scrutiny of her knowing eyes. Could she sense the cacophony of contradicting thoughts that were tiring me out? I could hardly summon the effort to tell her I had experienced nothing but a dream—a very vivid dream, but a dream, nonetheless. Had Holmes joined us in the parlour, he would have uncovered the puzzle of the empty chair in an instant and laughed at our gullibility. Yet another part of me believed the answer wouldn't be so ordinary.

"Palo santo sticks then," Mrs. Stillaway declared. "Can you go fetch them from the back?" she asked her niece. When Marieta left, her eyes met mine. "You're frightened."

She was right but admitting it would only make the feeling seem more real. I shook my head and mustered a laugh. "I'm fine. It was just a dream."

"Perhaps … but you are *not* fine." There was a moment of hesitation, and then she drew a deep breath, having made up her mind about something. "The people you came here with last time: how well do you know them?"

"Since the start of last semester," I said distractedly, wondering if I looked sickly.

"No, not how *long* you've known them, how *well* do you know them? We can know someone for a very long time and still not truly know them."

Feeling a bit mystified, I said, "I know Holmes quite well. I think I know what sort of person he is, if that's what you're asking." This was vaguely true, although my friend never ceased to surprise me occasionally. "The others, well, we live in the same house and run into each other quite a bit. We've shared meals and conversations, but I suppose I don't know them very well." I chose my words carefully; after all, the "others" included Mrs. Stillaway's own niece.

The lady was silent for a moment; she appeared to be thinking profoundly about something. The seconds stretched on long enough to make me wonder if she would ever speak. She did speak—only three words, in fact—but her murmured words, and her solemn expression, only unnerved me.

"Trust no one."

Alarmed, I set my cup down, my thirst suddenly gone. Marieta returned just then, holding a small terracotta ceramic bowl in one hand and a sturdy-looking stick of pale-brown wood in the other. Mrs. Stillaway carefully bagged the items and set them on the table.

"This palo santo stick comes from Peru, from the sacred *Bursera graveolens* tree," she said. "It's used in South America for healing and cultural ceremonies and has now become very popular in the West. The stick is lit, and the smoke is used to cleanse a person or place. You don't need to worry about performing the ritual itself. Marieta will take care of it."

I pulled out my wallet, but Mrs. Stillaway shook her head. "Unfortunately, the palo santo tree is being overharvested because of increased demand, so I don't sell the sticks. I'm also doing my part to not commodify native tradition. I present this to you as a gift." She pushed the bag toward me.

It was perhaps her grim face that propelled me out of the shop with so much urgency, with Marieta following wordlessly. I was impatient to return home, but there I met Arthur Gastrell's equally grim face. He was waiting in his favourite armchair, just as we had left him, looking flushed and nervous. He eyed the paper bag and the blackbird that emblazoned its front but said nothing as I joined him in the parlour. Together, we watched Marieta go upstairs, cradling the bag as though it were a child. She hadn't asked me to accompany her, which was a relief. I would avoid my room, and perhaps the entire second floor, for some time.

My stomach grumbled a few minutes later, reminding me of the late lunch Holmes had promised. It was nearly two o'clock, yet I had gotten no calls or messages from him. Texting for his whereabouts, however, would be useless since he neglected his phone most hours of the day. I imagined he was still in his room, his long gloved fingers twirling a test tube. Regardless, I decided I would search every other part of the house before I went upstairs; it was something to do, and I was in desperate need of a distraction.

I headed to the kitchen first. Holmes wasn't there, but in a large pot on the stove remained the last bits of minestrone. So, Mrs. Kerrigan had done something other than wipe tables that needed no wiping. Luckily, she hadn't stuck around to offer a serving of her scowls with the soup. I eagerly scraped up the remnants into a bowl, tested the edibility with a cautious bite, then ate the rest without bothering to sit down.

I then poked my head into the dining room; a few faces stared back, but I withdrew before any conversation could start — the last thing I wanted was to be asked why there were strange smells, and smoke, coming from my room. My search came to an end when I reached the library, not because Holmes was there but because the couches called to me. I stretched across one and closed my eyes. The faces of Marieta Charr, Elodie Willis, and Sherlock Holmes filled the blackness and blinked at me with matching sinister grins ... which one was I not supposed to trust?

*

Sleep has a way of mollifying one's problems. This was evident from the way I felt about my room a few hours later when I woke up, cheek pressed into the library couch. What a gullible dupe I had been! I had let a dream — and the imagination of a superstitious few — knock the reason out of me. Holmes would have been ashamed, but luckily, he would never find out. The palo santo, which I imagined had a strong aroma, wouldn't escape his incredible sense of smell, of course, but it was hardly suspicious to light some incense in one's room.

I made my way upstairs. A faint earthy scent hovered on the landing and grew stronger as I got closer to my room. The door was open, and I paused at the entrance, carefully scanning my humble abode. Marieta had straightened the chair and opened the window a crack, although the rough winter wind hardly swept away the scents of licorice and lemon that had settled in the space. The room was cold though and I rushed in to shut the window. Then I turned and slumped on the windowpane and surveyed the room again, every breath bringing an inner quiet.

But the peace died seconds later when my gaze landed on a spot of green nestled between the wall and the dresser.

I already knew what it was even before I reached into the corner and brought out the leaf. It was an elongated oval with depressed veins and smooth edges that ended in a point. I may have seen it around, but I was no botanist; to me it looked like a leaf from any old tree in the city. Yet the city was covered in snow and the trees slept barren. Wherever this leaf was from, it was warm, late spring or perhaps even summer.

I stiffened as a sudden chilling thought barged into my mind: It had been spring in Salem, Massachusetts, when Bridget Bishop had been executed. In fact, I had stood by a large oak in my dream.

I scrutinized the leaf. Was this the leaf of an oak tree? I had no idea, though a simple search on my phone would tell me. Yet I couldn't bring myself to do it. I was afraid and confused, and I could hardly stop my feet from running to Sherlock Holmes.

*

The human skull on Holmes' desk peered at me with more attention than my friend. From the manner in which he listened to my story, one would think he was bored. He slouched comfortably in his armchair, his feet propped up on the bed, and his eyes were half-closed. His fingers plucked carelessly at the strings of his violin, which lay in his lap, making desultory sounds here and there as I told him about the dream, my meeting with Arthur and Marieta, the trip to Tea & Tee, and, finally, the leaf, which I had hastily deposited on his desk, so eager was I to rid myself of the cursed thing.

Holmes opened his eyes languidly, watched me for a moment with an unreadable expression, and then, in the most sluggish of tones, said, "Tell me again, Watson, what Mrs. Bishop said to you."

I recited the three questions the poor prisoner had sprung on me as best as I could recall.

"Do the words sound familiar to you?" he asked, smiling faintly when I nodded in muted shock. How had he known? But he wasn't forthcoming with an answer. Instead, he plucked the leaf and examined it.

"It doesn't belong to an oak, Watson. I am not certain what plant it belongs to. Were it a poisonous one, I would surely have been able to identify it, so we can deduce that the leaf isn't poisonous."

"I wasn't planning on eating it," I said grumpily.

Although it was some solace that he hadn't laughed at my predicament, Holmes had still failed to provide any answers. I didn't ask him if he thought the leaf had come from Salem though; doing so would certainly provoke a fit of laughter, and I was in no mood to be laughed at.

"Very good then. Did you lock your door before you went downstairs to meet Gastrell?"

I shook my head. "No, I don't think I did. I was too anxious about the note."

"Was your window open or closed when you returned to your room this morning after our trip to the hospital?"

"Closed. Marieta opened it. But that leaf didn't drift in from outside, Holmes. There's nothing green left out there."

This point was ignored and the interrogation continued. "So, feeling the draft, you proceeded to close the window. In your peripheral, you spotted the leaf lying to your right. Hm, I wonder why Marieta didn't see it when she went to open the window. Perhaps the leaf was placed there after she was done or ..." He looked at me meaningfully.

"Are you insinuating that Marieta put the leaf there?" I exclaimed. "Why would she or someone else do something like that?"

Holmes' face hardened. "The answer is obvious, Watson: to make you believe what you experienced was real."

"That's what you said about the fridge. But why would someone want us to believe this–this nonsense?"

He shrugged. "That is a most excellent question, and I have yet to find the answer."

"Well, I don't think Marieta burned anything poisonous in my room. I felt rather good breathing in the palo santo."

"I don't know much about palo santo, but there is science at work here. Sniffing the scent no doubt releases a combination of dopamine, serotonin, and endorphins. Do not fool yourself into thinking it is anything mystical," Holmes said sharply.

"Oh, but there is *something* odd going on," broke in the carolling voice of Gwilym Lestrade.

I looked up as the door squeaked open to reveal his rat-like face. I wondered how long he had been hovering there and how much of our conversation he had heard. Holmes shot me an accusatory glare, reprimanding me for not shutting the door properly, and then greeted Gwilym with a smirk.

"It isn't good form to eavesdrop, Lestrade."

Gwilym shrugged and leaned into the door frame. "I was just passing by when your mention of Marieta Charr's name made me pause."

"Passing by?" Holmes' brow rose to a comical height. "Your room is on the ground floor. What reason do you have to venture up here?"

The answer was an ominous smile. "I'm glad we're thinking along the same lines in this case," Gwilym said.

"I've been watching Marieta ever since the incidents at Crooked Forest."

CHAPTER 21

Truth or Twaddle?

"My God, can there be some truth in all these stories?"

—Sir Arthur Conan Doyle, *The Hound of the Baskervilles*

I SWALLOWED. IT WAS NOW MY TURN TO RAISE A BROW. "You think she's responsible too?"

Gwilym shot a glance at the empty landing behind him, then, deciding it was safer not linger on the threshold—Marieta's room was just one door away after all—stepped inside and shut the door. Holmes' frown deepened.

"I can't say anything with certainty yet, but she's tied to every oddity that's happened." He then spotted the skull on Holmes' desk and grimaced. "If you don't mind—" His hand stretched past me and turned the skull away so it no longer grinned at us. "Now what was I saying … Ah, yes, Marieta Charr …"

Had I been in a better mood, I would have told him the skull was stolen property from the anthropology department. Holmes had promised to return it last semester but, realizing that he took comfort in talking to it, had failed to do so.

"She was present when the first dog was slain—I've confirmed that with Arthur," Gwilym went on. "And she was there the day of the second dog's murder. Then we have Christa and Elodie's, er, compromised states right here in Baker House." His face darkened. "Marieta Charr is tied to it all."

"How interesting," Holmes said, yawning. "You are a perspicacious chap indeed. Oh, don't forget her deep-voiced accomplice with the special talent of making himself heard without actually being present—for the most part."

The mention of the voice stirred fresh excitement in Gwilym. There was an unsettling glimmer in his eyes that conveyed both fear and fascination.

"Ah, yes, the voice. Disturbing, but not surprising. She dabbles in *weird* things after all," he said, his singsong accent sounding more melodious than ever. "I'm not saying I believe in sorcery, but who's to say she didn't conjure the voice?" Then he quickly added, "Through narcotics, of course. So there is no voice; her victims simply imagined it through the use of some hallucinatory drug."

Holmes managed to stifle the next yawn but made a show of doing so. "Very compelling, Willie. Do go on."

So great was our housemate's zeal that he didn't even notice Holmes' butchering of his name. "The first person to hear the voice was Arthur when he was lured into the woods."

"But he wasn't feeling well. Would he have accepted something to eat or drink from Marieta?" I interjected. "If he did, the drug must've started working in a very short time, although I suppose she could've given it to him hours before …"

Gwilym nodded with a sparkle in his eyes. "Leslie Alfredsson-Maine also heard the voice—"

"She has confirmed that she accepted no food or drink from anyone except for those sandwiches that were passed around," Holmes said airily, studying his fingernails. "They were obviously not the source of the drug since everyone ate them."

"Oh." Gwilym's face fell but brightened again almost immediately. "Well, we also have Christa, who felt unwell that one morning—"

"When Marieta was nowhere to be seen," Holmes interrupted. "Christa's other symptoms manifested hours later. I suppose Elodie is next on your list? You will recall that she, unlike her friend, wasn't at Baker House when she heard the voice. She was fine when she left the house, so how and when was the drug administered to her? To our knowledge, Marieta stayed in that night."

"What are you insinuating?" Gwilym asked slowly. "Th-that no drugs were involved?" His eyes brightened remarkably.

Although a hint of mischief lit his features, Holmes sounded nonchalant when he replied, "I am simply playing devil's advocate, mate. Elodie's blood tests detected no narcotic, after all." Gwilym appeared stunned by this news, but he recovered quickly; instead of looking chilled or even puzzled, his face shone with excitement.

"Why would Marieta do all this anyway?" I asked.

"The dogs were obviously some sort of sacrifice," our housemate explained. "And the girls ... well, revenge, of course! Christa has never treated her well, and Elodie, although much nicer, never intervenes. I don't know why she would hurt Arthur though; they've always seemed friendly with one another."

I've never done anything to her either, I thought. Gwilym seemed to be thinking along the same lines; he looked at me and then at the leaf in Holmes' hand. Something about his expression told me he had been present for nearly my entire conversation with Holmes.

"I'm not sure what tree that leaf belongs to," he said. "What's remarkable is the level of detail you remember about the dream. Very strange, don't you think, Sherlock?"

Holmes grunted.

"I suspect Marieta was somehow responsible for your dream, Janah. Did she happen to offer you anything to eat—"

"No," I said.

Gwilym shrugged. "It's all part of her plot: to stir fear, to make people feel as she felt when she witnessed her aunt's shop under attack."

"You know about her aunt's shop and the attack?" I exclaimed.

Holmes didn't seem pleased by this. Gwilym, on the other hand, looked like a peacock with its feathers unfurled: undeniably self-assured and proud. "Oh, yes," he said, nodding enthusiastically. "I bet you didn't know that Marieta witnessed the entire thing, hidden as she was in a back room." He leaned in conspiratorially. "She was off the entire winter semester afterwards, and when she came back, rumour had it that she was *different*, although I'd always thought she was bit of an odd—"

"Can you please stick to the facts, Lestrade?" Holmes interrupted. "Keep your suppositions to yourself."

Gwilym straightened, looking gravely insulted. "I've reported the facts, the culprit, and the psychological drivers motivating her actions. It's a simple case of post-traumatic stress. Marieta Charr is seeking revenge for the discrimination she has faced, her treatment for having certain religious beliefs, and for her aunt's disfigurement. I heard her face is horribly marred." His lips twitched. "Is it true? I believe you have both seen her."

Somehow, he had found out about our visit to Tea & Tee. I had never thought of Gwilym Lestrade as exceptionally bright, but perhaps his pedantism had overshadowed his intellect. He appeared to have a talent for unearthing information that nearly matched Holmes'. Still, his vulgar enthusiasm disturbed me.

When Holmes and I declined to answer his question, he asked another, "Did neither of you notice that the

Triple Moon—Marieta's tattoo—was one of the symbols in the snow near the blue fire?"

"We did notice," Holmes replied. "It is surprising you noticed too."

This made me pause for a moment. Although Marieta could have killed Stangers the dog and dumped his body before the adventurers had arrived, she couldn't have been responsible for the symbols in the snow and the blue fire—she had been with us then. I quickly reminded Gwilym of this.

"An accomplice, of course!" he chimed. "Or … well, if she's a practitioner of witchcraft, then I suppose she could manage without help."

"Are you a believer of magic, Willie?" Holmes asked wryly.

Gwilym coloured. "I, uh, no, of course not. It's rubbish, utter rubbish. I just—it's not a bad idea to keep an open mind, that's all. I mean, what if she's a descendant of the Salem migrants, the ones who settled in Crooked Forest?" He looked rather hopeful.

Holmes had no chance to taunt Gwilym's "open mind" since I interjected. "She's not a descendant. Her grandfather hailed from Boston, which means her ancestors remained in the States after the trials. His family didn't migrate here until the Civil War."

"But that's only one side of her family," Gwilym insisted. "Do you know anything about the other side?" When no answer came, he offered us a triumphant smile, which faltered a moment later when Holmes chuckled to himself and muttered what sounded distinctly like "fool."

"Well, then, I suppose we'll just have to agree to disagree." He offered us a farewell frown and reached for the doorknob, then stopped. Turning around slowly, he cocked his head at me when our eyes met; he was wearing a peculiar expression.

"The woman who threatened you in your dream: you said she had dark hair and a scarred face …" He paused thoughtfully. "Did you recognize her?"

I nearly recoiled as I recalled the face. The young woman's features were nearly as obscure as before, but Gwilym's question suddenly revived my realization from earlier. Those thick, raven-black strands of hair … and there, underneath the scars, were the high cheekbones. The slightly upturned nose was unblemished but had gone unnoticed before. It was Marieta Charr.

The horror on my face only renewed Gwilym's smugness; his suspicion was confirmed. He cast Holmes a cool look and then opened the door and slipped out. Holmes rolled his eyes and craned his ear toward the door.

"Ha! You hear that, Watson? He is returning to the ground floor. He wasn't passing by at all; that imbecile probably came up just to eavesdrop on us, then wasted our time with twaddle." He huffed loudly.

But I was less disturbed by Gwilym's interruption than he was. My gaze came to rest on the leaf on Holmes' desk; there lay the source of my agitation. That, and Marieta's scarred face and terrible threat. Before I could stop myself, I whispered, "It was Marieta. That's who I saw in th-the dream." Holmes threw me an exasperated scowl, which only compelled me to go on. "And yesterday, Elodie stared at Marieta and called her a witch just before she saw the dog-woman."

Again, there was no response; instead, he leaned over and rotated his beloved skull so that it could leer at us once again.

"This is all your fault," I snapped. "You said we were perfectly fine despite looking at the blue fire. And-and now—"

"And now you are experiencing phenomena that terrify you," Holmes finished. He picked up the leaf and twirled it thoughtfully. "I believe your trip to Salem was nothing more than a dream. You don't need to fear what you saw … but something nefarious *is* toying with us. Be very careful, Watson."

It was with this dark thought burdening my already taxed mind that I left Holmes.

The earthy scent of the palo santo greeted me when I entered my room, but I no longer felt comforted by it. I glanced around the room as I had done only an hour before; nothing was amiss. Pitch blackness reigned outside even though it was only six o'clock. Perhaps the darkness was what propelled me to bed without dinner. I lay wrapped in my comforter for some time, grateful for the warmth and snugness.

Yet I couldn't quiet my mind.

Despite Holmes' firm insistence that I hadn't gone to Salem, a fearful worry nagged at me. My own conviction was failing; I'd had dreams before, but none had been so immersive. I could still picture the townspeople, see the twitching of their nervous faces, and smell the countryside air. Worse still were the crystal images of Bridget Bishop and the scarred woman, who I couldn't help but think of as Marieta now. *Damn you, Gwilym*, I cursed.

If only I could find out where the leaf had come from. That would settle the business. My chances of coming across it through an internet search were slim though; there must be tens of thousands of tree species out there. Even if I restricted the search to trees in North America, there would be at least a thousand to sift through. Still, the tediousness of the task didn't stop me from pulling out my phone. There were many hours left in the day, and even though night had fallen, I wasn't certain I would fall asleep.

I had started flicking through some photos when I realized that my biased search assumed the leaf had come from elsewhere. The most logical assumption was that the leaf belonged to a tree in Toronto, and to confirm this, I could search for trees endemic to the city. But my mind protested once again. No deciduous tree would retain its leaves in the middle of winter, and considering the immense height of trees in general, I couldn't imagine someone growing one indoors.

Still, I ran the search, incited by a glimmer of hope. Perhaps there was an explanation I hadn't considered …

My tired eyes marked the half hour that elapsed then; my search had been fruitless. A nervous tingling reverberated throughout my body: Holmes had been wrong.

I quickly ran another search: *plants endemic to Massachusetts*. I could have replaced the state with Salem, but something about that frightened me. Another half hour tick-tocked by before I choked.

I had found the plant: the eastern flowering dogwood.

It was a small tree, growing only up to ten metres tall, with oval leaves, white flowers, and bark that resembled alligator skin. It was also endemic to southern Ontario, and even here, it lived in a select region southwest of Toronto, stretching from Oakville to Windsor. So, the nearest tree to occur in the wild was at least an hour's drive away. I shivered and put the phone away to stop myself from searching whether the tree grew in Salem.

CHAPTER 22

The Wrong Questions

"I conjure you by everything you hold dear to answer a few questions."

—Sir Arthur Conan Doyle, *A Study in Scarlet*

ALTHOUGH THE NEW YEAR HAD BEGUN TERRIBLY, THE DAYS that followed were uneventful—until Sherlock Holmes arrived at my door one Sunday evening, the day before the start of the winter semester.

"It has been awfully quiet these past few days, eh, Watson?" he remarked with undeniable regret and slipped in without invitation. He took a seat on my desk, even though the chair was unoccupied. I edged away from the windowsill where I had been mournfully watching the snowfall, which had started as a feeble sprinkle and was now turning into an icy barrage. My second winter in the city was turning out to be far more treacherous than my first.

"I mean that in relation to the investigation, of course," he elaborated. "The noise level in the house has increased considerably with the return of the holiday-goers."

He appeared to regret this as much as having no fresh leads in the case, but that was unsurprising. Earlier that day, Gwilym Lestrade's henchmen, no doubt incited by Gwilym himself for Holmes' rude dismissal of his ideas, had spilled spoiled orange juice on his newspaper — accidentally, of course. My friend had turned purple with fury, muttering, "*Un sot trouve toujours un plus sot qui l'admire*" as the trio had laughed diabolically, ignorant of the insult.

I softened a little at the recollection. "What do you want, Holmes?"

Holmes seldom entered my room. When he did, it was usually to wake me rudely or borrow something he didn't plan to return. There was most certainly an ulterior motive for his sudden appearance.

"Am I not permitted to visit you, dear Watson? To have a friendly conversation over a hot cuppa? I hope you aren't upset that I didn't take your otherworldly experience as seriously as Gastrell and Marieta did."

I ignored the last comment. "You seemed to have forgotten to bring the tea." He offered me a sheepish smile. "What do you really want, Holmes?"

"I have come to put your mind at ease, to undo the damage Gastrell and Marieta have done."

I raised an eyebrow. "Oh, really? What harm have they done me?"

"I accuse them of leading you to the false belief that something sinister infiltrated your mind and body and transported you to the moment Bridget Bishop met her death." He let out an exasperated breath. "You must admit, Watson, the notion makes little sense. History would have documented it had Mrs. Bishop morphed into a young woman and uttered a threat to a stranger no one else could see."

"Well, how do you plan to 'undo the damage'?" I asked, lacing the last three words in heavy sarcasm.

"With a book." His head swivelled around, searching for something. "Ah, there it is!" A single leap was enough to transport him from the desk to the bed, where he scooped up *The House of the Seven Gables*. He flipped past the introductory note and the preface, perused the first page of chapter one, then the next couple pages, before his face lit up. A grin now accompanying the satisfied gleam in his eyes, he pointed to a passage. "Read that, my friend. Well, don't just stand there, gaping at me! Read!"

I peered at the page curiously, and then understanding dawned on me. I read aloud, "Clergymen, judges, statesmen — the wisest, calmest, holiest persons of their day stood in the inner circle round about the gallows, loudest to applaud the work of blood, latest to confess themselves miserably deceived."

"You see? What Mrs. Bishop asked you in the dream was simply a derivative of this passage," Holmes exclaimed, shutting the book with a loud *twack*! "Your brain distorted what you had read to fit the narrative it was trying to deliver." He tossed the book like a frisbee; it bounced off the bed and landed on the floor. "I believe this strengthens my argument that you didn't experience anything supernatural."

His logic would have convinced me if a leaf from a tree that didn't grow in the city hadn't drifted into my room. For some reason, I couldn't compel myself to share my discovery. Holmes hadn't mentioned the leaf since I had given it to him; either he had tried to identify it and failed or he considered the task too trivial to devote time to … or he knew what I knew but had chosen to ignore it because *it* didn't fit the narrative *his* brain had concocted.

"But you said something nefarious was toying with us," I protested.

Holmes gave a grim smile. "Indeed, but nefarious doesn't always equate to supernatural, my dear. By the way, have you spoken to Christa since her, erm, little incident?"

I nodded. "She's been coming into the dining hall more regularly now for meals. We chatted at breakfast on Friday."

Our "chat" had constituted a cordial greeting, followed by an exchange of awkward glances as we each immediately recalled *that* night and the self-imprisonment of shame that followed, or perhaps she really had needed time to recover. Regardless, her hair shimmered its usual golden colour, and the pallor had left her face, although perhaps the blush on her cheeks lent a hand there. Still, she had appeared energetic and was no longer barking, so I considered her to be in good enough shape.

"She seems well," I told Holmes. "Elodie too, as a matter of fact. It's almost as if none of it happened."

"Yes, yes, that is all very good. I am glad the ladies have made a full recovery." He paused distractedly, then said, "Christa is in the dining hall as we speak, eating a late dinner."

I glanced at him inquiringly. Whether Christa sat alone or was strutting about town with Elodie glued to her waist was of no concern to me.

"We ought to go question her—about *that* night," Holmes pressed.

"We?" I made no effort to mask my suspicion. "You're inviting me to tag along? Why would you do something like that?"

Holmes looked affronted. "Why? Because we are a team, Watson! Holmes and Watson, consulting detectives. Doesn't that sound spectac—" My glare, which I am proud to say has the power to tame Holmes, halted his spurious proclamation before he could embarrass himself further. He spluttered, his mind undoubtedly racing to concoct more propaganda. At last, his shoulders slumped.

"I shall be most obliged if you would accompany me," he began, staring at the floor, "because-because people in this house *like* you, Watson. I will get the answers I am looking for if you are at my side." He took a step toward me, towering over me once again. "Shall I go on about how disagreeable people find me, or shall we do some investigating?"

My ego suitably flattered, I chose the second option, and we entered the dining hall a moment later to find Christa noisily slurping the remnants of her tomato soup. Breadcrumbs littered the tabletop and the spoon was untouched. She straightened at the sight of us and put the bowl down, looking a bit shameful that we had caught her feasting like a wild animal. To save face, she daintily patted her mouth with a napkin, and then looked at us inquiringly.

We seated ourselves at the table across from her. I was still deciding how to coax Christa into telling us what we wanted to know when Holmes asked bluntly, "So what happened to you that night?"

Christa groaned. "Do we have to discuss that?"

"Oh, I suppose we don't have to." He sprang up with remarkable speed. "Come, Watson, perhaps we can take a stroll in the park instead and wait around for Mrs. Kerrigan to hex someone else. They might be more willing to talk … if they survive."

I didn't stir. "What Holmes means to say is that we want to understand what's happening in this house. So far, two people have been—" I racked my brain for a word other than "hexed" and chose "affected. We don't want anyone else to get hurt."

Christa's hair-raising glare softened into subtle fear. "Oh, fine." She paused to gather her thoughts as Holmes sat down again. "I'm so glad you think it's Mrs. Kerrigan too. Elodie's starting to believe me too after what she saw. The question is what are we going to do about it?"

"*That* is the wrong question," Holmes interjected. "Let us start with the right questions. For example, do you use narcotics?"

Christa looked furious. "Did Elodie tell you that? I'm not a user and I was certainly not using that day."

"Those are contradictory statements, my dear Christa, but let us not delve into the matter. What did you consume the day of your attack?"

Christa shrugged, trying to recall. "I only had breakfast that day: a smoothie. Elodie had some of it as well so it wasn't the drink. Then that Kerrigan lady came into the room—"

"Yes, yes, we were there for that part of the story," Holmes said, waving his hand impatiently. "Did Marieta offer you anything to eat or drink that day?"

Christa gasped. "Do you suspect her as well? Maybe they're working togeth—"

"I'll take that as a 'no' then. Next question: are Elodie and Gastrell romantically involved?"

At this, Christa laughed loudly, unable to help herself. There was a demeaning tone to it that echoed in her speech. "No one would date a loser like Arthur. Elodie is nice to him because she's nice to everyone. Don't mistake that for interest. Anyway, she's in a long-distance relationship." Then she frowned. "What does this have to do with what happened to me?"

But Holmes seemed to think that too was the wrong question, even though I was also itching to know the answer. Perhaps he suspected the duo was plotting against Christa; yet, they too had suffered at the hands of the unknown perpetrator.

"You appear to take particular pleasure in teasing Gastrell," Holmes began slowly, a faint smile curving his lips. "I wonder … are you …?"

"Oh, jeez, no!" Our housemate made a disgusted face. "He's my cousin!" Then her face froze in terror as I blinked in surprise and Holmes smiled triumphantly. "Promise me you won't tell anyone," she commanded urgently.

Her glare may have wrestled Elodie or Arthur into submission, but I said, a little stiffly, "Why would you keep something like that quiet? So what if you and Arthur are related?"

Christa's cold exterior returned, and she eyed me as though I were a dirty child. "It would ruin my reputation. I can't be associated with that unsophisticated—ugh, what would my friends think?"

Ridiculous though her words were, she seemed to genuinely believe the credibility of these fears; my dislike of her grew to great new heights. Even Holmes looked at her with fresh annoyance as she disparaged Arthur some more, then deflected to how much "cooler" his sister was and how shockingly different the siblings were. Then she resumed her character assassination of Arthur and only halted when Holmes asked, "Did you hear that?"

We all stiffened, but the house was silent. Had Holmes feigned a noise to shut Christa up?

"What did you hear?" I asked.

He gestured at the dining hall entrance. "Footsteps. Someone may have been listening to our conversation."

Christa sprang to her feet, looking mortified. "We need to find out who it was!"

"Oh, don't bother. You won't catch them," Holmes said lazily. "They would have left the hallway by now." His pale face glowed with a slight but mischievous smile. "I suppose your terrible secret is out." He rose gracefully just as Christa slumped in her seat, looking as though her cat had died. "I believe we are finished here. Shall we, Watson?"

Holmes and I parted at the second-floor landing, having spotted no lurkers as predicted. Our eavesdropper, if there was one, had long since disappeared behind one of the many doors of Baker House.

CHAPTER 23

Pretense and Poison

"You would have made an actor, and a rare one."

—Sir Arthur Conan Doyle, *The Sign of the Four*

I AWOKE EARLY THE NEXT DAY, FEELING THE USUAL FLURRY of anxiety and excitement I always felt at the start of a new semester. I would be starting new courses, meeting new professors, and resuming a much-welcomed routine of lectures and homework. Before me lay a beaten path: familiar, predictable, and far from extraordinary. I was eager to forget Crooked Forest Adventures, the murdered dogs, Mrs. Kerrigan's possible sorcerous affiliations, and Marieta's possibly unbalanced state of mind and yearning for revenge. The nagging fear that I would start envisioning what wasn't there like Christa and Elodie hadn't left me either, even though I had felt perfectly normal in the days following the dream.

Encouraged by this return to normalcy, I breakfasted and dressed with remarkable energy that Monday morning. It seemed this skittish spirit touched all of Baker House; the residents bustled about like bees, splashes of coffee and bits of toast trailing them as they rushed to eat, drink, and get ready.

I took a seat in the parlour, feeling pleased that there remained more than an hour before the start of my first class, Old English. The subject was admittedly dry, but my afternoon class, Medicine and Literature, was something to look forward to, despite the costly monstrosity of a textbook I'd had to buy for it. The book occupied nearly all of my backpack and left no room for my laptop. Luckily, I wasn't in the habit of typing my notes. I wasn't looking forward to trudging around campus with that bulk though. Still, the thought brought a small smile to my face. It felt good to feel frustrated by trivial things again.

Had I started reading to pass the time as planned, I would have missed the nimble form of Sherlock Holmes hurrying past the entrance to the parlour. So great was his haste that he let the front door slam behind him.

Without thinking, I grabbed my coat and backpack and ran out of the house, not even feeling the gust of wind that whipped my ponytail around. Where on earth was he going? The lack of a backpack told me he wasn't speeding off to class, but he *was* holding something: a book, hardcover but small like a novel. I tilted my head to read the title as I crept up behind him.

"The Strange Case of Dr. Jekyll and Mr. Hyde?" I exclaimed, recognizing the cover. "I didn't think you would touch it."

It was the book I had gifted him for Christmas despite his disdain for fiction. His present had been equally inciteful: an ornamented snuffbox made of gold and enamel, a replica of one dated to 1770 and currently housed in a museum in London. It would have been a beautiful gift had he not stuffed it with snuff.

"Oh, hullo, Watson," he said distractedly. "I haven't read the book but have found another use for it. No time to chat unfortunately. I have an appointment to keep." His speed rose a notch, forcing me to jog to keep up.

Luckily, the sidewalk was clear of ice, and yesterday's snowfall had been heaved neatly to the edges.

Ignoring the textbook in my backpack, which dealt a blow to my back with each bounding step, I asked, "What appointment? Where are you off to?"

My friend sighed and slowed, perhaps sympathizing with my near-breathless state and flushed face. With some reluctance, he admitted to meeting a Professor Chastain at the Department of Plant Sciences. This wasn't surprising, for Holmes had an interest in botany, but why he felt compelled to take a Gothic novella with him to see a botanist puzzled me.

"Are you planning on discussing themes from *Dr. Jekyll and Mr. Hyde* with this Chastain?" I laughed. "Perhaps the duality of human nature?" This provoked a huff of annoyance, which encouraged me to continue being bothersome. "I would recommend Introduction to Literary Studies if you're interested in Stevenson's works. Professor Beussing did a stellar job—"

Holmes interrupted with a loud "humph!" and stopped in the middle of the sidewalk without warning, forcing the passerby behind us to manoeuvre sharply onto someone's lawn. After the man had cussed at us and walked away, Holmes let the book fall open.

Lying flattened against the page was the leaf I had plucked from my floor just a few days before, looking remarkably greener against its ink-and-paper backdrop. I stifled my gasp, but the damage was done. The paranoia and angst I had pushed away so triumphantly flooded my insides.

"You're going to ask the professor to identify it?" I asked, remembering my own discovery days before.

Holmes shook his head. "I've already done that myself. The internet is occasionally useful for such investigations."

"The eastern flowering dogwood," I blurted.

"Excellent, Watson, excellent." He beamed. "Now if you will stand aside, I—"

"Then why are you going to see —"

Holmes sighed resignedly. "I presume you are coming along? Well, then you shall see."

It turned out Holmes didn't have an appointment with Dr. Auguste Chastain. We arrived at his office in the Plant Sciences building to find the door shut. Instead of trying the doorknob and entering should it turn, which was typical Holmesian behaviour, my friend gave two loud knocks. I was starting to wonder whether anyone was inside when I heard a shuffling of papers, followed by a loud thud, an angry stomping of feet, and a stentorian roar. Holmes was gracious enough to give the man a few seconds to compose himself before pushing the door open.

In the middle of the room stood a ruddy man with a small head and an elephantine body garbed in a brown tweed jacket, a matching flat cap, and dark pants. The hair that poked out of his hat was as white as the snow outside, though not a wrinkle rumpled his face. His eyes were unusually small and didn't seem to open beyond a slit, cursing his face with a permanent suspicious expression. His meaty paws, which he had been shaking in uncontrollable agitation, froze at the sight of us.

"Ah, Professor Chastain, may we come in for a moment? I was hoping you could help us with a plant," Holmes said cordially.

Recognition flickered in the man's eyes, although they remained unwelcoming. "Can't you see I'm busy?" he barked in a thick accent. "Come back later."

Somehow, Holmes interpreted the command as an invitation to enter the small, stuffy room, made even smaller by a large oak desk, a bookcase of encyclopedias, and stacks of books and papers that cluttered every horizontal surface. Some papers lay on the floor as though they had been flung in fury. More commonplace of a botanist's office were the nineteenth-century illustrations of flowers and leaves, as well as the more modern-looking diagrams and photos of microscopic cross-sections, that covered the walls. I took an immediate liking to the old drawings, although they embellished the space as much as the poster of the periodic table in Holmes' room. The plants on the windowsill at least offered some colour.

Professor Chastain stared at us belligerently as Holmes took a seat at the desk. I remained standing, feeling quite uncomfortable and ready to sprint for the door. But a book, half of which sat precariously off the desk, caught my eye, and without thinking, I leaned over and pushed it to safety.

"Don't touch that!" the professor snapped. "It's a translation of Ibn Bassal's *The Classification of Soils*, one of the most important botanical contributions of the medieval Muslim world!" But my little rescue appeared to have softened him somewhat. He heaved his bulk into his chair and faced us squarely.

"What do you want, Monsieur Holmes?"

My friend let his book fall open atop the clutter on the desk. The leaf shimmered, and the professor glanced at it briefly before his interest died and his agitation returned. Holmes opened his mouth, no doubt to redirect the man's attention back to the leaf, but I intervened.

"It looks like we've come at an inconvenient time. Is something wrong, professor?"

Professor Chastain blinked at me miserably before wailing, "*Ouais*! The exams have been stolen!" His outrage freshly renewed, one large fist shot out and pounded the desk. I cringed as *The Classification of Soils* skidded to the edge once more. The leaf trembled. Sighing, Holmes leaned back in his chair.

Luckily, the outburst was short-lived, and the professor, having realized he had disclosed something he shouldn't have and perhaps feeling a little embarrassed, sunk into his chair like a deflated balloon. Something compelled him to speak again a moment later though; his narrative was directed at Holmes, which made me wonder if he was aware of Holmes' reputation.

"The final exam for one of my senior biology classes went missing today. I'd graded them in December. Half the students had come to pick up their exams before the holidays, so only about twenty or so were left. Earlier this morning, someone pulled the fire alarm, and I exited the building along with everyone else. My door was unlocked but closed. I didn't notice the exams were gone until a student came to get hers about twenty minutes ago. The entire pile was gone!" He inhaled loudly, wheezing, before exhaling equally as loud. "*Mon Dieu*, what will I do?"

"Why would someone steal the exam papers for a class that's already finished?" I wondered aloud. "Do you reuse your exams? Maybe this person is taking the class this semester or will be in the near future."

"If that were the reason, Watson, the perpetrator would have simply photographed the exam with their smartphone or borrowed it from someone who has already taken it," Holmes said.

Professor Chastain added, "Anyway, I change the exam questions every semester."

"Then why take them?" I asked.

"The solution is obvious," Holmes replied, but there was no sign that an explanation would follow. In fact, he stifled a yawn and looked unmistakably bored.

The opposite sentiment echoed in the professor's voice. "Help me, *je vous en prie!*"

"Ah, professor, but I am engaged in another matter—"

"And I will help you with this other matter, whatever you need!"

"Whatever I need?" A smile slowly crept onto Holmes' face. "Such as access to the greenhouse?"

Professor Chastain stuttered, "Ah, b-but that's restricted to staff and—"

"Oh, that's unfortunate," Holmes said. "Let's go, Watson." But he didn't rise from his chair.

The professor hadn't noticed that and wailed piteously again. "But wait, you said you needed help identifying this plant." He pointed a corpulent finger at the leaf.

"That is *not* what I said. I already know it is *Cornus florida*, more commonly known as the eastern flowering dogwood. I should very much like to see live specimens since the tree is facing imminent extinction."

Professor Chastain sat in contemplative silence for a moment. "Well, I'm sure I can't turn away a student so interested in plants," he finally said. "I suppose I can tell the greenhouse staff you are my research assistants. *Ouais*, it's settled then. You shall see your trees, Monsieur Holmes."

Holmes grinned triumphantly and murmured to no one in particular, "Ah, so there *are* specimens of *C. florida* in the greenhouse." The professor nodded vigorously, which appeared to swell Holmes' self-contentedness even more; he shot me a holier-than-thou glance and chuckled. *I told you so*, the glance said.

I was more relieved than annoyed by this. At last, I could quell that fantastical idea that had plagued me for nearly a week. The leaf hadn't travelled with me from Salem; I could say that with certainty now. Someone had plucked it from a dogwood tree in the greenhouse and planted it in my room, just as Holmes had said. I didn't understand Holmes' insistence on visiting the greenhouse though; seeing the trees for ourselves would reveal little, but apparently my friend thought otherwise.

"On to your little problem then," Holmes said to the professor. "Let me assure you that the exam papers will show up soon. We must give the perpetrator some time, although how much will depend on whether you use only checkmarks and x's when grading or also leave explanatory comments."

Looking puzzled, the professor said, "*Mais non*! I rarely leave notes. Who has the time?"

"Excellent, the perpetrator won't need to spend time studying your handwriting then. You should expect the exams back in a day or — *what*?" He looked baffled by our blank faces. "Is the solution not obvious? Oh, very well. I shall explain.

"You see, the whole plot was contrived to change a grade. We have approximately twenty suspects, that is, all the students who have yet to pick up their exams. We can reduce this list further by seeing who of this twenty has failed the course. They will be most desperate to change their grade."

"But I've already submitted each student's final grade!" the professor exclaimed.

"But there is time to edit the grade, yes?"

"Well, this Wednesday is the deadline."

Holmes said with satisfaction, "Then, by Wednesday, the exams will be returned to you."

"And then?" I piped in. "How will the student boost their grade, and how will we find out who it is?"

"Essentially, the thief is going to rewrite the exam and imitate the good professor's hand to give themselves a higher grade. Hence, one of the exams returned will be a forgery. Then they will come to pick up their exam and feign confusion at the discrepancy between the exam grade and the final grade, forcing you —" he looked pointedly at the professor " — to admit that you mistyped when entering the exam grade, which consequently led to a miscalculation of the final grade." He grinned. "*Et voila*, you are duped and the clever student passes."

"But where will the student get a blank copy of the exam?" I asked.

Holmes shrugged. "It can be easily created with whiteout and a photocopier."

"*Incroyable!*" Professor Chastain exclaimed, although whether he was referring to the intellect of his student or Holmes was open to speculation. The professor, mollified at last, looked at us happily. "I am most grateful to you, young man." It appeared he wholeheartedly believed the little whodunnit would unfold exactly as it had been described to him.

Holmes waved a hand modestly. "It is the only explanation that fits the facts." Rising, he said, "To the greenhouse then?"

The professor nodded. "I will make the call. You can head there right now."

He gave us instructions on how to find the rooftop greenhouse. We offered our thanks and rushed outside and into an elevator, which took us to the seventh floor. We ambled down a corridor that veered left, then right, and finally ended at a door that stood ajar. I peeked inside, then entered.

The room beyond was small and looked even busier than Professor Chastain's office, with its stacks of binders and folders, random papers, posters of plants, and actual potted plants that had been haphazardly placed by someone with no flair for décor. We went up to the counter, behind which sat a scrawny man with black hair, a large, unruly beard, and thick-rimmed glasses. I noted the name tag clipped to his shirt: *Samarth Narayan, Greenhouse Manager*.

"Hello, Mr. Narayan," I said since Holmes made no effort to speak. In fact, his gaze danced around the room as though he was searching for something. "Professor Chastain sent us. We're here to look at the eastern flowering dogwood."

Mr. Narayan nodded as he rose from his seat and gave us a once-over. I smiled pleasantly, which he didn't return. It was as though he sensed our deceit. Holmes had turned away, studying a diagram on the wall, his nose nearly touching the laminated surface. The gesture seemed to satisfy the greenhouse manager, and he whisked out a clipboard.

"Please sign in," he said stiffly before sitting back down.

The sheet, and those under it, were filled with an account of all those who had stood where I now stood, the hurried handwriting an obvious indication of their impatience to enter the greenhouse. I, on the other hand, wasn't so eager to saunter through the many glass rooms, weighed down by humidity and earthiness. Yet here we were. Holmes looked every much as thrilled to be here as an actual botany student. Sighing, I signed and then passed the clipboard and pen to Holmes as he approached the counter with a bounce to his step. He signed with an exaggerate flourish, nearly knocked over the plant on the counter, then laughed sheepishly.

All of a sudden, his giddiness disappeared, and he stared at the broad green leaves of the plant on the counter. He raised his right hand, examined it, then started to furiously rub it.

"Good lord, man!" he exclaimed. "Is that dieffenbachia?" He gestured wildly at the potted plant as though it was something vile and contagious.

"Wha—" Mr. Narayan could hardly utter a word in the two seconds that elapsed because Holmes' voice rang out again, much louder this time.

"Why would you have such a plant on the counter? Don't you know that even brushing against it could cause severe symptoms? My hand is burning! Look at it!" He held out his arm, and sure enough, the back of his usually pale hand was bright red. "Ingestion could cause death!" Holmes continued shouting, all the while forcibly condemned to scratching the bruised skin.

Mr. Narayan looked irked. "The dieffenbachia is poisonous, but it rarely causes serious—"

"Your divorce is no excuse for your carelessness, Mr. Narayan!" The poor man blinked at Holmes, astounded. "I shall be filing a complaint with the department head. Let's go, Watson. Who knows what other dangerous plants he has absentmindedly put around the office! I need to get a nurse to look at my hand."

He hurried out the door and I trailed speedily after him, catching only a shard of the muttered cussing that escaped the mouth of the miffed Mr. Narayan.

Holmes' agitation ceased considerably by the time we were in the elevator. In fact, the flush had receded from his face, leaving behind a pale exterior that twitched excitedly at intervals. By the time we exited the Plant Sciences building, his spirits were perfectly restored. He hadn't scratched his hand once since we had left the greenhouse office.

"What was that all about?" I asked.

Holmes blinked. "What do you mean, Watson? That wretched plant did this to my hand." He held up his limp hand, which was slowly turning pink again but due to the frosty weather this time.

I cast it a wary look. "Did you have to bring up the man's divorce? It was a bit rude—wait, how did you know anyway?"

But Holmes waved the question away. "Mr. Narayan's divorce plays an integral role in the case, my dear. So very integral. You see, divorcees tend to bury themselves in work." Before I could question this further, a grin fit for an imp lit up his features. "Such a shame our trip to the greenhouse didn't come to be, but allow me to make it up to you. How about I treat you to that unpalatable mint tea you like? The Village Idiot, tonight at seven o'clock?"

I grew even more suspicious, but he looked at me with such eagerness that I relented.

"Capital!" he exclaimed. "You had better hurry, Watson. You don't want to be late for class." Just before he turned to go, he added, smiling faintly, "Oh, and Watson, I'll sweeten the pot with the name of the person who put that leaf in your room."

He spun around before I could say anything and sprinted down the path. I stood for a minute, watching him become a speck in the distance. It was only then that I realized he had the sign-in sheet and clipboard tucked under his arm.

CHAPTER 24

Holmes Bewitched

"This murder would have been infinitely more difficult to unravel had the body of the victim been simply found lying in the roadway without any of those outré and sensational accompaniments which have rendered it remarkable."

—Sir Arthur Conan Doyle, *A Study in Scarlet*

THE EVENING BROUGHT WITH IT JANUARY'S CUSTOMARY biting cold, even when the wind reposed. The darkness was somewhat alleviated by the lit shop windows I passed and the bright lights of cars and streetlamps. It was nearing Holmes' appointed time of seven o'clock when I found myself straggling down the bustling street The Village Idiot called home. Baker House was only two blocks behind me, yet I was stiff as an icicle when I stepped into the pub.

Luckily, the air inside was thick and warm but saturated with the smell of fish and chips and spilt pints. A gentle murmur of voices and faint folk music playing in the background filled me with comfort that faded when I remembered why Holmes had invited me here.

I spotted my friend sitting at the head of one of the larger tables, face alight with a vivacity that made me wonder if he had already emptied a couple pints. In fact, he held a dimpled glass pint mug in his hand and took a generous gulp as I approached, his face shiny with sweat and exhilaration.

"Oh, hullo, Watson, good of you to join us!" He gestured grandly at the table where Arthur Gastrell and Gwilym Lestrade sat. "Forgive us for starting before the entire party arrived, but I couldn't resist when Gastrell most generously offered to buy the first round." To the bartender, he shouted, "A pot of Moroccan mint tea, if you please!" He nodded knowingly at me and winked.

I took the seat next to the one that Holmes' backpack occupied and faced Arthur and Gwilym, both of whom wore matching expressions of puzzlement. I too was bewildered; Holmes hadn't mentioned he had extended the invitation to others from Baker House, and … and he was also acting stranger than usual.

Some minutes elapsed. My tea arrived, and I had started sipping, wondering who else would come, when Christa and Elodie, arms linked and shivering from the cold, shuffled in. They shot the rest of us a quizzical glance before unlinking and taking the seats next to mine and Gwilym's. It wasn't until after Marieta glided to the table and seated herself at the tail end that Holmes stood.

"Welcome all," he said excitedly. "I am delighted you were all able to come." He made no effort to speak quietly, and his voice reached all who were seated in the vicinity. Some men at a nearby table craned their necks to look at us. The following proclamation made us lean in closer in curious anticipation: "I have summoned you here tonight to unveil the perpetrator behind the macabre happenings we have been subjected to since late December."

Holmes glanced at our curious faces with immense satisfaction. But then, without warning, his expression changed. Gone was the prideful smile, replaced instead with something I rarely saw on Sherlock Holmes' face: shock. At first, I thought Marieta was the source of his stupefaction, but no, something beyond her had paralyzed him. All I saw was a scattering of empty tables and chairs.

Holmes blinked, then shook his head ever so slightly and reached for his drink. His gaze, however, still lingered on whatever it was that had caught his attention, and he knocked over his glass. Cold beer gushed out and we all pressed into the backs of our seats as the spill stretched across the table, threatening to stream onto our laps.

"Oh, how clumsy of me," Holmes said distractedly and threw some napkins on the tabletop. "Where was I … ah, yes, the perpetrator …" He cleared his throat and forced his attention back to us. "Yes, yes, the curious happenings …

"Our narrative starts with the slaying of the dog, Drebber, followed by that of the dog, Stangers. The inverted pentagram, the mystical symbols in the snow, the blue fire, the man's voice heard by both Gastrell and Leslie Alfredsson-Maine, the latter's near sacrif—" Holmes stopped abruptly; his gaze had once again returned to the empty tables and chairs behind Marieta, taking our attention along with him this time. When we turned back synchronously to look at him, we saw that his eyes had widened in disbelief. He swore softly but then seemed to remember his audience and regained some of his composure. However, he sounded flustered as he continued.

"We went to Crooked Forest Adventures to solve the case Gastrell brought to us but left in a disturbed state of mind and with no resolution. Perhaps you even came to believe that something sinister followed us home, for soon after, Christa fell ill, followed by Elodie." He gestured at the two ladies before his gaze fell on me. "Then Watson here was spooked by a vision so life-like it led some of you to turn to time travel as the explanation.

There was talk of witchcraft, the devil, and a mysterious book …" He inhaled sharply then and shouted, "No! I won't sign your blasted book!" Holmes screamed before stepping back and knocking over his chair.

Paralysis overtook his legs; his eyes bulged, and he waved his arms around as though shooing a fly. "Stay away from me!" Shock, disbelief, and fear distorted his features.

"Holmes!" I cried, springing to my feet and reaching for him. At last, my fingers caught one of his flailing arms. My unrelenting grip had a surprising effect on him: in a brief moment of calm, my friend gazed at me. "It's her, Watson. The woman with the head of a dog." Then the paralysis gave away and his feet buckled, taking me down with him.

"Holmes!" I screamed. "Talk to me, Holmes!" His limp body rested against mine. I cradled his head, blinking back tears, unable to take my eyes off his closed ones. All the patrons had rushed to our aid, forming a tight, suffocating circle around us.

"Everyone, move away!" I hollered. "He needs air." My voice turned into a hoarse whisper. "Wake up, Holmes. Wake up."

The voices around me grew faint; someone shouted for an ambulance, but I barely heard, so haunted was I by the sudden collapse of a man I had thought indomitable.

It was that drawling voice of his that brought me out of my trance. "Oh, don't bother with an ambulance. I am perfectly all right." His eyes remained closed, but a faint smile was starting to form on Sherlock Holmes' pale face. At last, his grey eyes looked up at me.

"Holmes!" I exclaimed.

"Oh, Watson, you are crying," he said softly, looking touched. "I shan't mislead you for a moment longer." He sprang up and helped me to my feet.

One by one, the restaurant patrons returned to their tables, some irked by the interruption and muttering insults, others craning their necks to look at Holmes, still curious about his sudden collapse and immediate recovery. Our housemates also reclaimed their seats, but Holmes kept me standing alongside him at the head of the table. His hand snaked across my back and gripped my arm affectionately.

"Here, ladies and gentlemen, is a friend you can trust with your life," he proclaimed. "The type of friend who will keep you from falling or fall with you. Watson is the epitome of goodwill and trust ... but there is one person at this table who is *not* a good friend."

Holmes released his hold of me and then bent forward, resting his hands on his thighs. He locked eyes with Arthur Gastrell.

"Did you think you can bewitch Sherlock Holmes?" he asked quietly. "One sip was enough to tell me the beer was laced with something." He straightened, wearing a grim smile. "No one can bewitch me." To the rest of us, he confirmed the thought his words had stirred. "Yes, Arthur Gastrell is responsible for everything that has happened."

"But he brought us the case," I exclaimed.

"Indeed, but that doesn't exempt him from the suspect list. In fact, by the time we left Crooked Forest, I was convinced of Gastrell's involvement in the ordeal, but there was much to be uncovered." He peered down at Arthur. "Will you confess, or shall I narrate from the beginning?"

Arthur shuddered in response as though a pair of disembodied, cold hands had violently shaken him. His face expressed surprise, but also dread and guilt. Yet I found I couldn't quite believe the truth of what Holmes was saying. I sat down and breathed in the cool mint aroma that drifted from my teacup. It did little to ease my nerves.

"All right then," Holmes said. "I do believe I have a firm grasp of the salient points." He cast Gwilym a cool look before continuing. "It was the mention of an atrocious act—and the devil—that brought Gastrell to

Watson and me that day. It was perhaps a spontaneous decision on his part, fuelled in part by my own urging to reveal what was troubling him. And what a fanciful tale he told us!"

"So why did he invite us to Crooked Forest?" Gwilym asked.

"For applause, of course," Holmes exclaimed. "Did anyone notice how annoyed Gastrell looked when he told us Crooked Forest had managed to keep the first dog's killing out of the press? Of course, he was irritated—his handiwork had gone unappreciated! Hence, he invited us to cause a stir—free passes for all! We would uncover nothing, but we would carry news of a second slaying and more sinister incidents back to the city."

Holmes smiled grimly at Arthur, whose gaping expression confirmed the prowess of Holmes' oracle-like exclamations. "You went to work early that Saturday morning, poisoned Stangers, and made your preparations. The only problem was that you didn't know which trail the dogsledders would take that day. The safety checks hadn't been done yet, so you randomly picked the one leading to the right. The odds were in your favour. That trail had been used the day before after all. However, it was the left one that had been cleared.

"But, ladies and gentlemen, fortune was on Gastrell's side. It was sheer luck that Alberta den Nomot, novice that she is, turned right at the fork of the dogsledding trail. We wouldn't have discovered the slaughter otherwise." Holmes' gaze narrowed as he shot yet another dirty look at Arthur. "Or did you mislead her by telling her the right path was safe?"

There was no answer from Arthur. He had assumed a superficial impassivity, although there was something intense in the way his eyes shone: not with relish like Holmes', but with anxiety. The rest of the group made no attempt to control their shock, except Marieta Charr, who looked the picture of equanimity. Gwilym was half-propped on the table, leaning in as far as he could without his sleeves soaking up the spilt beer to ensure he didn't miss a word of what Holmes was saying. As for Christa and Elodie, each wore identical expressions of mortification.

"How delighted you must have been when Alberta radioed in the discovery! But you didn't have much time to savour the victory; you now had only twenty minutes to shoo away that Amira girl, draw the witchcraft symbols in the snow, and prepare the great blue fire. I would admire your efficiency if your purpose hadn't been so nefarious. That clear liquid you were trying to put out the fire with wasn't water but white sambuca, a colourless anise-flavoured liqueur, which gave the flames their blue colour and made them climb higher. What a sight it was!

"However, you did pay a price for using sambuca as an accelerant. Perhaps you are allergic to anise? Despite the dizziness and vomiting, you went on propagating stories of cursed fires. I knew straightaway the fire was a hoax though. I smelled the sweet odour of anise when I was near you despite the overpowering stench of your vomit, though I didn't yet suspect you. I did wonder if someone had used some kind of anise-flavoured liqueur to make the fire blue though. When little Amira came in drenched, she became an obvious suspect. I sniffed her gloves, but they smelled like mud and unwashed pups.

"I had little time to continue sniffing around though because it was then, under the cover of being unconscious, that you tormented your next victim: Jibril Özdemir. You obviously drugged him with his own stash of DMT." Holmes chuckled. "Being a recreational user, Özdemir recognized the effects and even managed to name the drug when he was lucid enough, which everyone mistook as 'Dimitri.'"

Looking around the table, he added, "An easy mistake to make, I suppose; Komarov is a brute, and one automatically feels he is capable of great violence."

Christa looked as though she was about to protest, but Holmes went on without pause, his penetrating gaze fixed on Arthur again. "You then left a most sinister note: *The next will be sacrificed.* Such an ominous touch! Poor Watson was in such a frightful state when I found her."

Although he was correct, I felt belittled by his words and would have protested had I not been so eager to hear the rest of the story.

"You did leave behind a clue, and for that, I thank you." Holmes reached into his backpack and pulled out a clear plastic bag housing the "hellhound" hair. "I found this near Özdemir. Komarov confirmed it didn't belong to any of the dogs at Crooked Forest, which left two possibilities: a real hellhound or a costume, most likely a mask."

A flicker of fresh emotion appeared on Arthur's face, but he said nothing.

"I doubt it was your intention to leave the hair behind; it probably fell off your mask, yes?" Holmes said. "The hair, though it looked real and certainly nonhuman to the naked eye, could be tested, which wouldn't help boost the credibility of the story you were trying to propagate. I did get that hair tested and it was unquestionably synthetic. There had been no dog at the scene. Poor Özdemir's drugged brain exaggerated what he saw.

"Next, I ambled through the crowd in the Great Room, not only to extract information, but also to see if anyone smelled of anise. No one did, which is what made me realize … it was only around you, Gastrell, that I had first caught a whiff. The pail you used as you pretended to put out the fire would have provided definitive proof, but you wisely disposed of it. I did give you the benefit of the doubt though. For the briefest of moments, I contemplated a different scenario: one where you used a bucket someone had already filled with sambuca and left to be used to put out the fire. Alas, you confirmed filling it yourself.

"So I returned to you and searched your pockets looking for clues, though there was nothing incriminating. But your sleeves and gloves, they revealed it all! They reeked of anise. No doubt some of the sambuca splashed on them as you threw the bucket into the firepit."

There was no room for denial now, but even then, Arthur didn't refute the accusation or offer an explanation. His lips were pressed into a stubborn line.

If Holmes was hoping for a confession, he wasn't getting one anytime soon, although that didn't seem to ruffle him at all. He was enjoying the rapt attention. "Of course, I had no idea you were aware of my nosing around," he said. "*You* knew that *I* knew that you were responsible for the blue fire. It was only a matter of time before I linked you to the more macabre events.

"Then Leslie Alfredsson-Maine appeared, wishing to speak with me. Watson, you no doubt felt hurt that she wouldn't divulge the matter in front of you. The truth was that she didn't dare speak in front of Gastrell. You see, she had seen him awaken and then resume his fainting act. She thought it suspicious naturally, although she hadn't the slightest clue he was involved in so much more." He cocked an eyebrow at Arthur. "Did you know, Gastrell? No? Well, how fortuitous it was that you ended up choosing her to be your sacrifice!

"Here we reach the climax of Gastrell's plot: his disappearance and that of Ms. Alfredsson-Maine. She was intended to be the sacrifice, as I mentioned, and Gastrell had to disappear to carry out the sacrifice and dispose of the incriminating parka and gloves.

"The plan was to steal off with anyone should the opportunity present itself, wasn't it? You were in the kitchen when you caught Ms. Alfredsson-Maine alone in the corridor, searching for the bathroom. You masked your voice and started whispering her name to lure her into the kitchen. As she approached, you grabbed a pot or something else heavy, and exited via the back door, leaving it open. She came outside, just as you had hoped and *whack*!" Holmes, in his excited state, swung his hand like a bat. "A blow to the head and she was out cold. Now it was just a matter of dragging her body to a spot in the woods, painting some symbols, then off to the Humber River to rid yourself of the parka and gloves."

There was more admiration than admonishment in Holmes' voice as he went on, "When we found you, oh, the charade you put on about the mysterious voice in your head! Simply marvellous! The theatre has lost a fine actor. You had Watson fooled from the start and even made me doubt my deductions for a moment.

"At last, we found Ms. Alfredsson-Maine, and she too had a fantastical tale to tell, one that had been scripted by you, Gastrell. She too heard a voice … rather clever of you to use her retelling to make your own seem more credible."

It was at this point that my conviction in Holmes' story faltered. The red paint at the ritual site had been fresh, yet Holmes' inspection of Arthur had found nothing. Surely some trace would have clung to Arthur had he drawn the symbols, particularly since he had been pressed for time. That much was evident from the hasty way the perpetrator had arranged Leslie. I voiced this, but the twinkle in Holmes' eyes didn't flicker.

He said, "You forget the missing winter accessories, Watson. It is highly probable that the gloves, in particular, would have had paint on them.

"Despite the destruction of pertinent evidence, by the time I left Crooked Forest Adventures that day, I was convinced Gastrell had played some part in what had happened there. The perplexing question was *why*. I needed more data to figure that out. One cannot make bricks without clay, so I set out to find some clay."

"You need to give some credit to the tea-leaf readings," Christa said, still eyeing Arthur with loathing. "Marieta's 'unfaithful friends' message was true. She did consider him a friend, but in return, he made her a target."

Marieta stiffened, apparently reminded of what she had endured at Crooked Forest at the hands of Dimitri and his mob. She cast Arthur a stony look, which, in a flash, disrupted his attempts at stoicism; his lips trembled, and blinking rapidly, he bowed his head in shame.

"The snake in my cup had the same meaning," I added.

"Even the devil in my cup was a clue," Elodie said.

Holmes laughed derisively. "Pshaw! A coincidence! Anyway, Marieta's tea leaves hardly resembled a dog, and every stringy bit of tea leaf looks like a snake," he exclaimed. "And what of my formidable enemy? There was no sinister, unhinged woman involved. You may also recall that the devil appeared as the culprit behind Christa's purloined necklace. The devil did *not* take the necklace. *He* did!" Holmes shot a long finger out at Arthur.

To Gwilym, Holmes said, "Willie, old boy, this is where some psychology entered the case." Then he turned to Christa. "You believe in protective charms and firmly believed the necklace would protect you from harm. You felt safer with it in your possession. If it were to be taken, you would again feel vulnerable. Not only did he know this little tidbit about you, but Gastrell also *wanted* you in such a state, for you were to be his next victim." Turning to us, he continued, "Had Mrs. Kerrigan not left the door to Christa's room open, he would have found another opportunity to steal it. Mrs. Kerrigan took the blame, and the lack of protection, along with Mrs. Kerrigan's threats, made an easy victim of Christa."

Christa's face went red, and she glared at Arthur.

Crossing his arms, Holmes faced Arthur once again. "And what a deplorable state you put her in! Barking and whimpering like a dog, seeing what wasn't there, and all in all, making a grand fool out of herself—what a treat it must have been! If I had only turned and looked at your face, all would have been confirmed then. Tell me, Gastrell, how did you do it?"

But he didn't wait for an answer. "It was obviously a drug, although as Watson noted, none of the usual signs were present. Yet it was potent enough to make Christa bite into her own hand and believe someone else had done it and to invent the ominous Red Book." He paused for breath. "What did you use?"

Gwilym opened his mouth in protest, no doubt to admonish Holmes for earlier dismissing his narcotics theory. Christa, however, interrupted angrily before either he or Arthur could utter a syllable, although I was certain the latter wouldn't talk even if we gave him hours to confess.

"Why me?"

We each offered her a hard stare in answer, but it was Holmes who replied, "Because you have always treated Gastrell terribly, possibly since childhood." To us, he added, "You see, Christa and Gastrell are cousins, a secret Christa kept hushed for fear her reputation would be tarnished should her popular friends find out she was related to, ah, I'll refrain from repeating the insults. I'm sure Gastrell has heard them enough times."

Christa's mouth opened in protest, no doubt to deny what Holmes had disclosed, but he was too quick for her. He said to Arthur gently, "I don't blame you there, Gastrell"—Christa's features morphed into a hideous scowl—"but it was quite wrong to let the blame fall on old Mrs. Kerrigan once again. You were probably happy about that though, eh? She is a sour crone. But why did Elodie suffer the same treatment? She has always been kind to you, has she not?"

I didn't expect Arthur to answer, but the question at least stirred him. He looked at Elodie with an unreadable expression. Was he silently asking for forgiveness? No, that didn't seem to be the case. Worry, fatigue, and bewilderment mingled in Elodie's return gaze. I understood her feelings instantly; she was begging him to speak, to put an end to this ghastly business once and for all.

And he obeyed.

CHAPTER 25

A Methodical Revenge

"I knew of their guilt though, and I determined that I should be judge, jury, and executioner all rolled into one."

—Sir Arthur Conan Doyle, *A Study in Scarlet*

"BECAUSE," ARTHUR GASTRELL BEGAN SLOWLY, "SHE always just stood by. She never did anything to stop Christa. She's just as bad."

At last, here was the confession, albeit an indirect one, but it revealed as much as an open declaration. My shoulders slumped. I still couldn't fathom the notion that Arthur had slaughtered two dogs, abducted a woman, and tortured his housemates with a narcotic. Holmes, however, looked delighted. With an inexplicable stubbornness, I decided I wouldn't accept the confession until every detail had been ironed out.

"And how do you explain the iciness in Christa's room that night?" I asked Holmes since Arthur was staring at the spilt beer miserably. It was difficult to tell whether he would speak again.

Holmes shrugged. "I can't be certain, but in all probability, Christa opened the window in her delirious state. There is no telling how much time passed before the barking started, bringing Elodie rushing to Christa's room. She must have closed the window shortly before Elodie's arrival. We arrived soon after she did, so the room retained the icy temperature. I assure you, Watson, a nefarious entity was *not* responsible."

"But how is it possible that both Christa and Elodie experienced the same symptoms as the ones reported centuries ago?" I pressed on. "How could the drug control what they would see?"

Gwilym opened his mouth, but Holmes quickly interjected. "It wasn't the drug but their minds that projected what they saw. I am reminded of something Mrs. Stillaway said: 'What we see is what we manifest.' She was referring to what supposedly appears in one's cup, but I refer to what one *thinks* they see in their environment is a product of what the mind has absorbed.

"There was an awful lot of talk about the trials. Elodie has already confirmed she researched the topic upon her return from Crooked Forest. Did you as well?" he asked Christa, who nodded guiltily. Holmes offered us a self-satisfied smile.

"We all did," he said, "but the rest of us didn't ingest a powerful narcotic, which brought a distorted version of history to life. Mrs. Kerrigan appeared as the antagonist in both of your, er, experiences simply because she already occupies the role of villain in your minds. She is generally disliked by all in Baker House. Your minds picked the obvious choice for the role of the witch.

"Watson's mind, on the other hand"—he flicked a wrist at me—"vilified Marieta, whose association with Wicca has been supplemented with wild rumours since the start of the semester. Another obvious choice to play the villain." Wearing a prideful smirk, he added, turning to Gwilym, "Is that what you were about to say, Lestrade? I think I have summarized the salient points rather neatly, without a degree in psychology." Gwilym shot him a frosty glare, which only made Holmes beam in pleasure.

"The intriguing part isn't psychology but chemistry," Holmes went on, "for Elodie's blood work showed no sign of any drug. I would bet the same would have been true for Christa had she undergone a blood test. Hence, the drug Gastrell used cannot be detected in the blood unless one were to look for it. Quite ingenious, Gastrell! Will you continue to remain silent on this point? I only pry because I wouldn't want your genius to go unrecognized."

When the flattery failed to compel Arthur to speak, I stammered, "Did you drug me too? Is that why I—the vision—Salem—"

"That was just a dream, Watson," Holmes insisted.

But I paid him no attention. "So you just took advantage of the situation? You lied about not seeing me at my desk, then you planted the leaf in my room to make me believe what I had experienced was real … Why did you do it? I've never done anything to you."

I was surprised to see Arthur turn away, his lips pressed together. He seemed truly ashamed, but Holmes furnished me with an answer that cast our housemate in a terrible light.

"Because he was enjoying spreading terror and paranoia," he drawled and pulled out *The Strange Case of Dr. Jekyll and Mr. Hyde* from his backpack. A quick flick of the wrist parted the pages to reveal the leaf that had tormented me for days. "The whole of Baker House was in for the same treatment, Watson. Perhaps he would have expanded his operations to include the entire university. Diminutive, ignored, little Gastrell, now the master puppeteer! And you certainly succeeded—for a while."

To me, he said kindly, "I don't blame you, my dear, for entertaining the idea. He elicited the tale from your own mouth and then planted the evidence to make you believe. He purposefully chose the eastern flowering dogwood since it is only found in a small part of the province but occurs naturally in Massachusetts. Hence, it was a good selection to make you contemplate an extraordinary solution to explain why the leaf of a tree that doesn't grow anywhere in the city ended up in your room." He paused and I held my breath; his eyes shone in a way that made me suspect I had missed something. "Do you recall *seeing* the dogwood in that vision of yours, Watson?"

I shuddered as I recalled the vivid dream. I remembered the oak clearly; there had been others too, but had any been a dogwood? I thought hard, but my mind couldn't conjure a tree with white blooms. I looked at Holmes with uncertainty and he offered me a knowing smile.

"The tree is *not* endemic to Salem," he said. "You also failed to realize that the trees you see outside aren't the only ones in the city. Plants that aren't endemic to an area can be introduced—grown in greenhouses, for example—and it just so happens that we have one in the Plant Sciences building. And that is where Watson and I went after receiving confirmation that our greenhouse is home to the eastern flowering dogwood."

Reaching into his backpack once again, he extracted his third exhibit—the clipboard and sign-in sheets—and looked at us triumphantly. "It is standard protocol for all who enter the greenhouse to sign in. These sheets contain a dated and timestamped record of everyone who visited the greenhouse." He flipped through a few pages. "The list of visitors over the holidays included some graduate students, two professors, and a few food-science students growing fruit for the jams they'll be selling this semester.

"I hear you will be selling blueberry and mint preserves, Gastrell. Your name appears on these pages frequently as a result," he said. "But on the first of January, the day Watson supposedly went to Salem, your comrades didn't join you when you rushed over to the greenhouse at half past noon—when Watson and

Marieta were at Mrs. Stillaway's shop. Perhaps you thought the greenhouse manager wouldn't be working on a holiday, and you could slip in with your access card unnoticed. But he was there, wasn't he? You see, Gastrell, Mr. Narayan—the greenhouse manager—" he added for everyone else's benefit, "has recently experienced a divorce. He has been recuperating by burying himself in work. So, he was there when you arrived, and you were forced to sign in. Rather fortunate for me!" he added gleefully.

He picked up the clipboard and showed us the page for the date in question; there was but a single sign-in that day, and the signature belonged to Arthur Gastrell. As Holmes had said, the time stamp corresponded to the hour Marieta and I had been away from Baker House. Arthur hadn't fabricated the time since there had been no need to do so; he didn't think anyone would think to check the clipboard with most of those involved in the events contemplating a not-so-logical solution. A sudden flare of anger shook my core; he had been sitting in the parlour, awaiting our return, the picture of innocence, with only the flush in his cheeks to hint at his covert doings. What an idiot I had been!

"Well?" Christa said belligerently, tapping her fingers on the table. "Are you going to confess or what?"

Arthur cast her a miserable, pleading look, and then, with much difficulty, met our loathing eyes. "Yes, it was me … Sherlock is right about everything. I was responsible for all of it." His eyes glistened and he bowed his head again in shame. His apology was barely a whisper: "I'm sorry."

Holmes beamed. "Ha! And there you have it, ladies and gentlemen." He put his hand over his chest and bowed as though his audience had erupted into cheer and applause. We did no such thing, of course; we sat in silence, digesting the confession.

Still, my friend looked mightily pleased as he took his seat at the head of the table. Christa and Elodie both looked relieved, their troubles over at last. Gwilym was staring at Holmes with envy, which hadn't gone unnoticed by the latter; here was another reason for Holmes to hold his head high: the detective had ousted the psychologist. Surprisingly, Gwilym remained silent even though I had expected him to at least have a go at the psychological aspects of the case Holmes hadn't touched on. In fact, it was Marieta Charr who tried to unveil the sticky emotions that had set in motion a slew of crimes.

"Tell us your side of the story, Arthur," she said with her customary gentleness. "Start with what happened at Crooked Forest." Her soft tone didn't convince Arthur to speak right away though. In fact, a long silence followed as he stared with unblinking red eyes at nothing in particular. At last, he raised his head slightly, though he refused to meet our gaze.

"They were always harassing me," he muttered bitterly. "Snide comments, playing tricks, shoving me into snowbanks—all under the guise of good fun. I complained to management, but nothing changed. I wanted them to pay ... and I wanted to ruin the reputation of Crooked Forest Adventures."

He went on to explain how Alberta den Nomot, who would ramble incessantly about the Salem Witch Trials, had inspired an idea for revenge. Naturally, he thought real witches and the theory of the northward migration was rubbish, but still, what if he could fabricate their presence? It was with intensive research and careful planning that he set his plan in motion. He chose Drebber as his first victim because the poor dog was terminally ill.

"But the company covered it up, called it an animal attack even though it obviously wasn't, and forbade us to tell anyone," Arthur spat with fresh anger. "I was forced to choose another dog, but this time I would make sure the story would make its way back to the city. So I invited you all, but my ulterior motive was to bring you,

Sherlock Holmes, to Crooked Forest. I've watched you all these months, and I know what you're capable of."

Although modesty wasn't one of Holmes' virtues, the smugness on his face was fleeting. "You knew of my talents but were not afraid I would sniff out the true culprit?" he asked.

Arthur shrugged. "I decided I would mislead you as best as I could and leave no evidence as I brought the 'witches' back to life. In the end, even if you managed to point the finger at me, it wouldn't matter … because mob mentality doesn't listen to reason. It's dictated by fear and paranoia."

Holmes laughed grimly. "Look around you, Gastrell. I have convinced each person at this table of your guilt."

Indeed, each of Holmes' guests wore an expression so wintry and accusing, a weak-kneed person would have shivered in shame and fear. Arthur did exactly that. He nodded helplessly and mumbled another apology.

"I supposed your crimes escalated because even the second slaying went unreported, not even one measly paragraph in the papers," Holmes went on. "You decided human subjects were required. That would give you the attention you sought. You would eventually link what was happening at Baker House to what had passed in Crooked Forest."

Again, Arthur nodded. "I drugged Christa and Elodie with a variant of jimsonweed that I grew in the greenhouse. It can only be detected in the blood if you test for it."

"I think we've heard enough," Christa declared with vehemence. She stood and stamped her feet. "Call the police!"

Arthur gasped and shrunk in his chair. Elodie, seeing his petrified face, shook her head pleadingly at her friend and grabbed her arm, yanking her back into her chair.

"How could you say that?" she cried. "He's your cousin!"

"He murdered two dogs," Christa hissed.

"Ah, yes, the poor animals," Holmes drawled. "You care so much about animal welfare, don't you, Christa?" He smirked. "How many were sacrificed to make your coat, I wonder ..."

Although Christa's hands jerked as though she would stretch across the table and throttle Holmes, Elodie managed to keep her friend still.

To Arthur, Holmes queried, "Was Stangers sick as well?" After receiving a forlorn nod, he asked an odd question: "And are you done?" When Arthur blinked quizzically, he elaborated, "Are you done with your revenge, or do you plan to continue wreaking havoc?"

The question startled Arthur, but he stammered quickly, "I'm done, and I regret it all. I wish I'd never —" He couldn't bring himself to name his terrible doings. A single tear escaped his eye, instantly blunting our loathing. Even Christa's temper faded.

Holmes sat meditatively for a minute, and I anxiously wondered if he was going to heed Christa's demand to call the police. Admittedly, I didn't want to see Arthur hauled away in handcuffs even as I remembered Stangers' pitiful remains. Before me was a whimpering, shame-faced man whose features conveyed without a doubt a heartfelt regret over the two lives he had ended and the grievances he had caused those who had trusted him. I knew in that moment that I had forgiven Arthur Gastrell.

Holmes cast me a sidelong glance. "It appears Watson has accepted Gastrell's apology. If she thinks this delinquent deserves forgiveness, that is good enough for me."

The group's scowls fell on me, and I opened my mouth to protest, but no sound came out—since there was truth to what he said. I glared at him as I always did when he behaved omnisciently.

Holmes avoided my gaze. "Shall we call it a night then?" He stood and started putting his exhibits back into his backpack, then looked down at us with impatience, for no one had stirred. He let out a loud sigh of resignation.

"We can involve the police, but what evidence could I give them?" He looked at us expectantly, but no one answered. "There is no evidence Gastrell killed Drebber and Stangers or that he drugged Özdemir, Christa, and Elodie. There is only my claim that his parka sleeve and gloves smelled like sambuca since neither article can be produced. Hence, there is no proof he was responsible for the blue fire." Again, that look of admiration returned and he said to Arthur, "Whether you meant to or not, you have covered your tracks well, Gastrell."

Arthur's mouth opened in protest, unwilling to accept the credit Holmes was giving his intellect, when Christa bared her teeth.

"He just confessed to everything! Isn't that enough?" she cried.

Holmes shrugged. "There is no written and signed confession. Perhaps by the time the police arrive, Gastrell will have changed his mind about confessing. After all, he risks criminal charges and expulsion from school."

"But we have his name on the sign-in sheet," Gwilym exclaimed. "He planted that leaf in Janah's room."

"I don't believe you can be held criminally responsible for plucking a leaf from a tree and using it to scare someone," Holmes said with a laugh. "It would be written off as a practical joke."

"Are you proposing we do nothing?" Gwilym grunted, outraged. "Actions have consequences!"

"Naturally," Holmes responded. "Gastrell, I don't think the ladies will ever feel safe with you in the house. I suggest you vacate Baker House. That will be your punishment."

Arthur looked aghast. "B-but I've lived there for two years. It's my h-home—" He interrupted himself, his face steeped in misery, before hanging his head in defeat. "I'll leave in the morning." He stood and put on his coat, looking dazed, then walked away under the watchful gaze of the restaurant patrons.

Holmes clapped his hands. "Oh, please do return to your fish and chips, everyone! We were just helping Watson here by acting out the final scene of the novel she is writing." He leaned over and squeezed my shoulder amicably.

Holmes and I left The Village Idiot shortly afterwards, trailed by Marieta. I slowed my tread along the salted sidewalk, forcing Holmes to walk less briskly; it felt rude to let Marieta walk home by herself. As she caught up with us, an icy blast of wind hit our faces, making us shiver as we waited for the walk signal to blink on. At last, the wind simmered down, and our walk, which had been a quiet one, resumed.

When we reached Baker House, I stepped forward and unlocked the door, wondering whether Arthur was already upstairs packing his bags. With a heavy heart, I stepped inside, only to jerk back in alarm and crash into Holmes.

"What is it, Wa—" Holmes cried, setting me upright. His gaze fell on the carpeted floor of the vestibule, and an amused understanding dawned on his face. "Ah, the accursed cat."

There it lounged on the carpet as majestically as always, not even slightly apologetic for startling me with its glowing silver eyes, and very possibly pleased with itself for causing a stir. I gave it a hard stare. Marieta brushed past us, and the cat sprang to its feet and sprinted into the parlour.

As we climbed the steps to the second floor, I asked, "The cat—was Arthur involved in that too?"

Holmes shook his head. "An unrelated incident, I daresay. It probably came in through an open window. Its sudden arrival was coincidental, but you took it as an omen of misadventure because you were already in a mental state of foreboding, Watson." He paused, smiling faintly. "That cat is strange, but I find cats in general are very strange."

EPILOGUE

I SHOULD HAVE RESTED EASY THAT NIGHT. THE SINISTER business was over; more importantly and most reassuringly, a human hand had orchestrated the plot that had imparted so much anxiety. I was free to focus on my studies and not be plagued by ritualistically slain dogs or housemates who spoke of disembodied voices and saw visions of beastly women. Arthur was banished from Baker House, and I would never need to return to Crooked Forest. Even the cat, I was sure, would soon be discovered by our cranky but completely normal housekeeper and ejected.

Yet why did that feeling of foreboding Holmes had mentioned continue to weigh on me?

A few hours had passed since the rendezvous at The Village Idiot. A warm shower had done nothing to ease my spirits; I was still digesting all that Holmes had said, replaying his explanations and recalling Arthur's childlike shivers. A light dinner had followed my shower, although I could no longer recall what I had eaten. I had then absentmindedly tucked myself under the covers, and there I lay for what seemed like eternity, reflecting and fidgeting and fighting the feeling that something felt wrong.

In fact, several things felt wrong, and as I trailed a convoluted web of thoughts, I began to see the holes in Holmes' story.

I recalled what he had said about Arthur's unease about not knowing which trail the dogsledders would use that fateful day. But had he seemed anxious? No … no, Arthur had seemed perfectly cheerful as he had welcomed us to Crooked Forest. There was that little incident with Dimitri Komarov, but who wouldn't feel flustered after getting shoved? Surely by the time Arthur had greeted us, he would have known which path the dogsledders would take … yet it hadn't bothered him that his handiwork wouldn't be discovered.

Next, there was Jibril Özdemir's attack, which I was certain Arthur could have played no role in. I had been sitting with him the entire time before venturing down the corridor that had led to my discovery of Jibril in the kitchen. Arthur would have had to slip through the front door unnoticed — an impossibility with all those people in the Great Room — enter the kitchen through the sliding doors, incapacitate Jibril with the drug, pull on a hellhound mask to torment the man, and leave as he had entered, all in the twenty seconds it had taken me to walk down the corridor. If the words of a delirious man could be trusted, Jibril had pointed beyond the counter to signal how the "witch" had exited; whoever it was had left through the kitchen's main entrance, seamlessly melting into the Great Room crowd *before* I had turned into the corridor.

And last was my own terrifying experience of reliving Bridget Bishop's hanging. Just as I could recall the dream with perfect clarity, what followed too was etched in my mind. Arthur had lingered by my door, looking like he had seen a ghost *before* I had told him anything about the dream. How had he known I had been through something so terrible beforehand?

Yet Arthur had confessed to all that he had been accused of. Why would he do such a thing? Was he trying to protect an accomplice? Or perhaps he was innocent but knew the real perpetrator whom he felt the need to protect …

I sprang to my feet and turned on the lights. There was one clue I could use to shed some light on the matter. Running over to my desk, I glanced past the laptop and heaps of textbooks and rummaged through the loose sheets of paper. My search grew frantic as I started opening the drawers. *Had I lost it?* I wondered; it was only a tiny piece of paper after all. It was very possible it had been unknowingly tossed into the garbage can.

Fortunately, I was spared from going through my garbage. I found the note Arthur had written to me — summoning me to the parlour after that wretched dream — in the bottom drawer. Two bounding steps brought me to the nightstand that held my phone; I grabbed it and brought both the note and phone back to my bed. My hands shook in anticipation, but I managed to steady my finger as I swiped through my photo gallery.

Amid the photos of winter scenery I had snapped at Crooked Forest was the one Holmes had asked me to capture of the sinister note on the cabinet wall: *The next will be sacrificed.* My friend hadn't felt the need to consult the message, and I had forgotten having ever taken the photo. But now, to me at least, it seemed to be the most important clue there was.

I held the phone and Arthur's note side by side. Just as I had expected, the handwritings did *not* match.

I put the phone and note away and slumped under the covers again, although my feet itched to bound up the stairs to Arthur's room and demand an explanation. But he would tell me no more than what he had revealed at The Village Idiot. Perhaps I was well-liked at Baker House, as Holmes had said, but I lacked his persuasiveness. If he couldn't compel Arthur to talk, then I had little chance. Regardless, I knew one thing with certainty.

Sherlock Holmes had been wrong.

TO BE CONTINUED…

About the Author

Jia Hartsiva currently works in academic publishing and lives with her family in Toronto, Canada. She has previously written for the business and popular science fields, although her heart lies in the world of fiction. She has a weakness for whodunits and a passion for Sherlock Holmes.

www.ingramcontent.com/pod-product-compliance
Lightning Source LLC
Chambersburg PA
CBHW032003050726
47590CB00006B/2030